'Beyond Reach? is a wonderful tribute to all those ordinary people who take action against the scandal of global poverty. For those of us who took part in the Make Poverty History campaign, it's also great to revisit the experience of that year' - *John Hilary*

'A gripping and inspiring story of forbidden love and the struggle for justice. In a hundred years people will look back on our culture of greed and realise books like this helped change the world' - *David Rhodes*

'A revealing story about a scandal of our time, witty, sharp - and above all urgent' - *Rosie Boycott*

'In this amusing novel, John Madeley links modern ethics and politics with the age-old issues of relationships and the meaning of life. All this, with serious intent, too' - *Tim Lang*

'In the tradition of *Saturday*, this outstanding novel weaves together the world of public events with the private world of individual lives' - *Carl Rayer*

'Be warned, this book could change your life' - *Ann Pettifor*

Author's note
In this book I try to write about a serious issue in a way that is revealing, interesting and enjoyable. It is a novel with a difference and I hope you find it both stimulating and a good read.

The national and international events described in this book are real and the author was present as a journalist at most of them. With the exception of Sne and Mbali, world leaders, politicians, authors, entertainers, actors, celebrities, church leaders and aid and development agency workers, the characters are fictitious. Any resemblance to anyone living or dead is entirely coincidental. The book is set in 2005.

Non-fiction books by John Madeley

Big Business, Poor Peoples: How Transnational Corporations Damage the World's Poor
50 Reasons to Buy Fair Trade (with Miles Litvinoff)
100 Ways to Make Poverty History
A People's World: Alternatives to Economic Globalization
Food for All: The Need for a New Agriculture
Hungry for Trade: How the Poor Pay for Free Trade
Trade and the Poor: The Impact of International Trade on Developing Countries
Land is Life: Land Reform and Sustainable Agriculture (co-editor)
When Aid is No Help: How Projects Fail and How They Could Succeed
Details on: www.JohnMadeley.co.uk

Royalties from the sale of this book are donated to agencies that are working to end poverty.

Beyond Reach?

John Madeley

Longstone Books Ltd
London

Published in the United Kingdom in 2009 by Longstone Books,
19 Barnard Road, London SW11 1QT

Copyright © John Madeley 2009

The right of John Madeley to be identified as the author of this work
has been asserted by him in accordance with the Copyright, Designs
and Patents Act 1988

Cover and illustration by Dimitri Crysto

A catalogue record for this book is available from the British Library.

Printed and bound by ImprintDigital.net

Printed on FSC-certified paper made from trees grown in sustainable
forests

ISBN 978-0-9554373-7-3

Contents

1

New Year's Day 2005

Two orphans. Sne and Mbali. At the end of a comedy programme that she rarely watched, they were to change Sara's life.

Sne and Mbali. Two young African children, heartbroken and sobbing, trying to comfort each other after their mother and father had died of AIDS.

The programme was a docudrama but the children were real. The TV screen showed their tears, their fear, in stark reality. And Sara cried bitterly with them. Tears that cascaded down her cheeks and were to start a chain of events she could never have foreseen. A dramatic end to a day that had started in the haze of a morning after the night before.

Sara and William Openshaw had something of a reputation for their New Year's Eve parties. They had moved from their native north-west of England to a town some twenty miles north of London. And in the north-west, everyone celebrated New Year's Eve. One big party, in the streets, in people's homes; you hardly needed to ask where you were going, what you were doing. You got together with others and partied.

But in their first year in the south, New Year's Eve came and went, and Sara and William wondered who had died. While the town centre was busy enough, their own neighbourhood seemed lifeless. So the following year the Openshaws threw a northern-style New Year's Eve party. They invited neighbours, friends, work colleagues, and asked them to come and bring anyone who was not doing anything. And bring a bottle. For all that, not many came, about twenty or so. Open invitations aroused suspicion in some in the south. "Bit much isn't it?" a neighbour had remarked, with more than a hint of disapproval. But those who came enjoyed it, and the party was judged a success. The Openshaws decided to make it an annual event.

New Years came, New Years went. The parties had become popular. As Sara and William wearily cleared away the mess and surveyed the scene of devastation in the late morning of New Year's Day, they wondered if their parties were such a good idea after all.

Dark-haired, good-looking, slim, exuberant, frisky yet down-to-earth Sara had met William at a redbrick northern university. Five years older, and an inch or two taller than five-foot-sixish Sara, William had been a late starter at university, having tried several jobs after finishing his A levels. Not quite a mature student, but with enough maturity to attract Sara, the angular William had been entranced by Sara's rich brown eyes and flirtatious manner.

Older and more experienced than most other students, William had fancied his chances of becoming president of the union. Inglorious failure was the outcome. Hardly surprising, as he had expected to become president without any campaigning. Out of eight candidates, William came eighth. Sara at least made it onto the union executive.

In the mid-1990s, soon after their first child Chloe was born, they moved south, William taking up the offer of an adequately-paid job in a ball-bearings company. And Sara became a full-time mum until soon after their second daughter May was born. She took a job as a part-time nurse at the local GP's. This suited her fine, giving time for other interests. When they moved South, Sara made an effort to lose her north-western accent, while William had stubbornly clung on to his.

Sara scrubbed at the carpet. "Bloody red wine," she muttered, her head pounding as she leant forward. Lips pursed she muttered: "There's a cigarette burn on the sofa, too. I thought I'd made it clear, no smoking indoors."

William stood in the doorway, his face bland and expressionless. Among the pile of unwashed dishes in the kitchen lay the inevitable remains of paper hats, crackers and party poppers.

Sighing, Sara sat back on her heels, noticed that several of the Christmas cards had been knocked off the shelf. She stood, her knees aching, picked them up and found a letter inside one of them from a couple she had met briefly some twenty years ago.

A welcome diversion. She read in one paragraph: "We were delighted when our elder daughter, Harriet, told us in August that she was expecting a baby. We took a bottle of champagne out of the cupboard. But our delight turned to dismay when she informed us that her husband, Donald, was not the father. We put the champagne back in the cupboard."

William went into the kitchen, began washing up, his tuneless whistling grating on Sara's nerves and exacerbating her thumping headache. She switched on the radio – Radio 3. Classical music, all very soothing, just what the nurse ordered.

Sara had trained as a nurse soon after completing a degree in English. It was a close-run thing with journalism. Editing the student newspaper at university had given her a taste for writing short, newsy articles. A gap year had ended with a month of playing record requests for a hospital radio. Playing records had not been enough; she wanted to be more centrally involved in hospital work.

As she listened and hummed along to the music of Strauss, Sara recalled a seminal event in her life, the premature death of the grandfather she had adored as a girl. A forty-a-day smoker he had died of lung cancer in his late fifties, nudging Sara further towards a career in nursing and turning her into an anti-smoking activist, which in turn had rapidly widened to the health of the planet and the health of its many and varied populations.

William, elbow-deep in soapy water, had other things on his mind. Ball bearings. Ball bearings were always on William's mind. After a degree in economics he found a job as a management trainee with a ball-bearings company. And ball bearings became his dramatic passion. He was reckoned by friends to be the only person in England who was enthusiastic about ball bearings.

Dog-tired and planning an early night, something happened that evening that was to change Sara's life. Slumped in a chair, she switched on TV for no reason in particular, flicked around the channels to see the opening shots of the programme "The Vicar of Dibley". A melodious choir was singing "The Lord's my shepherd". Sara came within a second of switching off. But something caught her attention. The Dibley vicar, Geraldine, was about to be forty, an age that Sara was also nudging. The Parish Council was trying to think of an appropriate present. Ideas were tossed about − like renting the services of Mel Gibson for an hour, or perhaps having a truckload of anti-ageing cream delivered, Geraldine being of ample proportions.

The actors prattled on, humorously enough for Sara to stay with the channel, and to see a quite heart-rending final scene. A television is switched on to show Sne and Mbali sobbing. One by one the actors then stand silently in front of the camera wearing white armbands which read "Make Poverty History".

Make Poverty History, yes, Sara remembered reading something about it, Towards the end of 2004, around fifty non-governmental organisations, including Friends of the Earth, Oxfam and War on Want, had launched a campaign for 2005 under that name.

According to these groups, 30,000 children a day were dying from poverty-related disease, one every three seconds. 2005 apparently offered a series of opportunities for Britain to lead the global fight against poverty. Not least because in July the UK would host the annual G8 gathering of the world's most powerful leaders. Gordon Brown had said that leaders would discuss "the most important issue of our generation − world poverty."

Sne and Mbali, thought Sara, this is about them, about children like them.

William had slept through it all. Sara left the room, went up to their bedroom and cried bitterly for those two children and for other children in that predicament. She knew that she could not put this behind her. Not one for New Year's resolutions, Sara made one in tears that she vowed to keep in practice – that not a day would pass in 2005 when she would not do something, however small, about making poverty history. It was Saturday night, tomorrow she would start by talking with friends about it. And next week buy a white band, and e-mail Tony Blair.

Sara realised that what the programme had done was to move her concern for people who live in poverty from her head to her heart. In her head it jostled for attention with many other things. In her heart, it was a more important part of her, it was something she cared deeply about and could not and would not let go. But that was not the only matter that in the course of 2005 was to move from Sara's head to her heart.

★ ★ ★

It was a statement he had to make, but it nearly killed him. A statement for a cause that when 2005 dawned he didn't know existed. But when the Reverend Simon Copplestone, assistant curate at St. Luke's church, met his boss that New Year's Day he was handed some papers that were to prove fateful. Papers about a campaign called Make Poverty History.

"All the churches and mission societies are behind this, also Christian Aid, Tearfund, etc.," said St. Luke's Vicar Bernard, "and they say 2005 has a number of events that give people the opportunity to influence policy. So would you make this your thing for the next twelve months?"

It was a command not a request. "Well I don't know anything about it, but I'll try," was the only response Simon could make. Make Poverty History, sounds grand, would be great, he thought as he walked back home on a blustery January day. In the study of his semi on a modern housing estate, he went to the campaign's website. He read of the children who died each day as a result of poverty. Of how the resources and knowledge were available to stop it. "Help us to literally change the world . . . join us now, get a white band," he read.

Could he find time for it, he wondered. Tall, slim, prematurely losing more hair than he liked to admit, a good listener and a good if plummy speaker, 33-year-old Simon had been at the gaunt building that was St. Luke's for three years. In a home counties' town some twenty miles north of London, the church he served was a typical product of Victorian England. "They made them by the mile and chopped them off by the yard," was a fair description of late-19th century St. Luke's.

But it's people not a building that make a church and Simon's work with people was beginning to bear fruit. He had started a group for parents, toddlers and babies, set up a youth group and given young people a part in the services. He had taken a group for a week to Taizé, a Christian community in France. And encouraged the choir to accept girls for the first time.

Believing that the church should go out to meet people where they are, Simon had started holding short services outside a local supermarket. And whereas many churches in the early part of the third millennium were reporting falling numbers, St. Luke's was bucking the trend.

An only child from a privileged background, father a barrister, mother a company accountant, the Reverend Simon Copplestone knew nothing of poverty. It was a career in marketing that he pursued after a first-class honours degree in Philosophy, Politics and Economics at Oxford. For two or three years all went well. But Simon grew restless. He felt that he wanted something more out of life than being a cog in a selling machine, tackling problems that tens of thousands had worked on and solved. He wanted a challenge, but was not sure what it was.

His life was to change when a friend invited him to his church to listen to a visiting preacher who seemed to make sense. He began attending church regularly and was soon a youth leader. Doubts about marketing as a career began to creep through, doubts expressed to the church's vicar who told him that he could be a suitable candidate for ordination. Simon had decided to let his name go forward. He was accepted and opted to go for training at a theological college near Oxford. Brainy, well-read, easy to get on with, Simon was considered by friends to be a bishop of the future. But the assistant curate had a problem: he was busy, but lonely. The busy-ness of his life served only to mask the loneliness. In his three-bedroom curacy house there was just him and Flick. His cat.

Simon hadn't planned it that way. He was not a confirmed bachelor, it was just that his encounters with women seemed to be confirming it. While talented and clever, Simon was a disaster area when it came to women. He simply lacked judgement, falling hopelessly in love with a succession of unsuitable females. After a few inconsequential relationships at university, he had had a number of disastrous relationships – he counted four in all.

St. Luke's didn't help. An acute shortage of suitable, marriage-age women was all too clear. A recent church survey had found that the largest age group was the seventies to seventy-nines, followed by the sixties to sixty-nines. More encouragingly this was followed by the zero to ten group, reflecting a thriving Sunday club. There were young mothers and young women whom he helped prepare for marriage. But marriage for Simon seemed as out of bounds as these women.

There was the hazard of the occasional late-night phone call from one or two middle-aged-plus, lonely women, requesting an immediate clergy visit. But Simon's training had included how to cope with these situations. The reality was that there was hardly a single woman at St. Luke's between the ages of twenty and forty.

Back home from meeting Bernard, there were messages on the curacy answering machine, someone crying off from a Bible reading tomorrow, a request for details about the youth group, someone who was bereaved and wanted to see him. The New Year's Day holiday it may have been, but not everyone was able to take a holiday from events. Simon, however, preferred it that way.

The calls were not an interruption to the day. Rather, they were what his days were about, they showed that he was needed, had a role to play. They confirmed his ministry, meant that he was with people, they combated the loneliness.

It was evening before he was back home to cook a meal, and then slump in an armchair and listen to music. Flicking through the television schedules he noticed that tonight would be the final episode of "The Vicar of Dibley". This was a programme that some clergy were not keen on, as the vicar, they believed, was something a caricature.

But the blurb said that tonight's programme would have a Make Poverty History theme. Interesting, might learn something, I'll take a look, he thought. He too saw Sne and Mbali. Yes, he thought at the end of it, I really have to do something about poverty this year. I must put something back into the society from which I have taken so much, he thought, but what, and have I the time? Simon was to find that he did have the time. And to find a great deal more, although almost paying the ultimate price.

2

Yours in Hope

Sara's first thought was to speak with Agnes. And to do it the very next day, January 2nd. In the early 1970s, at the age of four, Agnes had come to Britain from Uganda with her parents to flee the despotic rule of Idi Amin. The youngest of five children, Agnes had more first-hand knowledge of poverty than anyone Sara knew. Despite the early poverty, Agnes achieved well at school and was now a social worker, mother of a three-year old boy and helper at a Sunday group for three-to-five year-olds at St. Luke's church.

"Make Poverty History? No I've not heard of that. Poverty where? There's more of it around here than a lot of people think," was Agnes's blunt response to Sara's opening question.

"Right, right," Sara played for time, a bit startled, wasn't quite expecting that. She explained that it was a special campaign for this year to mount a concerted effort to end poverty, and that the tsunami which hit Asia on Boxing Day had showed the vulnerability of poor people. "But Agnes, you know better than I do that millions of people are vulnerable in ways that don't make the headlines. Tell you what, can we look at the website? Explains it better than anything I could say." www.makepovertyhistory.org was duly summoned to the computer screen.

"Make Poverty History is a unique UK alliance of charities, trade unions, celebrities, campaigning groups and faith communities who are mobilising around key opportunities in 2005 to drive forward the struggle against poverty and injustice," it said.

Three demands were central to the campaign, they read: More and Better Aid, Drop the Debt and Trade Justice.

The campaign, the site went on, was the UK's contribution to "an international effort called the Global Call to Action Against Poverty". It said that 2005 would see a truly worldwide effort "where groups from countries on every continent will come together at key times to take action to end poverty." This activity would be drawn together in a movement "that world leaders cannot ignore".

"So this is about poverty in developing countries. Nothing to do with the people that I see sleeping rough in shop doorways in a rich capital like London," Agnes was again blunt and challenging. It was a valid point, but this time Sara was ready.

"Agnes, if you are talking about ending poverty, you're talking, aren't you, about tackling poverty wherever it exists. Yes, there's poverty here, but read on down the site – a child dies every three seconds as a result of poverty. You wouldn't deny, would you, that the scale of poverty in Africa and its effects on people are far worse than in London?"

"No of course not, but don't make it one-sided, Sara. Don't make out that Africa's a basket case. Remember, Britain has problems too, that's all I ask. I help at the town's drop-in centre for the homeless once a month, you should come some time, and I can tell you there is poverty here, right in the middle of the affluent south-east. But ok, let's look at the issues. 'More and Better Aid', hmmm, what does that mean?"

"Let's read what it says, shall we?" Sara was relieved to move on.

"The developed world has a responsibility to fund international development programmes," it read. The UK had previously committed itself to giving 0.7% of its gross national income in development aid. The promise was made in 1970. "Some 35 years later," it went on, "we are still waiting for the promise to be kept."

And: "The Chancellor says the UK should finally reach the 0.7% target by 2013. Yet by 2013, some 45 million people will be newly infected with HIV. Only half of Africa's children will complete primary school and one in six will die before their fifth birthday."

"So, you see, this is about us meeting our responsibility to you," Sara was more buoyant.

"Yes, but when you give aid, who do you give it to? You know there are some rich dictators on the African continent. And there's a feeling that at least some aid money has found its way into their greasy pockets. Don't be naive Sara, it's happened."

Sara knew that Agnes had the first-hand experience that she herself lacked. Sara had campaigned on poverty, globalisation, global warming, the environment. She had been a member of the World Development Movement, War on Want and the Jubilee 2000 Drop the Debt movement. She had served as the local press officer for all these groups, but did not have the experience of life and conditions in a developing country.

"OK, but notice that the campaign's about more and better aid," Sara countered, "look at these paragraphs . . ."

Aid must also be given in ways that help poor people, not donor-country firms, read the website. "Aid needs to focus better on poor people's needs. This means more aid being spent on areas such as basic health care and education. It should no longer be conditional on recipients cutting health and education spending, or opening up their markets. Aid should support poor countries' and communities' own plans and paths out of poverty."

"At last, something I warm to," Agnes laughed, an infectious laugh that made Sara feel they were at last connecting. "But you know I still have this concern that giving people aid can make them dependent."

"But isn't aid a matter of supporting the efforts that people are making themselves to get out of poverty, where perhaps a little help from outside can make the difference between developing and staying poor?" Sara was delving deep into memory for something she had read in a report.

"What's this Drop the Debt then?" Agnes moved on, "this Jubilee 2000 stuff. The first time we met, you were collecting signatures in the high street for a petition that wanted Western governments to cancel debts in 2000 as a fitting way to mark the new millennium, you said. It didn't work then did it? Why should it work now?"

Sara conceded that debt was not cancelled as they had hoped – but cancelling it, she pointed out, would surely have made a bigger contribution to humanity than building a Dome. And at least the Jubilee 2000 campaign persuaded governments to make a start, she said, and some countries did have their debt cancelled, with positive results.

They looked at the website again. "Debt Relief Works!" it proclaimed boldly. "In Benin, 54% of the money saved through debt relief has been spent on health, including rural primary health care and HIV programmes. In Tanzania, debt relief enabled the government to abolish primary school fees, leading to a 66% increase in attendance. After Mozambique was granted debt relief, it was able to offer all children free immunisation. In Uganda, debt relief led to 2.2 million people gaining access to clean water."

"You know Agnes, I think I'm right that Uganda was one of the first countries to have debt relief. It's working isn't it?"

"It's working in a way. It is true we had some, by no means all, of our debt cancelled in the late 1990s. But then what happened? The world price of coffee collapsed. And do you realise that coffee is the only export earner for tens of thousands of Ugandan farmers? I remember Ugandan papers saying that the fall in coffee prices more than wiped out the benefit of debt relief."

"God, I didn't know that!" Sara was shaken. "That's awful. I suppose it takes us to trade justice. Let's see if there's anything about coffee here."

"Sorry, I've been very inhospitable Sara, can I get you a coffee – Ugandan of course!"

Coffee was welcome, very welcome. This was hardly a normal way to spend a Sunday, thought Sara, but if she wanted to keep that resolution, she needed to be there.

Trade justice. Both women confessed they had barely heard the term. Fair trade, yes, but what was trade justice?

The UK government, read the website, should fight to ensure that governments, particularly in poor countries, can choose the best solutions to end poverty and protect the environment. It should make laws that stop big business profiting at the expense of people and the environment.

The women shrugged, who could object to any of that, wondered Sara, apart from big business. But what about coffee?

"The UK government is committed to free market responses to global poverty," they read on. "The relentless pursuit of trade liberalisation, privatisation and deregulation has continued in the face of mounting evidence that they entrench and do not overcome poverty. The impact on poor people and our collective environment has been disastrous."

"Well there's the coffee, Sara," said Agnes. "Coffee is traded in free market fashion. No controls, no management, the price is left to the dictates of supply and demand, and the farmer is on the receiving end. That's free trade for you. The snag is it does not free farmers from poverty."

"And there seems to be worse. Says here that the European Union is threatening African, Caribbean and Pacific countries with 'Economic Partnership Agreements' which require poor countries to open their markets to virtually all European goods within ten years. This would force ACP countries into unfair competition with rich European corporations," read Agnes.

The roof took the strain. "That's immoral, that's stupid," she raged. "The EU is doing that to us. Look, how can we end our dependence on coffee if we can't diversify and build up our industries? How can we do that if we have to compete with European, American, Japanese goods? We need space to grow, and we need to decide for ourselves, not be dictated to by anyone."

Anger, fury, passion, the worlds of the two women had met. They sat in silence, quietly fuming. Sara broke the silence: "So will you join me in campaigning on this? How about organising a meeting of people round here who are interested? We could then start planning, get press attention and begin to make an impact. You have connections at church don't you? People there should be interested, surely?"

"Yes, they should be. We have this clever young curate called Simon. Bit posh, talks with a plum in his mouth," Agnes laughed infectiously again. "But he's OK really, and some of his sermons are quite good; he seems aware of social issues. He also helps at the drop-in centre. Could be interested. I'll have a word."

"Good, and could I use your phone to ring my economist buddy, Peter? I'd like him on board and I want to ask him to look at this campaign through an economist's eyes."

Until the early 1990s Peter had been a conventional economist. His work on how the free market served the interests of all, rich or poor alike, was widely acclaimed. But he was given an assignment which dramatically changed his view of the world. The Washington-based International Monetary Fund asked Peter to join a team that would advise Russia on its policies in the wake of the collapse of the Soviet Union. The team lived in Moscow for six months and came up with a classic text – one they could have written without leaving London or Washington. All the usual stuff was there. In non-economic language it amounted to two fingers to the state, demolish controls, privatise everything, let the market rule.

Yet for Peter it made a difference being in Moscow, a big difference. Because he began to realise that imposing unbridled free-market solutions on a country emerging from state control was insensitive. That it was like telling a football team to stop kicking a ball and take up cycle racing – overnight. He felt it was too brutal, that something less harsh was needed. But his reservations were brushed aside. Yet as Russia developed, as a few made millions, even bought top English football clubs with the proceeds, many more people remained in deep poverty. Was the free market the answer, or was there another way, something in-between state control and the market? Were there alternatives to economic, corporate-led globalisation? It was questions like these that now occupied Peter's academic work.

"Make Poverty History, yes, something in the paper the other day about it. Has a website does it? OK I'll read it. Why don't you and William come round tomorrow for a drink and we'll have a chat." For Sara, Peter's response was enough to propel her home through the damp January streets.

Peter and Charley (Charlotte at work) had lived together after a mutual interest in fell-walking brought them together. Both in their early fifties, they lived to some extent rather separate lives. A high-ranking civil servant, only slightly below the very top echelons, Charley sometimes spent the night at a hotel in London near her office rather than take the last train home. And Charley said little about her work, even changed departments without telling Peter. And she kept well away from his interest in party politics. Civil servants must be impartial. Even Peter couldn't say for sure how she voted.

Charley's weakness was that she was hopeless at holding her drink. After two glasses of wine she had been known to spill some very indiscreet beans. But at least she was aware of the weakness, and Charley's left hand often seemed sown to the top of her glass. To keep her lips buttoned up about government matters, Charley drank alcohol with the greatest moderation. So at 4.00 a.m. at the Openshaws on New Year's Day, Charley had been the only one there who was stone-cold sober.

"Happy New Year for the second time Sara," said Peter, opening the door the following evening. "Can I get you anything – wine, tea, coffee, me?"

"*You* of course, except you'd get quietly, or not so quietly, murdered. I'll settle for tea, thanks."

"Where's William?"

"Along in a jiff. Couldn't drag him away from the end of a bank holiday football match on TV. Hi Charley. Do you expect Blair to survive the year?" Mischievous, and the discreet smile of a reply was all that Sara expected.

"OK Peter, Make Poverty History. What do you think? Does what they're saying make sense? Just how much can more and better aid, debt relief and trade justice contribute to ending poverty? Do they get to the causes of poverty?"

"Wow, big questions. Let's unravel them. First of all, the analysis on the website. On the whole I'm impressed. It doesn't cover everything, you couldn't expect it to, but it's clearly been put together by people who know their stuff and it covers most of the main issues. I'm glad it stresses that companies trade, not governments. Two-thirds of world trade is between transnational corporations. I think it should have more on this, because these corporations are unregulated and are basically running the show."

And Peter went on to explain why the power of the corporations meant that there was no such thing as free trade; why it was wrong to force trade down the throats of developing countries, when Britain has used all sorts of devices to protect itself and still did. Justice in trade dealings would allow poor countries that same right.

"But the causes of poverty are many." he said. "People are poor because they have few, if any, material assets. They don't have land, or maybe not enough land to grow the food they need, or not enough money to buy food. They have poor soils, they're made poorer by the desert taking over land, by armed conflict, poor health, HIV/AIDS, illiteracy, etc." And Sara's mind went back to Sne and Mbali.

"But it amounts very largely to lack of resources," Peter went on. "And yes, trade justice, debt relief, more and better aid – they won't do it all of course, but they could increase the resources to lift people out of poverty. On trade justice, remember that most of the poor are smallholder farmers who have little or nothing to trade. But their problems are often compounded by cheap subsidised food dumped by Western countries and sold below the cost of production onto local markets, against which they cannot compete."

Sara sipped her tea, looking at the occasional leaf blowing through the garden on a cold afternoon, listening as Peter shared his experience and knowledge.

"Remember also, Sara, that poverty will not end on the stroke of midnight, December 31st 2005. What a New Year's party you would have if it did! The reference to the millennium development goals on the website is good because this puts it into context. The main millennium development goal is to halve extreme poverty and hunger by 2015. If you could halve it by that date, then why not the other half by 2030? So you're talking about a 25-year campaign – at least. Are you up for it?"

"Wow, I did have a funny feeling that it would not only be this year! But how can we walk away from this when the poor can't walk away from their poverty?"

"Be warned, Sara, that governments can be slippery customers, the Blair government's a model of it. They will say and tell you all sorts of things to make you happy and then do the very minimum. Governments will take some shifting. Business has huge influence with them."

Raising his voice, Peter went on: "In fact it's not only civil servants who run the show, is it Charley? You're in a conspiracy with big business."

At which Charley, raising a demure eye from her copy of *The New Yorker*, drawled her longest statement of the year so far. "You may say that, but I couldn't possibly comment."

"You know, I've heard that before somewhere," rumbled Peter. "Anyway Sara, that's how I see it. What's next?"

And Sara explained that she planned to organise a meeting in the town to launch a local Make Poverty History campaign. "Will you come," she asked, "and say pretty much what you've just said to me? Before that, I plan to buy a couple of dozen Make Poverty History white bands, get these round to friends, sell them for a quid, or give them away, and start to organise. And I shall write to Mr Tony Blair when I get home."

"Well best of luck to you. My views on Blair are unprintable, as you know. Anyone with any principle would have resigned after misleading us – I'm in a polite mood today – about Iraq. To think I knocked on doors for Labour in 1997, and again in 2001 – more fool me. Never again until he's gone! Although I'm not as smitten as some with G. Brown."

The doorbell rang. William sheepishly stumbled in with a "Sorry, good match, couldn't miss the end. Have I missed anything here?"

"No, we've just decided you're running the country, that it's all your fault . . . that you dictate government policy, that you're unregulated and out of control," Sara laid it on as strongly as she could.

"Oh, nothing much then," William wasn't rising to that one.

"As I hinted at breakfast, but you were not listening, I'm thinking of launching a Make Poverty History campaign in the town," said Sara.

William was used to Sara's campaigning. "Good luck. If you don't mind, I'll get on with my ball bearings. I'll make a donation though."

"Are not all ball bearings much the same, William?" asked Peter. it was a question that Peter lived to regret.

"Certainly not," said William, and proceeded to expound at length about stainless-steel bearings, plastic bearings, thin-section bearings, miniature bearings, thrust-ball bearings, vibration deep-groove radial ball bearings . . .

"You know, I reckon if anyone told you that you are all balls, you'd see it as a compliment," said Peter, in a rare moment when William paused for breath.

An exasperated Sara came back to the issue. "Make Poverty History isn't a fund-raising campaign. It's *us*, not our money the campaign needs. And, dearest, it does want you. We need business people. The campaign is not anti-business, it is anti the abuse of power."

"Fat chance of me having any power to abuse," William grunted.

"Power corrupts," Peter began, "but absolute power" . . . "is much more fun." It was Charley who added the end, a novel twist to the usual, "corrupts absolutely". And left the others gasping.

"Well, you should know," Sara was the first to recover. "Charley, you will let us know from inside government what's going on this year about Make Poverty History?"

"You may ask that, but I couldn't possibly comment." Charley was positively enjoying this.

"I'm going home to e-mail Blair. Are the girls still next door? Time to get them home. How do I explain Make Poverty History to a seven-year old?"

"Good question. I need notice of that one," Peter replied.

Dear Mr Blair,

Happy New Year. I hope it is a happy one, both for you and for the many millions of people who are poor. Because this year you can do something special about their poverty. Only recently you have spoken of your concern about poverty. I was pleased to read that. You have just taken over the presidency of the G8. Good. I am expecting you to use your influence with other world leaders to make this a year when tackling poverty has the very highest priority in your policies.

I ask you to make a real contribution this year to making poverty history, in Africa, everywhere. I need not remind you how urgent this is, that a child dies every three seconds because of poverty.

I urge that we increase our aid to the United Nations 0.7% target and do so this year, not at some future date. Also that the debts are cancelled, not just of a handful of countries, but of the sixty or so countries who need it. And I want to ask that you stop pushing free trade on the poor. The poor want justice in trade, not free trade. Trade liberalisation has been disastrous for the poor; there is mounting evidence that it does not overcome poverty.

I ask you also to regulate the traders, the transnational corporations. At present I feel the tail is wagging the dog – that these companies are too influential in determining policy. Again there is evidence that the impact of many of their activities on the poor is disastrous. I believe there is an urgent need for regulation.

I ask too that EU governments stop imposing free-market Economic Partnership Agreements on Africa. These so-called partnership arrangements are survival of the fittest – in practice, the richest. EU companies have the funds to exploit the new market opportunities. It's they who stand to benefit, not the poorer countries. Yet this is supposed to be the year for Africa. As you hold the presidency of the EU later this year, please use your influence to offer African countries an alternative form of partnership.

Prime Minister, do please take advantage of the opportunity that
2005 offers to make poverty history.

Yours in hope.
Sara Openshaw

   And Sara began the process of immersing herself in the issues.
She had to know more, understand more, be ready for bland replies.
But events were underway that she was unable to understand.

3

The Meeting

Back-to-work day, the Tuesday after New Year's Eve. Business as usual. Except that the busy GP's surgery in town, where Sara worked on weekday mornings as a nurse, was twice as busy after the holiday.

"I'm going to Kenya on safari for two weeks, nurse. Will I need any injections? I've heard there's malaria. What about anti-malaria tablets?"

"I should have had a flu jab earlier, better late than never I suppose. Have you any left?"

"Firm's asked me to have my health checked as I'm going abroad. Could you give me an MOT and a health certificate?"

Sara had heard requests like these many, many times. It was an exhausted woman who cycled the mile or so home just after one o'clock. And back to planning the local launch of Make Poverty History. Glancing at the paper she noticed that an estimated 11 million people had watched "The Vicar of Dibley" on New Year's Day. The programme was fourth on the holiday's ratings list. And that meant, she felt, that many people would have been moved by Sne and Mbali.

A venue and a date for the meeting had to be decided. The venue was no problem as the GP's surgery was built on land where an old community hall once stood. The doctors were given permission to build a surgery on condition that it was a two-storey structure and that the upstairs was a large room for community use. At reasonable prices. And there was a discount for surgery employees.

But the date . . . Agnes had suggested they choose a date in late January, and just hoped that most people who were interested were free to come. Tuesday 25th January being OK for Sara, Agnes and Peter, it was duly chosen.

And the planning . . . "There are now over seventy organisations behind Make Poverty History, up from fifty-eight a week ago," Sara told Agnes on the phone. "Going through the list, all the main churches are there, also some trade unions. Let's invite them to send as many people as they can, and let's print some posters and get them up everywhere, in the library, the doctors' surgeries, the churches. Don't suppose he'll come, but let's invite the MP as well."

And how the evening should go . . . "There's a Make Poverty History powerpoint presentation. How about if I introduce the campaign, we have the presentation and then hand over to Peter for him to talk about the economics side. Not for too long mind. And Agnes, how about if you say something about Uganda, the debt, the coffee you told me about."

"OK, but let's have something lighter too. Tell you what, those Make Poverty History bands. I've already seen different ones around, some from shops and some home-made. How about a fashion show of bands?"

"Great idea. Then a break, fairtrade tea and coffee etc, then questions, then plan the campaigning, discuss what we actually do. Will you look at the website and see what they suggest? And I will prepare a news release to tell the press what we're doing."

Saturday, January 8th found Simon working on a sermon for the next day. Could he find anything new to say about the wise men, he wondered, the people the church thought about at this time of year? Still pondering, he was conscious of a letter dropping through the door and noticed Agnes walking down the street. The letter was an invitation.

MAKE POVERTY HISTORY
Invitation to a meeting to launch a campaign in the town

This year we have a real chance to do something about the poverty that takes the life of a child every three seconds. A coalition of churches, charities, trade unions and campaigning groups has launched a campaign to Make Poverty History.

Events in 2005 mean there is a unique opportunity for us to be the generation that says poverty must be brought to an end. In March a significant report will be published by the Commission for Africa. In July, Britain will host the G8 gathering of the eight most powerful world leaders. July also marks the twentieth anniversary of Live Aid. The gap between the world's rich and poor has never been wider.

Our leaders are influential players on the world stage. They have the power to cancel the debt, to change trade rules and give more aid to those who most need it.

Come and let's discuss how all of us can make a contribution.

The Surgery, High St. 7.45 p.m. Tuesday 25th January. Enquiries, queries to Sara Openshaw, 99478401, or to Agnes Mwakakwe, 99477448

Hmm, I've done nothing so far about Make Poverty History, other than buy a white band, better go to that meeting, he thought. Back to the wise men. Simon liked new angles. He prided himself that he liked to ask questions, raise issues, that were fresh and novel. He liked to explore parts of the Bible that people overlooked.

So he had studied the Old Testament Apocrypha, in between the Old and New Testaments. Containing some controversial passages, this is omitted from many bibles. Simon found that many at St. Luke's had either never heard of it, or just knew it as "the bit in the middle of the Bible".

But Simon was now looking for a new angle on the Three Wise Men. He had read recently that they were not quite all they seemed. They were called Magi – but could that mean they were magicians who cast spells on people? An evil bunch of rotters? And that gold, frankincense and myrrh were not gifts as such, but rather tools of their wicked trade. But, the Magi had been moved to repent of their trickery, and had travelled east to place these gifts at the feet of Jesus in an act of relinquishment. This was where their wisdom lay. Simon thought he would go with it. "Are we all we seem?" he prepared. "Are there not wicked things that we need to lay at the feet of Jesus and leave there? Where does wisdom need to break into our lives?"

After preaching the sermon the following day, he wasn't sure if his rather conservative congregation knew quite what he was talking about; or liked having their time-honoured view of the wise men stood on its head. Simon was torn between feeling pleased that he had given them a new angle, or concerned that he had been too clever by half.

In the Monday post came another invitation:

MAKEPOVERTY**HISTORY**
CHURCH LAUNCH
2005 IS A YEAR TO CHANGE THE WORLD
ALL YOU NEED TO DO IS FIND OUT HOW

Saturday 29 January 2005
11am–4pm
Bloomsbury Baptist Church
235 Shaftesbury Avenue, London

Will you help **MAKE**POVERTY**HISTORY**? Do you dare to believe that it's possible? Come to the church launch of Make Poverty History, an ecumenical event to mobilise and inspire people of faith to take action throughout the year.

An impressive list of speakers then followed. "Come along and get inspired and get active," it went on. "Find out how you can get involved individually, locally or nationally."

"Better go to that too," thought Simon. "Get some good ideas from the Christian angle. The congregation is going to expect that when I talk about it."

"There's no way I can escape this," he thought as the local paper dropped through his door that evening. "Make Poverty History campaign to be launched in the town," read the main page-two headline. 'The tsunami that has hit Asia is truly awful and has become known to the world. Less well known is that a hidden, silent tsunami is effectively happening every week,' say the campaign's organisers Sara Openshaw and Agnes Mwakakwe."

Agnes, thought Simon. Yes of course, great that she's involved. Sara? Oh yes, she's the one who has New Year's Eve parties. Interesting combination.

"Every three seconds a child, somewhere in the world, dies from a disease connected with poverty . . . This year we have a real chance to do something about such gross poverty," it went on. "So come to the meeting, support the campaign!"

Following her invites and the press release, people were responding to Sara to say whether they would be coming. The date did not please everyone. "Such a shame you have chosen a date in the Week of Prayer for Christian Unity," wrote one cleric. And from another: "Do you realise that we mark the conversion of St Paul that day?"

Sara responded with "sorries", but reflected that Christians from all the churches could do worse than unite behind this campaign and show unity in action. And that maybe some would be converted, on St Paul's Day 2005, to making poverty history.

For a cold January evening it was a pretty good turnout, some forty or fifty people coming to the surgery's comfortable "Upper Room". Ready to hear an uncomfortable message, they wanted to find out what they could do about it.

Sara and Agnes were there early, getting the powerpoint presentation right, putting up posters, laying out material received
from the different agencies behind Make Poverty History. And
one of the first to arrive was Simon.

"Hi Simon!" shouted Agnes from the other end of the room.
"Good to see you; come and let me introduce you to Sara."

"Hello Simon, thanks for coming," said Sara. Their eyes met . . .
and stayed together a little longer than eyes normally do. Simon
felt held, unaccountably held, by something in the wide dark eyes
looking at him.

"Good to be here," he blurted, "and thank you for organising
this."

"Have a good look at the material around, there's some stuff I
think you might find useful here," said Agnes. "If you don't mind,
we'll get on." Others arrived and quiet chatter soon filled the
room.

"Heavens, he's posh isn't he?" giggled Sara, when the two were
well out of Simon's hearing, "But bloody nice all the same. Those
eyes! The way he looked at me. For a second the world kind
of . . . stood still. Fascinating!"

"Sara behave yourself. Yes, he is nice – and is known apparently for his terrible choice in women!"

The meeting began. Sara welcomed everyone and made some
opening remarks about the campaign, nervously at first, but soon
picking up. Simon kicked himself for noticing the confident,
attractive way that Sara was speaking rather than what she was
saying. "Behave yourself you fool, she's a married woman," he
told himself. It wasn't to be the first time in 2005 when he was
glad that Sara could not read his thoughts.

The powerpoint presentation began, consisting of a number of
slides. The first had the image of a boy fetching water.

"Students in the future would marvel at the state of the world
in the early 21st century. A world where 1.1 billion people don't
have safe water," Sara read out from the accompanying script.

The second slide contained an image of malnourished children.
"Yes, we have a world where 150 million children are malnourished.

In sub-Saharan Africa and South Asia, child malnutrition levels are rising, with devastating impact: stunted growth, impaired development and slowed learning," Sara went on.

Slide three showed a pregnant woman. "A woman dies in childbirth every minute," Sara paused to let that sink in. "Half a million women die this way each year and almost all those deaths could be prevented. Maternal death rates are much higher where women don't have access to healthcare. A woman in sub-Saharan Africa faces a one in thirteen chance of dying in childbirth over her lifetime, compared with one in 4,100 in an industrialised country like ours."

And so the slides went on. An image of vaccination to show that disease could be prevented. A slide with the text of the millennium development goal to halve world poverty by 2015. Then an image of a classroom, to highlight the need for primary education for everyone.

The final slide was captioned "2005: the year to make poverty history." "2015 is only ten years away. This year, 2005, the countdown begins," said Sara. "And the UK is now in an unusually influential position. In a year that holds special summits on global poverty, our Prime Minister will be president of the EU and host of the G8 summit of world leaders. And Tony Blair has already said that Africa and climate change are at the top of his agenda.

"Make Poverty History is part of a wider campaign, the global call for action against poverty. There will be activity all over the world. So let's together make poverty history – this year," Sara concluded.

"I'd like to introduce economist Peter Riley to tell you more about aid, debt and trade, the basics of the campaign."

So Peter told them more, and in turn introduced Agnes. If there was some fidgeting when Peter was speaking there was certainly none when Agnes was on her feet.

"Africa is not poor, it is potentially rich," she went for the shock treatment. "It has been made poor because of you, and yes, because of me. Because we pay Africans a pittance for what they grow, because we exploit them, yes, because of the way we live. I plead with you all, let's stop it."

A white-band fashion show and a tea and coffee break followed. Time for questions.

"I take what you say about the need for more aid, debt relief and trade justice," said an elderly man on the front row, "but surely the problem in many of these countries is corruption. Dictators are stacking away millions. What are you doing about that?"

Peter took this one: "Where there is poverty, corruption is more likely to be found. Tackling poverty is also tackling corruption. And corruption exists at more than one level. The really big corruption takes place internationally and is practised largely by transnational corporations. It often involves huge sums of money. And it distorts priorities. This sort of corruption is growing largely as a result of the rapid privatisation of public enterprises. This has been pushed by Western creditors and governments and carried out in such a way as to allow corporations to operate with increased impunity.

"Transnationals, effectively supported by Western governments, are engaging in corruption on a vast scale. Our government is not doing nearly enough to stamp this out. There are very tight controls on aid and debt relief, and there is no case of debt relief funds being misused. But yes, corruption must be stamped out wherever and whenever its exists."

"Surely these countries are poor because people have too many kids," said another. "So, what are you doing about population?"

"What, at my age!" cracked Peter, getting the best laugh of the evening. But Agnes answered this one.

"Where there is poverty, people tend to have large families. I know from Uganda that not all will survive. Most African countries can't afford old-age pensions. So children are seen as an insurance, yes, their pension. The way to reduce population growth is to beat poverty. In fast-growing economies of Asia, population growth has declined markedly. In areas severely affected by HIV/ AIDS, it's under-population that's the problem – notably lack of young people, especially men, to farm the land. It's happening in some coffee-growing areas in Uganda."

"Is not the government behind the Make Poverty History campaign?" was the next question. "Gordon Brown's talking about a new 'Marshall Plan' for the developing world."

"No, not yet. It has still quite a way to go," said Peter. "It's what government ministers are not saying that's significant. On trade issues, for example, the government is stressing free trade, the dropping of barriers to trade. Ministers are not telling us that trade liberalisation in the past ten years has been ruinous for many developing countries, obliging them to open up their markets at a big cost to their farmers and industry. It has ruined livelihoods. So while the government says free trade, we say trade justice.

"In fact just before I came out this evening there was a press release on the web from War on Want, the World Development Movement and Friends of the Earth, commenting on a speech that Gordon Brown is going to make tomorrow about poverty.

"According to WDM's director, the UK government has hijacked the language of development campaigners to hide its promotion of ultra-free market economics, privatisation and deregulation which is serving the interests of transnational corporations. UK government policy, says the WDM, "is a major barrier to the fight against poverty. The government is failing developing countries over international trade. Their current policies make it part of the problem, not the solution."

"Could we get on with what we can do locally?" was the next comment.

"Fine," said Sara, "please do write this down. If you have no pen and paper there's some over here. I have a list of ten things and this is just for starters.

"One, please sign the sheet that's coming round with your name, address and e-mail if you have one. We will then circulate this to everyone here. Put a cross by your name if you don't want your details divulged.

"Second, we all have networks of friends, Please would you network about this like you have never networked before. Make sure that everyone you know is aware of Make Poverty History and its importance.

"Third, hands up those who are wearing a white armband? Hmm . . . only about a third. To the others, buy a band please, there's some on the tables here, and flash it! It can start conversations galore.

"Four, go to www.MAKEPOVERTYHISTORY.org and sign up to support the campaign. The site will tell you about all sorts of things that are going on.

"Five, write to the Prime Minister and urge him to take action on poverty this year. Tell him that words are not enough, that you want action. There's a prepared letter on the Make Poverty History website but it's fresher if you write in your own words. Stress the need for trade justice, not free trade. He doesn't seem to understand this." She didn't play that for laughs. But got a pretty good one.

"Six, write to the Chancellor, tell him to increase aid and write off the unpayable debts of developing countries – this year. "Seven, local campaigning. There's loads of things we can do. Like holding meetings, talking to local groups, staging street theatre, handing out leaflets to shoppers. I'd like to start a small committee to work on these. Do send me your ideas.

"Eight, there's a firm making large Make Poverty History banners, ideal for hanging on churches. Please think of where you could hang one.

"Nine, write to the local paper about the importance of this. I will write a press release on this evening but the more letters it gets the more coverage it will give us.

"And ten, come if you can to some events that are taking place soon. Next Thursday, 3rd February, Nelson Mandela is speaking in Trafalgar Square around lunchtime about Make Poverty History. Should be a fantastic occasion. I'm planning to go. Let's get a party together. In April, from the 10th to 16th, there's going to be a week of action for trade justice. Please put Friday 15th April in your diary. An all-night candle-lit vigil in Westminster is planned, kicking off with a gathering at Westminster Abbey, then moving to Downing Street. We're promised loads of stuff to keep us busy through the night.

"And then an even bigger one, On July 2nd, the Saturday before the G8 meeting, which this year is at Gleneagles in Scotland, there's going to be a big rally and march in Edinburgh. Special trains may be running from London. Or we could hire a coach. Let's all go up there and take our families with us. So do put it in your diary. Any questions?"

Yes, where do you get your drive, your energy, your appeal from? Simon would have liked to ask. What flair, what enthusiasm this woman had. He reflected how, in the 18th century, Methodism's founder John Wesley had been accused by the Church of England of the 'sin of enthusiasm'. Good job Sara wasn't around then, he smiled to himself.

But the audience had a lot to take in and there was silence. "OK, come back later informally if you want to. In the meantime, a committee. The three of us here are prepared to serve, I'd like three more." Two hands eventually went up.

"Thank you. Anyone else?" Silence again.

"Simon, how about you?" A kind of magnetism had swung her round to face him. Should I have used his first name rather than Revd Copplestone, wondered Sara, when I have only just met him? But yes, on occasions like this, people are equal. There are no ranks.

"Well er . . ." Flattered as he was that Sara was asking him, he knew he could not say yes, just because she had asked him. "I am not sure. I do have rather a lot on right at the moment. Can I think about it and let you know?"

"Yes, of course," Sara smiled. That accent! And the way he spoke. So precise.

"Thanks for coming everyone, let's meet again in about a month's time, shall we. I'll circulate a date." So Sara closed the evening. An evening when it was not only the cause under discussion that was advanced.

★ ★ ★

Bloomsbury, January 29

African singing and dancing greeted participants, some six hundred in all, as they arrived at the church for the launch of the church campaign. After finding a seat, Simon went through the impressive list of speakers, Joel Edwards of the Evangelical Alliance, Martin Drewry, Christian Aid, Stephen Rand, Jubilee Debt Campaign, among them.

"Today, we call on our leaders to act to make poverty history," Peter Price, Bishop of Bath and Wells began the meeting by saying to deafening cheers. "Today we call for a new morality. Put the poor first – above all the demands of the world's financial systems and our own self-interest."

Joel Edwards asked people there to remember that Christians should come together to make poverty history because the poor are in God's heart. He said: "It is right for the church to engage in such life-and-death matters as global poverty."

The Chief Secretary to the Treasury, Paul Boateng, addressed the event, speaking of his own childhood in Africa. He warned that the fight to end poverty would demand sacrifice by all, before saying that the world faced failure over the Millennium Development Goals, and the progress being made wasn't remotely good enough.

A Christian Aid worker, Martin Drewry, was in Sri Lanka nine days before the tsunami struck. "If we had known it was coming," he said, "we would have done everything possible to save lives, move people to higher ground, build barriers, whatever. But if we had known it was coming and done nothing, well, how could we have done nothing? We know that poverty is not just coming, it's here, that we have a silent tsunami every week. How can we do nothing?"

"How can we do nothing?" it was a thought constantly going through Simon's mind. As the day went on, the speakers, the questions and the discussions increasingly inspired him. To the point where he made up his mind – he would not only accept the invitation to join Sara's committee, he would go home, tear up the sermon he had prepared for tomorrow and start again – and preach on the need to make poverty history. But first he had to share all this with someone, and there was only person he wanted to share it with: Sara Openshaw.

It was around six when Simon rang the doorbell of 27 Barnlady Road, praying that Sara would answer. Before anyone answered, two small faces appeared in a front downstairs window. Chloe and May. "Who's that?" said one of them. 'I think it's that bald man who takes prayers at school, Mr Copples something, said the other. "Mummy, Daddy, someone at the door."

Bald, I am not bald, a few hairs missing perhaps but not bald, thought Simon, recalling nonetheless the adage that people who overhear conversations about themselves rarely hear anything good.

Mr Copples . . . who on earth . . .? Sara answered the door.

"Simon!" she exclaimed, gobsmacked. "To what do we owe this honour? An official clergy visit at this time? Well don't just stand there. Come in."

Bowled over by the welcome, he tried hard not to look into Sara's eyes, but it wasn't possible. "Keep your mind on why you're here," he told himself.

"No, no, certainly not an official visit," he blurted out. "In fact I have just come from the churches' launch in London of Make Poverty History. It was all so inspiring I wanted to tell you about it, and to say that if you will still have me, I would like to join the committee."

"Of course. But Simon, slow down, you're so excited, you're talking so fast, I can barely understand you. Look, can I get you a glass of wine? Just relax. I'd love to hear about it. Simon, let me introduce you to William – and to Chloe and May, who go to your school."

Bald indeed! It wasn't easy to speak slowly, so enthusiastic was he about the events of the day. Simon tumbled them out, grateful for the wine, even more grateful that Sara was listening to him in the way he had listened to her earlier in the week.

"I am with you, right behind the campaign now," he ended by saying. "Today has convinced me. And count me in for Nelson Mandela next week, please. I shall go home, tear up a sermon I'd prepared and preach on this tomorrow."

"Wow, that's fantastic, Simon! You know I'd like to come and hear you, but we've promised to take the girls to a theme park . . . But as they go to your school, we ought to come more."

"No no, only come if you want to, do not come because you feel you ought to. Do not get a hardening of the oughteries." So precise, but he's got a sense of humour, thought Sara. They laughed. It was a good point at which to leave.

"Heavens, he's posh isn't he?" said William after the door had closed.

"Yes, but I noticed it less this time," Sara responded. "And it's not his fault is it?" They laughed again. Sara had not meant to defend the assistant curate of St. Luke's, but was damned if she was going to hear anything said against him. Feeling elevated that Simon now cared passionately for the cause of ending poverty, part of her also wondered why it was to her door that he had felt the need to come.

4

In the Square

"You expect me now to begin at least every other sermon I preach with a quote from the Apocrypha. And I do not want to disappoint you today." The assistant curate of St. Luke's warmed to his theme the morning after Bloomsbury.

Simon was aware that today was Candlemas in the church calendar – a day when the church remembered the presentation of Christ in the Temple. But the sermon that he had prepared for it was discarded. The message of yesterday, the immediacy of making poverty history, the passion that he now felt for this cause, was too powerful not to use. Preaching on the needs of people was more important than preaching to conform with the Church's calendar. For what was the Church but the body of Christ? he reasoned, and bodies today were starving.

"So from Sirach, also called Ecclesiasticus, chapter 4, verses 3, 4 and 5: 'Do not add to the troubles of the desperate or delay giving to the needy. Do not turn your face away from the poor. Do not avert your eye from the needy.'"

"Yesterday, I went to the launch in London of the Church's arm of the campaign to make poverty history. This unique campaign was launched in the town last Monday. You may have read the news item in the local paper. Agnes over here is one of the organisers. Agnes, thank you for what you're doing.

"I say a unique campaign, because over 130 organisations have come together for this, including the Church of England, Christian Aid and the Mothers' Union, because they believe that it is time for a concerted effort to make poverty history, in a year when substantial progress is possible.

"2005 is unusual," he said and went on to tell the congregation why. "With 30,000 people a day dying from poverty-related disease, the campaign is pressing for changes in trade rules, for debt cancellation, and for more and better aid.

"What struck me at yesterday's meeting was that some 600 people had come from all over the country, ordinary people like me, with little power themselves, but joining together in the hope of influencing the policies of the world's most powerful leaders. The weak trying to shame the strong, coming together to make a difference.

"The Prime Minister has received over 20,000 letters about poverty since the start of this year. They encouraged him to speak about it at the World Economic Forum in Davos last week. But words are not enough. 2005 is a year for action." So Simon shared with the congregation some of the highlights from the previous day.

"Roy Searle of the Baptist Church told the meeting that he had a dream: that in forty years time he would go to a museum with his grandchildren. The museum would tell the history of poverty. It would tell of how Christians joined forces with others in the early part of the 21st century to declare that poverty had gone on long enough, and persuaded those in power to make it history.

"And if we think, 'Good idea, but it would take a miracle' – yes, but miracles begin to happen when we say yes. Weak we may be, but God makes use of the weak of this world – provided that the weak say yes. All through the Bible we see examples of God using the weak. Moses appears to have been an awful speaker. Seems doubtful that the Church of England would have made him a vicar." And Simon got the hoped-for laughter.

"Jesus chose twelve fishermen to be his first disciples, people in a weak position in society. Saint Paul said that God's power is made perfect in weakness. God uses the weak. God turns our weaknesses into his opportunities. Yes, we sang that in a hymn earlier.

"I am asking you now if all of you will say 'yes' to making poverty history this year. I come back to my text for today: 'Do not avert your eye from the needy.'

"What can I do, you might ask? I have a sheet here with ten things we can do. Please take one from me at the door. This special year presents us with unique opportunities, Poverty will not be wiped out in 2005, but the year could be a milestone to that end.

"Said a young Christian from Africa yesterday: 'You are my friends, you are my family. Africa and her people need you. I appeal to you to make poverty history.' Amen."

Simon knew that not everyone would like this. He was hardly looking forward to coffee in the hall after the service. It didn't take long . . .

"Reverend Copplestone," Beryl Candford limped up to him. "I have to say that I found your sermon totally inappropriate for Candlemas. I want spiritual direction, not this social stuff. Why, if it wasn't for my leg, I would have got up and walked out." Simon kept his feelings under tight rein.

"Well Mrs Candford, I am sorry you feel that, but I do have to preach the message that God lays on my heart. And world poverty, a child dying every three seconds, that really is a spiritual matter, you know."

"Bah! Poppycock! Socialist nonsense! People should help themselves the way I have always done. Be self-sufficient," she replied, taking a sip of the Ugandan coffee without a hint of irony. But Beryl turned out to be the only one to criticise.

"Great sermon Simon! You know you really came alive today. I have never heard you preach so passionately. You really care about this, don't you, and it shows," said another. And yet another said something similar. And while most people said nothing, as usual, Simon's handouts were all taken.

"That was good Simon, really good," said Agnes. "Have you a copy? I'd like to give Sara one." Simon could barely hand over a copy fast enough.

"Simon," it was Sara on the phone the following day. "Agnes dropped in a copy of your sermon. Loved what you said and would like to include an extract from it in my press release today. I'm trying to bombard the local paper with stuff so that we get something in every day if we can. Is that OK?"

"Yes, yes of course it is. Thank you." Bewildered, Simon had never seen any sermon of his quoted in the local paper before. He wondered whether he had a ghost of a chance of keeping up with this woman.

"Oh, and Thursday: Nelson Mandela. Most people of course are working; one or two people in London may go straight there. But from here, so far it's just you and me and Jean, a volunteer at the Oxfam shop and long-time anti-apartheid activist who's longing to see Mandela. Just turned eighty, I gather. Could we get a train around 12.00? Meet at the booking office in the station?"

On page 2 of the local paper a headline ran: "Curate urges flock to help make poverty history." Beryl wouldn't like it one little bit, thought Simon, but the piece accurately reflected what he had said. Before Thursday, I have to sort out my mind, he told himself. "I need to have a proper friendship with Sara, one that remembers who she is: married, a mother, and who I am: assistant curate at St. Luke's."

As she left work on 'Mandela in the square day', Sara's thinking was on much the same lines. This slightly balding, rather posh man had somehow broken through her natural defence system. The way he had looked into her eyes when they first met, it could have happened a second ago. There was something intriguing about him, "but I have to remember who is he, his position; who I am, my family."

One month into the campaign and Sara felt that she was keeping her resolution. Every day since the start of the year she had done something to promote Make Poverty History. The local paper did not use all she sent in, but her strategy of sending news releases virtually every day, ringing the paper, getting to know the editor, was all paying off.

This week was a big one. Mandela on Thursday, a meeting of G7 Finance Ministers at the weekend. Supporters had duly been asked to mail Gordon Brown to urge that ministers increase aid and drop the debt.

★ ★ ★

The three for Mandela met at the station, Sara managing an hour or so off, Simon cycling in at the last minute, Jean taking the bus and getting there early. Sara was wearing trousers with a fetching coat, making Simon's heart miss a beat. As for Simon, no clerical collar was in evidence.

On the train into London they munched sandwiches and talked about the campaign. Jean was keen to switch the conversation and tell them how this was a very special occasion for her. How she had spent many hours, years ago, picketing with other members of the Anti-Apartheid Movement outside South Africa House in Trafalgar Square. Now she was going to hear Nelson Mandela speaking in that same square. He was her hero, she couldn't wait to hear his voice booming over the very pavements where she had picketed.

"How things have changed," said Sara, "Once we wouldn't touch South African goods. Now we buy their wine – their fair-trade wine too. We had some on New Year's Eve."

"Yes, I've heard about your parties," said Simon, "I hear they are very good."

"Well, this is the rumour we try to spread," Sara responded, a touch defensively.

Thousands of people were already in the square when they arrived. The three of them found a spot not too far from the platform, and waited. And as such events often do, it started late.

"If you will keep my spot, I am going to make a little pilgrimage to South Africa House, to stand for a moment in the same place where I stood years ago." And with that, Jean left them.

They were alone for the first time. Nervous smiles accompanied a silence that was broken by Simon.

"Sara, can I say, without being patronising I hope, that I was full of admiration for the way you organised the meeting and presented the campaign last week. For all you are doing, the way you are getting press coverage. You have such energy. You are such an inspiration. Agnes calls you superwoman."

"Thank you," she laughed, "but I am not superwoman. I am very disorganised at times. I can be bossy, short-tempered. My job's demanding, I have two lively girls, all apart from Make Poverty History, and I get tired, sometimes very tired, when my energy just seems to leave me. This year, well so much has happened, the adrenaline has flowed like crazy and I've barely had time to feel tired. But, I'm liable to crash out." Why had she been so frank, so open, she asked herself? She barely knew this man, but here she was opening up to him.

If he was surprised at Sara's openness, Simon did not show it. His reply was at a high level of pastoral concern.

"Sara, when you feel that happening, you must take a break. Forget the press releases. Rest. You must not burn yourself out." Concern, real concern. Now it was Sara's turn to look into his eyes and to sense a genuine pulse of that concern.

"Thank you for your concern, yes of course I would. Don't worry about me." Simon wasn't worried about her, but, among his concerns, Sara was rapidly going up his list. It was Sara's turn to switch the conversation.

"I see you're not wearing your clerical collar today. Why's that?"

"Because, well, the collar says something about me that is not me. It might tell people that I am judging them, frowning on them. Which I am not. The collar, it kind of confirms a clerical stereotype, which I want to get away from."

"Well yes, but if I needed help and saw someone wearing a clerical collar, I would go to them. It would tell me there's someone I could speak with."

"Good point and that is precisely why I wear it some of the time. I cannot decide which of the two is more important." They laughed. And as Mandela had still not appeared, Sara put another question.

"Tell me, why are you the assistant curate? On St. Luke's notice board, it lists the vicar and the assistant curate. Who's the curate?"

"Well the vicar is the curate, he has what is called 'the cure', the care, of souls. And I am his assistant. Yes, it is a bit confusing I grant you. It is said that God moves in a mysterious way his wonders to perform, but, I tell you, the Church of England runs him a close second." They laughed again.

"So God's a man then." Sara couldn't resist this one.

"Well, God came to earth as a man, Jesus, yes. This is a central Christian belief. But, above all, God came as a human being. When you have a day or so to spare, let us talk that one through." More laughter. But the body language they enjoyed was beginning to run even deeper than the laughter they shared. Jean came back and, soon after, the man they had come to hear appeared to a tumultuous welcome.

"I am privileged to be here today at the invitation of the campaign to Make Poverty History," began Nelson Mandela. Roars . . .

"As you know, I recently formally announced my retirement from public life and should really not be here." Laughter. "However, as long as poverty, injustice and gross inequality persist in our world, none of us can truly rest. Moreover, the Global Campaign for Action Against Poverty represents such a noble cause that we could not decline the invitation.

"Massive poverty and obscene inequality are such terrible scourges of our times that they have to rank alongside slavery and apartheid as social evils. The campaign for action against poverty can take its place as a public movement alongside the movement to abolish slavery and the international solidarity against apartheid. And I can never thank the people of Britain enough for their support through those days of the struggle against apartheid. Many stood in solidarity with us, just a few yards from this spot." At which Jean leapt into the air like a teenager. Those long years – made it all worthwhile.

"Through your will and passion, you assisted in consigning that evil system forever to history," he went on. "But in this new century, millions of people in the world's poorest countries remain imprisoned, enslaved, and in chains. They are trapped in the prison of poverty. It is time to set them free." Louder roars. "Like slavery and apartheid, poverty is not natural. It is man-made and it can be overcome and eradicated by the actions of human beings." Yes, yes! someone shouted – Sara.

"And overcoming poverty is not a gesture of charity. It is an act of justice. It is the protection of a fundamental human right, the right to dignity and a decent life. While poverty persists, there is no true freedom." A quiet murmur of "hear-hear", "absolutely".

"The steps that are needed from the developed nations are clear. The first is ensuring trade justice. I have said before that trade justice is a truly meaningful way for the developed countries to show commitment to bringing about an end to global poverty. The second is an end to the debt crisis for the poorest countries. The third is to deliver much more aid and make sure it is of the highest quality.

"In 2005, there is a unique opportunity for making an impact. World leaders must now honour their promises to the world's poorest citizens. The G8 leaders, when they meet in Scotland in July, have already promised to focus on the issue of poverty, especially in Africa. I say to all those leaders: do not look the other way; do not hesitate. Recognise that the world is hungry for action, not words. Act with courage and vision." Roars again.

"I am proud to wear the symbol of this global call to action in 2005. This white band is from my country . . . Sometimes it falls upon a generation to be great. You can be that great generation. Let your greatness blossom. Of course the task will not be easy. But not to do this would be a crime against humanity, against which I ask all humanity now to rise up.

"Make poverty history in 2005. Make history in 2005. Then we can all stand with our heads held high. Thank you." The crowd went wild, wild . . .

"Mr Reverend Simon Copplestone. I want to die on this spot!" shouted Jean above the din in the square. "This is the highlight of my life. Nothing, nothing, will ever surpass this. Take me Lord! I command you to fix it, vicar!"

"I will do no such thing, Jean," Simon shouted back, hardly noticing his sudden elevation. "And I am sure the Lord does not want to know either. You heard what the man said: Let your greatness blossom. Yes you, you have got to campaign to make poverty history this year. No matter what age you are, you have as big a part to play as anyone."

Jean threw her arms around him and hugged him for all she was worth. Then hugged Sara. They all hugged each other, then danced around in a tight circle like the demented witches from Macbeth.

So moving was it all that as they made their way from the square, Sara was hardly aware that she had hugged Simon. As for Simon, he just felt happy. And Jean was still high above the clouds. It was too much for Jean and on the train home she was asleep within minutes.

"Isn't she great? I hope I'm like that when I'm eighty-one," Simon said with a smile, which Sara returned.

"Simon, in the square you thanked me for the way I presented the campaign last week, for what I'm doing. Well I want to say how I liked what you said to Jean. You made her feel so important, it was fantastic." Simon glowed.

"Is that the secret of your success?" she went on. Sara had no intention of giving the game away, telling him how he had made her feel important just by looking into her eyes. She knew the compliment hid the reality: that she was falling for this man. Superwoman? Never. Weak woman, stupid woman more like, she thought. Undecided whether to feel bad or enjoy it, Sara just had a dreadful feeling that Simon was reading her like a book. And an awful hope that he felt the same.

"Well I don't know about success, I don't have much success to report." They laughed, Jean woke up.

"What a day! Thank you Sara for organising this," said Jean at the station, giving her a parting hug as she headed for the bus. Sara and Simon cycled together for a while, before taking different routes, Sara with a parting "will be in touch after G7 Finance Ministers meet this weekend. Let's hope there's some progress. And the committee meeting – I'll ring to fix a date," Do it soon, he thought.

Sne and Mbali had got her into this, thought Sara, had driven her into action. But she had a feeling that the continuing drive would come from someone that she had only recently met.

5

Spilling Beans

The headline was encouraging. "G7 Finance Ministers open door to 100% debt relief," began a Christian Aid press release on the internet. Sara's heart leapt. Great. They're listening. The campaign's working.

"Last week the G7 Finance Ministers agreed for the first time to the principle of 100% debt cancellation for the world's poorest countries. This is good news. But what are the chances of them actually delivering?" it went on.

"Gordon Brown put on a brave face, describing the meeting as an 'historic breakthrough'. He hopes the meeting will be remembered as the '100% debt-relief summit.' But there's a lot of work ahead to translate these fine words into action."

Yes . . . keep your feet on the ground, Sara, there's still a helluva lot to do. Peter rang.

"Sara, there's something on the Treasury website you ought to see. It's a speech the Chancellor of Exchequer made last Friday – the opening day of the G7 meeting mark you – to a conference called Advancing Enterprise 2005. And you're not going to like it any more than I do."

"Over the last year I've made it my business to meet as many businesses as possible," the Chancellor had said. "You've told me about the importance of removing all barriers to an enterprise culture . . . we are prepared to remove any unacceptable barrier, legislate any necessary reforms and introduce far-reaching new incentives."

"Regulation," he had gone on, "[is] a problem raised in every industrial country for many years . . . for all businesses large and small we have removed or reformed over 400 separate regulations . . . we will continue to remove barriers . . . putting every new and existing regulation through strict new tests for their impact on enterprise and competitiveness . . . I want to consult at every stage with you, the businesses of Europe."

This just shows who's running the show, thought Sara. It's all about removing regulations rather than regulating transnational corporations to protect the developing countries that Brown says he cares about. And there was something on free trade . . .

"Britain was the pioneer of free and open trade . . . [hell, that's a half-truth, she thought. He didn't say we protected like mad when it suited us and still do]. Now to take advantage of the vast opportunities global markets offer we must lead the way again in breaking down international barriers to trade and commerce."

So it's more free trade, she thought, more of the same. Brown does not get it. He's just not into joined-up thinking. Livid, boiling, she rang Peter to thank him, and to let off the steam coming out of her head. Yet another press release was dashed off, this one denouncing the double-standards of the government. Then a phone call to Simon, Agnes, again to Peter and to the others who had agreed to be on the committee.

"Look I want to suggest an early meeting. We have a lot to do." They met on Friday that week. Friday was Simon's day off, but he cared little about that. He wanted not just to get stuck into the campaign, about which he'd had some new thoughts, but simply to be with Sara again, to see if he could unravel mysteries, to make some sense of what was happening.

After a report back from the Mandela meeting, from the church's launch, and a discussion of the G7 and what the committee believed was Brown's duplicity, Sara was in full flow.

"We need to organise. I've identified five different areas and I wonder if we could take one each. First, we need someone who can co-ordinate work on persuading those in authority to change policies which hurt the poor – sending e-mails, letters and and so on. Secondly, one of us should concentrate on raising awareness of the issues. I would love to take that because it covers press work."

"You got it," said Agnes, to unanimous nods.

"Thank you. I'm planning to write punchy articles on the issues as well as press releases and letters to the editor. Third, someone to encourage people to get to know more about the issues. There's a lot of goodwill for this cause, but there's a need for more information, for people to know more. Fourthly, can someone volunteer to encourage people to use their purchasing power to buy goods which help the poor? Surprise, surprise, I am thinking of fairtrade goods."

For Sara was into fairtrade products in a big way. Originally it was just coffee, tea and bananas. More recently, fairtrade mangoes, sugar, fruit juice, honey, chocolate, biscuits and wine were on her shopping list. And she was also buying fairtrade clothes.

"While sales of these are small at the moment, they're a symbol of what the world trading system could become – a system based on fairness, a good return for all who produce them," she went on.

"Fifth, I see more and more warnings that the way we live is hurting the poor. That the way we use energy is contributing to climate change, which is making the world a harsher place for the poor. So one of us needs to encourage people – OK I'm thinking big – to change the way they live, yes, to challenge ourselves. Save energy, save a life, let's say. Simon could this be your thing?"

"Well yes, except there is something else I've been thinking of," he responded. "Many, if not most of the people who came to the meeting last week and signed the sheet are from the churches. And for Christians the starting point of any activity is prayer.

So what I would like to do is to start and lead a prayer group. You might think that is not action, but I assure you that it can lead people to action, action in surprising ways."

"OK, fine, so that's six areas, one each. Brilliant. Let's see who does what . . ."

And a press release of the meeting was afterwards soon on its way. As for Simon, he felt pleased that he had got onto prayer and away from fixation with Sara. He rang her the following day.

"Sara, I have been thinking. I would like our church council to hear more about Make Poverty History and to give the campaign its formal support. I could speak about it, but there is something in the Bible about a prophet not being without honour except in his home country – not that I claim to be a prophet you under-stand – and I think it would be better if someone like you came and told them about it. What do you think?"

Talk to the church council? Sara felt her heart sink. She knew she could not say no, but the prospect filled her with some alarm.

"Simon, it's kind of you to ask me but I don't know if I'm up to things like this yet. That meeting we had last month, everyone who came was interested. They were there because they wanted to know more. That might not be so with your council. They might ask me questions that I can't answer."

"I understand, but bring Peter if you wish and I will invite Agnes too. Our council is made up of all kinds of people. Some of them care deeply about spiritual matters, some social issues, some finance, some administration, some everything. You will be fine. Between us, we can answer the questions, I am sure."

"Is your council like the Vicar of Dibley one?"

"Well the group in Dibley is a parish council. We are an elected church council – although the last time there was an election, well I gather that J. F. Kennedy was in the White House. Our council can be ten times worse than Dibley's and it's meetings are always fifty times longer. How I envy their crisp meetings!"

"What's the date Simon? I can't say no." The date was in late February. The venue was a side chapel in the church, barely fur-nished, but with some curtains that were to come in useful.

When Sara and Peter walked in, it was to be greeted by a dozen or so people sat around in a neat circle. Simon had suggested that Sara bring in some humour near the start of her talk. So she began by holding up her arm with the Make Poverty History wristband.

"You may have seen these. In fact I see that one or two of you are wearing one. They're a symbol of the campaign to Make Poverty History, and I've found they start all sorts of conversations. I was standing in a queue the other day and a young woman next to me said: 'Do you mind me asking where you bought your wristband?' 'From the Oxfam shop,' I said, 'and you can buy them on-line.' 'Do you realise,' she said, 'that those armbands have become a fashion statement?' So for the first time in my life I am making a fashion statement! Well, fashions come and go; it's time for poverty to go."

It broke the ice, it removed the nerves. Sara was on her way, confidently, clearly, avoiding jargon, not talking down to them nor assuming they knew too much. She held their attention. Simon felt proud.

"You'll take questions, will you?" asked the chairman when Sara finished.

"I will try to answer questions," she smiled, "I cannot guarantee it."

"Yes, David," said the chair.

"Well this question is really for Simon. I hear what Sara has said, and I thank her for putting it so powerfully. But Jesus said the poor you will always have with you, It's in Matthew's gospel, chapter 26 verse 11. I'd like you to respond if you would Simon." Simon had expected this one. And was ready.

"Matthew records that Jesus said the poor you will always have with you. We cannot of course be absolutely sure that Jesus said precisely these words because Matthew wrote his gospel many years after Jesus lived. But let's take them as gospel – no pun intended. What Jesus did not add was – 'and that's the way it should be.' Not at all.

"His whole life shows concern for the poor: 'I was hungry and you gave me something to eat'; 'I have come that you might have

life and have it more abundantly.' Just two of the things he said.
God cares for us, body and soul. Look at the concern of the early
Christians for the poor, so much concern that we read in the Acts
of the Apostles that there were no needy persons among them.

"So maybe Jesus was reminding us that the reason there are
poor in God's abundant creation is because of human sin and self-
centredness – because we fail to love as we should. Because we do
not share." Simon paused.

"I am quite certain," he said, looking slowly and purposefully
around, at every person in the room, "that God did not take the form
of a human body in Jesus if he wanted to see that body starve."

Another pause. Those were his key words and Simon waited
for them to be grasped.

"There will always be the relatively poor," he went on more
lightly. "I will always be relatively poor compared with, say,
Richard Branson. What Make Poverty History is about is ending
the degrading poverty that traps 800 million people, that kills so
many children."

Sara lapped up the ensuing silence. What an answer, she thought,
what an entrancing answer. He had taken the bull by the horns,
even earned some smiles with the Branson remark, and had shut
them up on that one. More questions: corruption, population –
are you being fair to that nice Mr Brown? It was becoming
predictable.

"Sara, Peter, thank you for coming," said the chairman when
the questions had ended. Peter got up with apologies to say sorry,
he had to leave for another meeting.

"Sara, before I close the evening," the chairman went on, "is
there anything else you would like to say?"

"Yes, I'm falling in love with your cu . . . er, em, er, em curtains. Your . . . curtains. I just love your er . . . curtains. I mean,
if you ever sell them on e-Bay, I'm bidding!" Floundering, crazy,
in a hole, she dug even deeper. "And your building, I just love
these old buildings. If you ever sell it, er no . . ." She recovered,
slightly: "What I mean is, well er . . . it shows off the Make
Poverty History banner so well."

"Well how very kind of you Sara, how very kind," responded the chairman, bewildered. "Those curtains, yes I suppose they are quite nice. As for the building, well most of us think it's hideous. Perhaps that's the secret – cover it with banners." Laughter. Final prayers.

Sara looked for a trapdoor in the floor, certain there had to be one. Eyes not meeting anyone's, she was aware of Simon talking to her hair, with: "Can I offer you a coffee before you cycle home, Sara? The curacy house is not far."

I just want to get out of here and run, pedal, helicopter, anything, she thought. "Surely they've all rumbled." Why then did she hear herself saying "coffee would be lovely, thank you"?

A large glass of fairtrade wine, any wine, would be better, she thought, but, pending an instant escape, coffee would help.

"Afraid the house is a bit of a mess. Sorry, let's go in here." Simon ushered her into his study, picking up papers scattered all over the floor.

"OK – coffee, tea, something stronger perhaps?"

"I could murder a glass of wine," she said. Courage was returning.

"No problem, red or white?"

Don't mind as long as it's fairtrade, she wanted to say. But this was not the time for point scoring, certainly not after her own gigantic own-goal.

"White please." While Simon went out for the wine, Sara looked at his many books. Most struck her as thick and worthy tomes, but a rather different title caught her eye: *The Joy of Sex: A Gourmet Guide To Lovemaking*, by Alex Comfort. Interesting, she thought. Unmarried curate and all that. Wonder how often he reads that. Wonder how often he . . .

"I've poured you a large one, Sara. I have a feeling you need it."

"Thank you." Large one it may have been, but a good half promptly disappeared down Sara's throat.

"Oh God, er sorry, that's better. You know, talking to your committee was great, but it really took it out of me. I feel drained, absolutely whacked."

"I can understand that. Speaking to groups is like preaching, it's more demanding than a lot of people realise." Silence.

Simon picked up: "People on the committee were impressed by what you said, Sara, and must have been touched by the way you liked our curtains. The e-Bay bit baffled some of them though. I overheard someone saying at the end: 'Why should we sell our curtains at Herne Bay'. And your kind comments on our building. We don't get many of those."

No, but neither are many like you, she thought. He must have rumbled me. I should have gone straight home. Before she could reply, Simon followed on with a more direct: "Indeed, I almost wondered if you were about to say something else."

Sara drained the glass. He's well aware of what I was going to say, she thought.

"Sorry, I just wasn't thinking straight," at last she found her voice. "Does it ever happen to you, your mind kind of . . . well, disappears and you find yourself on the brink of saying something, you know, stupid. I'll check in at surgery tomorrow for a mind transplant."

Simon's laughter hid what he was thinking, that Sara had not so much almost given the game away, but blown both of them up, as well as undoing the work she was doing to promote the Make Poverty History campaign. Was she really about to add – curate? Was she serious? That was mind-boggling. Even if it was only a reflection of what he was feeling.

"Better go, got to prepare the girls' lunches for tomorrow before I go to bed. Thanks for the wine, it was great."

"My cat's missing," he said, opening the door. Simon wondered if he could risk a goodnight kiss on the cheek. It seemed safer not to. He couldn't guarantee he could stop at her cheek. The look into each other's eyes at the door was the kiss.

"How could I have come so close to saying that? You fool, you idiot! Why didn't I just announce it on prime time television?" she thought, wobbling back home. She swerved and nearly ran over a cat. "Get a grip. God, was that his cat?"

* * *

"Sara," it was Agnes at the door, not long after a still shaken nurse had returned from the surgery the lunchtime after the evening before. "What's going on? I know what you were about to say last night. What are you playing at?"

Agnes isn't the kind of person to condemn or judge, thought Sara. She's a good friend, I have to tell her.

"In confidence, and I really do mean in confidence. I just feel there's some chemistry. I feel something for Simon, and I think he feels . . . well, that we kind of reflect what each of us is thinking. And for a second last night my discreet mind – don't laugh – left me. Perhaps it was being in a church that made me want to be honest, I don't know. I nearly said what I was honestly thinking: that I am falling for this guy. OK , I then went to the very dishonest. Oh God . . . those curtains!"

"So let's get this straight. You honestly believe that Simon feels the same?"

"Yes. If the body language could talk. . . .yes, I think he might feel the same."

"Sara do you realise what you are saying?" Agnes was speaking quietly and trying to stay calm. "Simon is young, still a weeny bit immature, but with good prospects. You are married with two children and you're allowing yourself to fall for someone like Simon. You do realise that you're playing with fire? And that someone could get very badly hurt?"

"Agnes, I know, I know. I did not choose this to happen. It just happened. I can't explain why it happened. I am sorry, I really am."

"Have you told William?"

"No, but then I hardly saw him last night. I got back late – Simon invited me for a drink after the meeting. And William was off to work early this morning. In any case, you know what William's like. He's so laid back, if he fell off a log he wouldn't notice. I could have an affair with the Sultan of . . . wherever, and William would barely get off his ball bearings.

"He would be devastated if I left him though. But do you know something Agnes, I love William, it's just the bizarre attraction of opposites I suppose. I have no intention of doing anything to hurt him. What I feel for Simon is different. If it's love, it's somehow in a different category of love. Are you only allowed to love one person? I'm thinking aloud; I just have to work this through."

"Have you discussed it with Simon?"

"No, of course not. And neither has he said anything to me. Agnes, thank you for your concern, but don't worry. I will work this out. Coffee?"

"Thanks. But Sara I want you to promise me that you will not do anything mad, that you will come and talk to me, about anything. And please, please, guard your big mouth."

"Do you think they were onto me last night, members of your council? Must have been."

"Amazingly, I think you largely got away with it, although probably not with Bernard, the vicar. But you may have noticed that the average age of the church council is around seventy. Selling the curtains on e-Bay!" Agnes roared. "That really had them. They must have thought you were an expert in curtains. But Sara, Bernard may be quizzing Simon about it."

"Please can we forget about last night and talk about the campaign?"

And the campaign, they felt, was going well. On reflection, Sara thought there was even a positive side to last night. It had given her the confidence to speak more about the campaign. She decided to contact all the voluntary organisations and schools in town and offer to speak about Make Poverty History.

"We must meet again soon, Agnes – the committee –, and go through what everyone is doing. Look the Africa Commission report is due on 10th March. Our excellent source – Peter – says that he will have the report the day before. Can we meet then?"

She rang Simon about the meeting. But first wanted to know if his cat had turned up last night.

"Yes, he came in soon after you left, looking as though he'd had a fright."

"I'm afraid I think he did," Sara was as sheepish as she sounded. "Some fool of a cyclist nearly ran over him."

"Not you?"

"Sorry, can't you fix him up with a flashing light. I know, an illuminated Make Poverty History band. Er, sorry, bad joke. Look, can you mange a meeting on Thursday, 10th March, the day when the Africa Commission report is due? Peter says he will have it the day before. Good peg for publicity. We must react to it."

Yes, but how do I, how should I, react to you? Simon wondered when the phone was back on the hook after his usual yes to Sara's request. How should we react to each other? She almost gave the game away at the church meeting, she runs over my cat, he thought, she's consistent with every other love in my life: a disaster.

Except she is not a disaster, and neither could she be the love of my life, he told himself, but surely she can be *a* love, surely we can find a way of having a proper relationship, one we can both enjoy, where we show love while recognising that we are out of bounds to each other in a certain way of love. We just have to work this out.

Simon and Bernard met most days of the week. They said weekday services together, planned visiting, decided who was going to take the funerals, who was going to see couples preparing for marriage, and discussed other things that came along.

"Attractive young woman who spoke to us about make poverty history, Simon," said Bernard a day later. "Known her long?"

"Well not really, about a month I suppose. We met when I went to the meeting in town – you remember you handed me some details about it on New Year's Day and asked me to take an interest?" Bernard started all this, after all.

"Yes of course. And you are clearly taking a big interest. I think her children go to our school. She spoke well. But tell me, do you have any idea what she was talking about at the end?"

He's fishing, thought Simon, fishing so much he may as well get his fishing tackle out of the cupboard. "Well er . . . well." I have to tell him, he's no fool. If I can't tell Bernard who can I tell?

"Bernard, time for frank confession. We have worked together on this campaign, Sara and myself, and the fact is that we have become close. Perhaps a little too close. I think that maybe she was expressing that. But it is my fault. I should have seen this coming and avoided the possibility of anything like this. Perhaps I should withdraw from the local Make Poverty History campaign and then I would not see her again." Bernard's reply surprised him, although knowing Bernard as he did, not too much.

"No Simon, that what's you should *not* do. It does not help if you run away from a problem. You care about this campaign and I am delighted you do. You care a little more than you should do for Sara and yes, you do have to sort this out. But don't run. Where would we be now if Christians down the ages had run away from difficulties instead of facing up to them? And then turned them around into something positive. I am sure there is a positive way of working with Sara – you have to find it. And you know, I believe you do have a unique contribution to make to the campaign; you showed that at the meeting."

At which Simon not only breathed a deep sigh of relief, he resisted the urge to do what he badly wanted to do: hug the boss.

6

Four Going on Five

"OK, welcome, everyone, to the meeting. Peter has a copy of the Africa Commission report, which is out tomorrow. We're ahead of the game, thanks Peter. After we've discussed it, and decided how to react, let's look in turn at the different areas of our activity." Sara was in full flow.

"First the good news," said Peter. "You will recall maybe that the Commission was set up to consider the particular problems of Africa. Chaired by Tony Blair, in Africa it's known as the Blair Commission. Bob Geldof's a prominent member.

"The good news is that the report calls for radical changes in the relationship between African countries and rich countries. The condition of the lives of the majority of Africans is intolerable, it stresses, and it urges an improvement in these conditions through a change of policy in favour of the weak. Good.

"On debt, the report commits to 100% debt cancellation for all sub-Saharan African countries. Good. On aid, less good. While the Commission calls for an increase in aid to Africa of US\$ 50 billion per year by 2015, it does not set a timetable as to how to get there. Disappointing."

Peter went on to say how on trade, the Commission explicitly states that liberalisation, free trade, should not be forced on African countries. That countries should be allowed to choose when to open their markets based on their own development and poverty reduction plans. That was good, he said, completely at odds with the UK government's position.

He explained the Commission's call for increased spending on HIV/AIDS and for universal access to free antiretroviral drugs by 2010. "This means a shift away from private sector solutions to free health care for all of Africa's people," he said.

"Now the not-so-good news," Peter went on. "The Commission emphasises good governance, but says nothing about holding the bribe-givers to account, UK companies among them. Indeed UK law exempts UK subsidiaries from prosecution. So we've some work to do on this one.

"There's a glaring, although hardly surprising, omission. The Commission report does not call for new laws to hold transnational companies accountable for their impact on developing countries. It only calls for more adherence to international codes and standards on a voluntary basis. The problem is that none of these codes are legally binding. And the key thing is whether governments of rich countries accept the recommendations the Commission makes. We shall know that in the months ahead."

"So we have a lot to do to convince our government that it must implement the commendations," Sara responded.

"Exactly. I've looked at Christian Aid's reaction to the report. It says that the report represents a major advance on current economic thinking, but that without sweeping changes to current UK government policy, it will be just another piece of paper."

"Thanks Peter, let's decide what we do," said Sara. The committee worked out their strategy. They would encourage supporters, everyone they could, to write to the Prime Minister, urging the government to accept the report's recommendations, and pointing to its weaknesses and the omissions. They would press for more aid and debt relief to be given quickly and without conditions. They would urge the government to look again at its trade policy in the light of the report.

And Sara would, as ever, prepare a press release, and would do it tonight. The local paper would then have it first thing in the morning and might carry the reaction of local campaigners on the very day the report came out.

"OK, let's turn to the six areas of our activity," Sara went on. Not for the first time, Simon felt utter, breathless admiration as this human dynamo pounced.

"Agnes, you're co-ordinating the first area – persuading those in authority to change policies which hurt the poor."

"Yes, I can report that a lot of people have told me that they have sent e-mails and letters by post to Blair and Brown. But we need to do more, a lot more. I am asking people to think wider and to write to the heads of the World Bank, the International Monetary Fund and the World Trade Organization to ask them to look again at their policies as they affect the poor.

"I'm also asking people to urge the government to end its support for the privatisation of water supplies in developing countries. When private companies take over water supplies they expect payment. This may be fine in rich countries. But millions of the poor have no money. Defeating poverty and privatising water are opposites. A system governed by people's ability to pay will not bring water to people who live in poverty. This is free trade ideology gone mad. We should urge the government to stop this nonsense. Water should be a public good, not a private money-spinner."

And Agnes went on to say how she was urging people to press for a tax on international currency speculation, to call for stricter limits on emissions of the gases that cause global warming, and to buy a single share in a transnational corporation involved in developing countries. Also to campaign for an end to trade in armaments, urging the government to abolish subsidies for the armaments Industry, "armed conflicts being a main cause of hunger," she said.

"Thanks, Agnes, for all you're doing, it's fantastic. Raising awareness of the issues, that's me. OK, in addition to press work,

I've spoken to the council of St. Luke's church . . ." Simon and Agnes kept their heads firmly down . . . "and I have written to all the local organisations to offer them a speaker on the issues. I've had a few requests already and I'd like to draw up a speakers list, so it's not always me. I'm talking with a local theatre group about organising some street theatre, to dramatise our message. I'd like to devise a Make Poverty History exhibition and ask the schools and library to take it for a while. I am also looking at the idea of a rich world–poor world meal, a march between the churches, a multicultural carnival . . ." And so she went on, the ideas pouring out.

"Oh, and please everyone, do persuade as many people as you can to come to London on the evening of Friday 15th April for the all-night trade justice event. Should be fun."

"Encouraging people to get to know more about the issues, that's you again, Peter."

"Yes, I am trying to encourage people to read more about development, to read the newspapers of developing countries, for example, which are readily accessible on-line. Also to join agencies such as the WDM and War on Want, and also to make friends with someone of another race."

"Nicki, you're encouraging people to use their purchasing power to buy goods which help the poor. How's it going?" This time Sara asked the question rather less buoyantly. She knew that she was beginning to flag, badly flag.

"Fantastic," said Nicki, who had volunteered at the initial meeting to be on the committee, "though I'm only just becoming aware myself of the enormous range of fairtrade goods. I am trying to explain to everyone I meet that when they buy a fairtrade product they're helping someone to edge out of poverty. I'm now trying to persuade shops in the town to stock more of these goods."

"Thanks Nicki. Over to you Howard." Howard, the other volunteer, a teenager on an environment course, had taken on the task of trying to persuade others to change the way they live to save energy and cut down their carbon emissions.

"Well for a start I am trying to encourage people to leave the car in the garage and to cycle, walk or use public transport," said Howard. "For long journeys, to take the train not the plane or the car, or to join a car club, or think of buying a hybrid vehicle that uses less fuel. I am suggesting they calculate their food miles, working out how far their food has travelled, to shop locally and buy local produce when they can. Also to use less energy in their homes. And there's loads of things people can do here. Like turning down the thermostat a degree or two, switching off electrical devices completely when they've finished using them, not leaving them on standby, buying household devices which are energy efficient, using low-energy light bulbs, installing loft insulation. And not filling their kettle to the brim but boiling only the amount of water they need."

Sara rarely felt outdone in the activity stakes, but at that moment she felt that Howard was leaving her standing. But at that moment, Sara had a headache, a bad headache of the kind she rarely had. It was a headache that told her something was wrong. What was wrong was that she felt utterly drained.

"Thanks Howard, that's great," she managed. "Simon, how's the prayer group?"

Simon had done little about a prayer group – so much had been going on, he comforted himself. And now he felt concerned about Sara who had slumped in her chair looking dreadful. And it took a lot for Sara to look dreadful, he thought.

"Well not much I'm afraid, but there's a Churches Together meeting next week and I will ask for someone from each church to join me in a group . . ." he tailed off.

"Sara–" Sara wasn't so much falling asleep, as on the point of collapse.

"Sara, what's wrong?" Agnes leapt out of her seat. The human dynamo was flat. Sara keeled out of the chair and hit the floor.

"She's done too much, the idiot. I've seen her like this once before. She's absolutely exhausted. Quick help me to get her downstairs. I'll take her home." Agnes's urgency compelled action from the others. As they trundled her downstairs, the little hair that Simon had stood on its end with alarm and concern. At least he managed a weak "Look, I'll do the press release. Leave that to me."

★   ★   ★

Simon wrote the press release next morning. And rewrote it, and rewrote it. He didn't seem able to match Sara's crisp style, her succinct way of putting things. But as the clock spun round to the 10.00 a.m. deadline for the local paper, an evening paper printed by 2.00 p.m. in order to get out to surrounding areas, Simon pressed the "send" button and hoped for the best. And he was desperately worried about that woman with the crisp style.

As for Sara, she slept, and slept. It was close to noon before she came round to see William sitting there.

"Welcome back, love. You know you have really overdone it this time. Last night Agnes was frantic with worry about you, and that posh curate fellow who came with her looked as if he'd seen a ghost. Anyway Agnes insisted that I take the day off, take the girls to school and look after you. You must never get like this again. How do you feel?"

"Awful, but better than I did last night. Hell, is that the time? Did you ring the practice?"

"Yes, of course I did. Forget about work. The practice manager gave strict instructions that you are to rest. And one of the team is coming over later to check you out. You've a nasty bump on your head where you fell. And they say that on no account are you to appear again at the practice for a week. Are—you—receiving—me? A week."

"A week? I can't do *nothing* for a week!"

"You *will* do nothing for a week. You will stay here and rest. I have to go to work on Monday so I will arrange lifts for the girls and ask friends to come round and see you." William was unusually active.

"Lifts for the girls, yes, but leave inviting friends for me, would you? Some of my friends can be hard work. They wouldn't be much of a rest. Look, would you ring Agnes, Simon, Peter and the others? They'll be worried."

Agnes had been ringing on the hour, every hour, William informed her. He duly rang around. The Friday evening paper arrived.

"Where's our story?" wondered Sara, having picked up very faintly that Simon was doing the press release. She searched and searched – until finally she found a small item at the bottom of page twenty-two, nowhere near the length they usually had. Just a few nondescript paragraphs in between the car ads and the "Would Like to Meet" column. Something's gone wrong here, she thought.

A weekend doing nothing, well, not exactly. It was beginning to worry Sara that the campaign was keeping her so busy that she was neglecting the children. She was not spending as much time with them, not listening to them as she used to, and the thoughts going round and round in her head about Simon didn't help. This weekend there would be no campaigning, no organising, this weekend was family.

"Mummy, these Make Poverty History meetings and things you go to. Can I come to them?" Chloe was confirming what Sara was thinking. She was neglecting them.

"Sweetheart, of course you can. Some of them you'd find boring, mind. But tell you what . . . get me a sheet or two of A4 paper would you and let's plan something for people your age."

"Cool." It was Chloe's favourite word, "May, are you there? Get me a couple of sheets of A4 paper would you?" Bossy madam, wonder who she gets that from, wondered Sara. No campaigning, but here she was stretched out on the lounge floor, planning something else. But planning it with the girls. Good.

"Tell you what. The second week in April is going to be something called Trade Justice Week. We want poor people to get a better deal from the world trade system, you know what that is, people in different countries exchanging goods with each other. The trouble is that at the moment, poor people don't get a fair deal from the system. They don't get paid very much and the rules are unfair to them. And we want our government and other governments of rich countries to put that right. So, some of us are going to London on the Friday that week, for an all-night vigil, around Westminster, Downing Street . . ."

"Oh, cool, can we come, please Mummy?"

"No darling, not to that. Neither of you could stay awake all night, and then you would need carrying. And in any case you've both got swimming next morning and you know you wouldn't want to miss that. But what we need is something local . . . here in town . . . let's think . . ."

And together they worked something out. They would ask the Make Poverty History committee to agree to a march between all the prominent places in town – the churches, the town hall, the fire station, the library . . . They would stop at each place and use a loudhailer to tell people what they were doing, and hand out leaflets about trade justice as they walked along. And everyone could come, whatever their age. They would do it on Saturday April 9th, on the eve of Trade Justice Week, in four weeks time. That would give time to plan the details . . . get press coverage . . .

"Here we go again," thought Sara, "I'm supposed to be having a rest." But planning with the girls, involving people like them . . . this is what it's all about. And it's people their age who are so cruelly dying of hunger.

* * *

Simon couldn't find anything about the meeting in the paper either. But then the editor had rung him and told him he couldn't understand half of what he'd written, that all those long words he'd used may have been fine in a theological essay but were useless for the local rag. A sub-editor would now have to rewrite it from scratch and see if he could salvage something, he was told. But, finally, Simon found it, right next to a "Man, early 30s, WLTM leggy, busty blonde for companionship only" advert in the "Would Like to Meet" column.

Sara's going to kill me for this, he thought, what a mess. Ah well, at least it's something, better than nothing. William's call came as a relief.

"I'd like to call soon," responded Simon.

"Yes, but leave it till after the weekend. She needs to rest." Simon rang mid-morning Monday. "Are you OK? Can I come round?"

"Yes, of course. Give me fifteen minutes though. I'm not dressed yet." But when Simon rang the doorbell of number 27, she was dressed and looking, he thought, not merely better than she did last week, but simply beautiful.

"An official clergy visit, this time is it, Reverend Sir? Visiting the sick in their deepest hour of need," she laughed. "Sorry, can I get you anything, tea, coffee . . ." She decided to leave out the "me". This was a clergy visit.

"Sit down and let me do it. William says you are supposed to rest and I agree. I can find the percolator, the tap, just tell me where the coffee and the mugs are."

So it was Simon who made the coffee while Sara put her feet up, looking down the garden at the emerging spring flowers, enjoying Beethoven's 9th symphony as a CD played quietly in the corner, with the familiar "Ode to Joy" bursting through. This is joy, she thought, this lovely man serving me coffee in my own home.

"This is great coffee," he said, "fairtrade of course?"

"Yes, and more. It's Machu Picchu from Peru. It's not only fairtrade, it's organic too."

"Must get some. Anyway, how are you?"

"Oh, I'm OK, a bit weak. I guess I just overdid it. You remember I told you at the Mandela meeting that sometimes I get very tired? I got very tired last Thursday. Anyway, I see the paper had a little bit in about the Africa Commission."

"Yes, Hmm. I made a mess of it. Sorry, the editor didn't like my press release. Lucky to get anything in, I suppose."

"Don't worry, at least it was something. I'll give you a lesson in writing a press release sometime . . . I was amused by where they

put it . . . right next to a 'man WLTM leggy, busty blond' ad."
They laughed.

It surely couldn't be him, could it? Sara suddenly thought. No, it couldn't be him advertising for a leggy . . .

"Well it wasn't me, it wasn't my ad," he said, then regretted it.

"Oh, and which was your ad, then?" she teased.

"I didn't have an ad," he said, a touch indignantly. "It's the first time I've seen that column . . . although I must admit it was quite interesting. Some of the things people want . . ."

"Well, there's no reason why you shouldn't have an ad, Simon. You're single, why not advertise – if you want someone that is, or are you happy single?"

How did I get into this? he wondered. How do I get out of it? The only woman he wanted was sitting in the room with him.

"Well er, I suppose I am just waiting to see what happens . . . although I do not really think anything is going to happen. The fact is that my love life is a bit of a disaster area."

"Oh really," Sara visibly picked up. "Oh do tell me more." But she never thought he would respond. She fully expected the reply.

"No, I am not telling you more, definitely not."

But Sara thought it was worth pushing. "Oh go on Simon, it's boring sitting here resting. Tell me about it . . . and don't leave out the spicy bits." Where Sara led, Simon, lamb-like, was sure to follow. He wanted to tell her.

"In strict confidence. On patient confidentiality terms?" he said.

"You have my word," she responded, surprised that Simon was willing to talk about it. Taking her legs of the floor and tucking them underneath her on the chair, and wrapping her hands around the coffee mug, she thought: "Patient confidentiality terms, yes, of course, but I'm going to enjoy this."

And so Simon told her about his love life. How there had been four in all. How first he had gone head over heels for Jocelyn, a women almost twice his age, who wore the most gorgeous clothes but who said little about where the money came from to pay for them. Give or take a fancy name or two, she turned out to be the madam of a London brothel. While this was back in his marketing days, Simon couldn't see there was any future in it.

Soon after came totally different Jenny. Sweet but cold. Simon dated her for two months without so much as a kiss, but he lived in hope. Then Jenny revealed her secret. "The fact is Simon, I'm gay. I've lived with Violet for years and we decided as an experiment to each date a man for two months to see if we are bisexual. Violet has found she is, and has moved in with him. I'll never forgive her, how could she! Simon, you're a nice guy but I can't bear you touching me, and I dread the very idea of you kissing me."

"Well thank you Jenny and goodbye, I thought," he said. "Shame I didn't get Violet!"

Then came Anita, a dreamy young woman, prone to fantasies. The extent of the fantasies was revealed when Simon read in the local paper that Anita had been arrested for trying to rob a bank with a gun that turned out to be a toy one. While the staff and most of the customers had stood there terrified, a young boy said to his dad that he had a gun "just like that one". Rumbled and panic-stricken, Anita dropped the 'gun' and fled, soon to be caught by bank staff and marched to a local police station. Accepting that Anita was more unbalanced than criminal, the judge handed out a suspended sentence and sent her for corrective treatment. It had been too much for Simon.

Next, at theological college, came lovely, devout Margaret. And Margaret could have been very suitable, the life partner he was looking for, explained Simon. All went swimmingly for a few months, until Margaret suddenly announced that she had been accepted as a novice in a religious order. She wanted to become a nun. He was devastated and visited the convent a few times, hoping that Margaret would change her mind, or perhaps not make it beyond the novice stage. But Margaret seemed so radiantly happy, it only made him feel worse. To be honest, he said, he wasn't sure that he would ever get over Margaret.

Sara's eyes widened as she listened to this one-man catalogue of disasters. While her eyes were widening, her inside was splitting, splitting with laughter.

"Oh Simon, I know I shouldn't laugh. I'm sorry, but this is priceless. I've not laughed so much since . . . oh, I don't know. I know you shouldn't laugh at someone else's misfortunes . . . sorry . . . but just to clarify this Simon . . ." Sara was positively enjoying this.

"First you fall for a madam, then you find yourself part of a gay experiment, then it's a bank robber, and then you find the woman of your dreams who goes off and becomes a nun . . .

"Oh you may as well laugh, better to laugh than cry. I did not think it was funny at the time, obviously, but yes, I see the funny side now. You know it is rather nice having someone I can talk to about all this who is not a regular at St. Luke's. Funny but I could never confide in a regular – not that I would want to deter you of course."

"Simon you are such a tonic. I feel better already. The assistant curate of St. Luke's has healed me! Away with the crutches . . ."

They sat there, finishing the Machu Picchu, looking down the garden. Four inappropriate women, thought Sara, poor Simon. But then – it hit her. It hit her that he could be falling for *her*, as she was for him. And that she, Sara Openshaw, was next on the list of his inappropriate women. And that she was the most inappropriate of them all, married, happily married, faithful to her husband, out of reach to anyone else . . . What was she doing now but adding to Simon's disasters? And this was not funny. I wonder if it's occurred to him . . .

No, Simon was not thinking that at all. He felt so happy when Sara was near him, he didn't consider the idea that she might be inappropriate.

"Well, I'd better go," he said, reluctantly. "Stay there Sara, I will let myself out." But should he kiss her on the cheek as he left, he wondered? Yes, she's now a friend, he told himself. No, this is a clergy visit . . . but then I give old ladies hugs . . . Yes, because she might be expecting me to; no, because she might pull away and I'd be devastated . . . yes, because . . .

I wish he'd get on with it and kiss me instead of standing there like piffy on a rock bun, thought Sara, a north of England expression for someone hanging about pointlessly, going through her head.

Her earlier thought about disaster areas, Sara put to one side. As Simon went forward to kiss her, her face smilingly moved towards him and her head tilted sideways just enough for a gentle kiss on the cheek.

"Take care," he said.

"I will. Thank you for coming and for sharing with me the way you have." Her eyes looked deep into his. "You have helped me to recover, you've no idea." Sara was back at work the next day.

7

Arrested

Lighter nights and warmer weather, April dawned full of promise. The Make Poverty History campaign was making progress. For campaigners, April offered opportunities to press home the message on trade justice.

The Openshaws had been to St. Luke's on Easter Day. With Christmas Day, it was normally one of the two days in the year they attended. They started cycling together at the weekend. And Sara wondered how spring might influence her relationship with Simon. She had a feeling they needed to talk. Where they stood with each other was unknown territory. They had talked on the phone about the campaign but not met since the morning when Sara was recovering. Both sensed it would be good to keep cool heads.

Simon for his part had started a Make Poverty History prayer group. On April 5th, the Prime Minister took a short ride to Buckingham Palace and asked the Queen for a dissolution of Parliament. There would be an election on May 5th. April would be full of electioneering. Good opportunity, thought Sara, to ask the candidates where they stand on Make Poverty History issues.

The march around town on the eve of Trade Justice Week was well supported. It just happened to be the marriage of Charles and

Camilla that day. But not too many were by their televisions. Starting off at the Roman Catholic church, a hundred or so people of all ages – from a nine-month baby in a pushchair to a ninety-eight-year-old in a wheelchair – went through the town holding banners in the air. "Trade Justice, not free trade" was the most popular.

The loud-hailer turned heads, the marchers handed out leaflets and chanted: "They say free trade, we say fair trade, they say liberalise, we say justice . . ." The Saturday shoppers were given something new to think about. Just what the campaigners wanted.

As they ended the walk, Sara took the loud-hailer and said to the marchers: "Listen, I'd like all the adults here and the older children, sorry girls, to come to London next Friday evening for an all-night vigil for trade justice. Millions of people all over the world are now calling for trade justice, not all of them will be in London next weekend of course, but there will be a candle-lit vigil in Whitehall, near number ten Downing Street, the biggest this country has ever seen. Throughout the night there's an incredible programme of activity, and a dawn procession, just as the sun comes up. So come and be part of making history!"

About twenty or so people were inspired to say "yes, where do we meet?"

"Let's meet at the station at 8.00 in the evening. Would everyone bring a torch or a glow stick? Also a candle in a jam jar to light as part of the vigil. Be prepared for any weather, bring plenty of warm clothes and waterproofs, just in case. Bring your own food and drink, although there will be refreshments available."

They met at the station the following Friday. Sara gave them more instructions. "Please make sure that you follow the instructions given by the stewards. The event has been developed in full co-operation with the police to ensure that everyone has a peaceful and safe night. Make sure you pick up a programme to see what's happening. A lot of different things are going on, so I don't expect we shall all stay together. But can we meet up at 8.00

tomorrow morning at St Martin-in-the Fields church and come home together from there?"

Thousands of campaigners were already milling around Westminster when the group arrived. It turned out that 25,000 people were there in all. Most of Sara's group headed first for Westminster Abbey and the opening event, a programme of songs, readings, guest speakers and the kindling of the vigil light. Sara, Simon, Agnes and Peter managed to squeeze together into a packed church.

Damian Lewis and Adjoa Andoh began by delivering extracts from the Peasants' Revolt of 1381 and the Pan-African Congress of 1945.

From the Peasants' Revolt they heard: "My good people, things cannot go well till everything be made common, and there are neither peasants nor gentlemen, but we shall all be united together, and the lords shall be no greater masters than ourselves. What have we deserved that we should be kept thus enslaved? What reasons can they give to show that they are greater lords than we, save by making us toil and labour, so that they can spend? They are clothed in velvet and soft leather furred with ermine, while we wear coarse cloth; they have their wines, spices and good bread, while we have the drawings of the chaff . . . And it is from our labour that they get the means to maintain their estates . . . who will hear us, or do us justice?"

A short section of the Pan-African Congress came next: "The delegates believe in peace. How could it be otherwise, when for centuries the African peoples have been the victims of violence and slavery?"

And from the Peasants' Revolt again: "We are determined to be free. We are not ashamed to have been an age-long patient people. We continue willingly to sacrifice and strive. But we are unwilling to starve any longer . . . We will fight in every way we can for freedom, democracy and social betterment."

From the Pan-African Congress: "We condemn the monopoly of capital and the rule of private wealth and industry for private profit alone. We welcome economic democracy as the only real democracy."

It was an inspiring start to the night. Sara's feelings of slight discomfort in the imposing and unusual surroundings of Westminster Abbey were far outweighed by the comfort she felt being so close to Simon. It was nearly midnight when Peter whispered: "There's a debate next door at St. Margaret's church – "Is Free Trade Fair?" Begins at midnight, going to be packed. Why don't we get in there quick?" And soon after they got in, the doors were closed. It was packed. The lively debate strengthened their view that free trade is not fair trade.

Then it was over the road to Westminster Central Hall, which again was packed. They heard Radiohead's Thom Yorke perform an acoustic set, which included a previously unheard song from their forthcoming album, as well as an old favourite "No Surprises".

Up Whitehall next for a 2.30 a.m. service at St Martin's-in-the-Fields. Bur first they lit their candles and joined in the all-night candlelit vigil in Whitehall. By the end of the service in St Martin's it was clear that Sara was beginning to flag. But it was almost four o'clock in the morning.

"Sara, you are looking very tired. Remember what happened last month," Simon was speaking quietly but his concern spoke volumes. "Vigil or no vigil, Sara, you need some rest. Look, stretch out on this pew."

So she stretched out, and the others did the same. For nearly an hour, they slept. Sara woke up, no longer tired but buoyant, quite frisky, even if half-asleep. And the three others too were waking up.

"I've slept with the assistant curate of St. Luke's," she yawned, stretching her arms into the air.

"What shall we do with her Simon?" Agnes too was still half-asleep. "Any ideas? I know! How about an assisted package to the Cook Islands, one-way of course?"

"Excellent idea, excellent," said Simon, omitting to add that if an assisted package to the Cook Islands could be found for Sara, he was damn sure he'd soon find one for himself.

"Si-i-i-mon," slowly and mischievously pretending hurt, Sara rested an arm on his shoulder, looking into his eyes. "I thought you were my friend. Don't send me to the . . . Cook Islands."

"Sara, have you been hitting the fairtrade wine? You sound drunk." It was the best throwaway response Simon could think of.

"I am not drunk," Sara playfully patted his face, "how could you? I haven't had a drink all night. But you're right, I suppose. When people are half-awake, maybe they do sound as if they're drunk." And Sara wanted the playful mood to go on.

"Si-i-mon, if you ever had a big shock, a really big shock, would that plum fall out of your mouth and would you speak normally? Do you think you would pronounce Bath properly, Bath, instead of baaaarth," she laughed, not expecting him to take it seriously. He tried not to.

"I don't even like plums. Anyway, I speak King's English."

"Gave you lessons did he? You're older than you look! Which King was this – King James, the one who wrote the old Bible?"

"No Sara, King James did not write the Bible, it was written in his time . . . you know that, stop it!"

"I shall find a one-way package for you Sara, if it kills me," said Agnes. But as for Simon, it was ages since anyone had been so playful with him.

"Break it up you two. Come on, dawn procession to Downing Street now," said Agnes. They moved down Whitehall with thousands of others. It was dawn on a Saturday morning, a time when Whitehall would normally be deserted, and here were 25,000 people. They had forgone a night's sleep to demand trade justice for the poor.

"God, please can those in power listen," Simon prayed as the sun came up. "May the sun rise on a new deal for the poor." On the train home he said that he'd better go and get some sleep, as he had a wedding at 12.30.

"Simon, this is very sudden. And you didn't even invite me! Who's the lucky woman then?" was Sara's crisp response.

"Not my wedding. Who would have me?"

Well I would, you gorgeous balding lump, if things were different . . . she thought, and that definitely remained unspoken.

* * *

"Major parties deserve ASBO for anti-social international policies," Sara read on the web. It was a press release from WDM,
Friends of the Earth and War on Want.

"This sounds good," she thought, and read on. "Anti-poverty
campaigners today served the leaders of the three major political
parties with an international ASBO demanding that they halt their
anti-social behaviour towards the developing world and the environment and that they stop bullying African countries in international trade negotiations."

The groups were accusing the three major parties of not doing
enough to stop rich countries, including the UK, behaving like
the neighbours from hell by forcing free trade and trade liberalisation policies on poor countries. According to the Home Office
the purpose of ASBOs, she read, is to: "target activities which
disrupt the lives of individuals, families or communities." Detailed
examples followed of the UK's anti-social behaviour towards
poor countries, including intimidation and harassment of developing countries in trade negotiations.

Then came the charge of mindless vandalism to developing
country economies. The example was given of Zambia. After
being forced by the IMF and World Bank to slash tariffs, the
Zambian textile industry could not compete with cheap imports
from industrialised countries, and the sector had all but vanished.

The government's support for the WTO's General Agreement
on Trade in Services (GATS) came next. "First and foremost an
instrument for the benefit of business," was how the European
Commission described the GATS. The government was using the
GATS, it was alleged, to bully poor countries into liberalising services such as water supply, if they wanted more aid and debt relief.

Wilful damage to the global environment followed. "The UK
Government has championed the introduction of genetically
modified food in direct opposition to the democratic wishes of
the electorate."

Got to do something on this, Sara thought, this is great campaign stuff. An idea flashed through her head. She rang Agnes,
Simon and Peter and yelled "ASBOs" down the phone at them.

"We've got to do something with ASBOs. Can we meet, like, say, five minutes ago?"

They managed to get together soon. Sara was in full flow.

"I've an idea. That the three of you dress up in large uniforms, costumes, and wear ugly masks. One of you will have 'UK government' on their back, one 'WTO' and another 'World Bank/IMF'. We'll go into the shopping precinct next week, and, in the nicest possible way, pretend to bully people around, very gently of course. We'll say 'you can't go that way, that's barred', 'you can't go in there', 'who do you think you are', we'll say 'stop what you're doing and do it this way'. Then I will come along with a big ASBO sign and slap it on your back, saying that this outfit has been served with an ASBO. Then we'll explain to people that this is what powerful institutions are doing to poor countries. What do you think? It's a bit like . . . what do you call it, a parable, isn't it Simon?"

"Yes, yes, I suppose it is," Simon was feeling as breathless as Sara sounded. "So what happens then?"

"We say to people: 'Under the terms of the ASBO I serve on you, I order you to stop bullying people, especially those who are weaker than you are'; to behave 'or else you'll be in worse trouble'. Then you turn round and show who you are. And we explain to the 'victim' why we're doing it and what he or she can do about it. We'll get some leaflets printed. And so we go on, like that."

"I think it would be best if we don't approach children. Bullying is a serious matter, that of course is the point we want to make. But only adults – right? Let's be clear on that," said Agnes.

"Definitely," said Simon. That was all he could manage, but alarm bells of caution were ringing in his head. So bowled over was he by Sara that articulation proved difficult.

"I am not completely convinced, but, well, it's a light-hearted way of getting the message across," said Peter. "I dunno what Charley will think, mind you. But, yes, let's go for it!"

They went for it. Three hefty, ugly-looking uniforms were stitched together, large ASBO labels were run off, they had a rehearsal. Sara prepared a press release, inviting a reporter and a photographer to come along. And they went for it.

The day they chose was damp, but the spirits of the "UK government", alias Simon, "WTO", alias Agnes, and "World Bank/IMF", Peter, were high as they padded into the shopping precinct in search of people to "bully". So good were the uniforms and masks that the three were totally disguised. Which, thought Simon, was just as well.

"You can't go through there sir, that's not allowed," said Simon to a man preparing to walk through a passage. Simon was doing his best to get into the skin of being the UK government.

"What do you mean, I can't go through there?"

"You can't go through there because I say so. I will tell you the way to go."

"This is mad. What are you talking about?"

"This is what you must do," said Simon. "You go to that bus stop, buy a ticket for £1.50 and the bus will take you to the end of the passage. I know that's only a hundred yards away from where we are now, but that's the way I order you to go."

The man went crimson. Sara appeared.

"Are you being bullied, sir?" she asked the "victim". "You are. Right you, UK government, I am slapping an ASBO on you." Simon turned round to show the man the UK government sign on his back.

"I do hope I didn't frighten you," he said, "but this is what our government is doing to poor countries. Not letting them do things their way. Offering them aid and debt relief on condition they do things the way our government says, bullying them. It deserves an ASBO. So we're doing this as a humorous way of drawing attention to what's going on. We want the government to end its anti-social behaviour towards poor countries."

"Well that's a relief then," said the "victim". "You mean that the government bullies countries like that? That's a disgrace!"

"Write to the government, to Tony Blair, to the election candidates and tell them, will you?" said Sara, handing him a leaflet.

And so the morning went on. ASBOs galore were handed to Simon, Peter and Agnes, and most people took the joke. Most rumbled them and were laughing with them, even before the "bullying" had come to an end. But Peter felt he had to report to Sara that not everyone was seeing it that way; that someone had told him he didn't like it at all, and would ring the police to complain.

The police. The words had barely left Peter's mouth when a police car screeched up, sirens wailing, into the precinct. Jumping out of his car, a policeman demanded of Simon: "What's going on? We've had reports that people in menacing uniforms are bullying frightened shoppers. That's you, isn't it, for one?"

"Oh no, officer, no! I am not really bullying anyone. I am pretending to bully them to make the point that our government is bullying poor countries. My two friends here are doing the same, except they are the WTO and the World Bank/IMF." The constable was distinctly underwhelmed.

"Pretending to bully is bullying in my book sir. And you madam," turning to Sara, "I have heard that you are handing out ASBOs. Who gave you permission to do that? Do you realise that you are impersonating the Home Office? This is serious. All of you, you're under arrest."

"What?" Simon almost dropped his accent. "You can't do this, officer. We are only playing parts. I've done nothing wrong."

"Are you resisting arrest sir? It will only make things worse for you, I warn you. Come on, the lot of you."

"Officer, this is a dreadful mistake. I'm the curate at St. Luke's church."

"Yes, and I'm the King of Cairo. Get in the car." A local reporter and photographer were there to record it all.

"What a story!" yelled the reporter. "Local clergyman held for bullying, resists arrest. Quick, I'll ring the paper, tell them to hold the front page."

★   ★   ★

It took some time, the police station was busy, but Sara was the first to be interviewed.

"You know, madam, we could throw the book at you lot for this. Bullying shoppers, handing out ASBOs, resisting arrest.

Come on, let's hear your side of the story. It had better be good."

"I take the blame for all of this, officer, it was all my idea. The Reverend Copplestone did not mean to resist arrest, I am sure. He was just so shocked. But I was only handing out mock ASBOs to my three friends. And we were making a serious point." And so Sara tried to explain what they were doing, said sorry for not consulting the police about it first, and pleaded that most people really had taken it well.

"And we did not approach children," she went on, "only adults. We had a very firm stance on this."

"Madam. We had at least three complaints about what you were doing and we had to investigate. You do realise, I hope, that bullying is a very serious matter."

"I agree officer, I entirely agree – that's exactly the point we were making. That it is serious, wherever it goes on, and that it's happening not just between people, but between rich and poor countries. And that millions of the poor are suffering as a result."

"Madam, the police are here to police society. We do not get involved in the rights and wrongs of political issues."

Simon was next for an interview, a shivering Simon, minus his costume which had been confiscated at the desk. And he had been waiting ages.

"Reverend Simon Copplestone, oh dear, oh dear! I am sorry we did not recognise you earlier sir – an understandable error if I may say so. But it seems, Mr Copplestone, that we have done those things which we ought not to have done. And that there is no health in us."

As Simon gasped on hearing a perfect rendition of the Church's Prayer Book confession, the officer went on: "I used to sing in your choir when I was a lad, morning and evening, long before you came here. Those words are ingrained in me. Reverend, how on earth did you get involved in this? Shouldn't you be setting an example, sir – a man in your position?"

"Officer, this is my fault and I really am sorry. If I may follow your excellent lead – I do truly and earnestly repent me of my sins, and intend to lead a new life. I am sure Mrs Openshaw will have told you of the purpose behind it. I joined in as I feel the same as she does about it, because I want to shame our government, the WTO etc. to stop their bullying. And most people in the precinct took the point well. Obviously not all."

The four of them were brought out to the desk, and stood, heads bowed.

"All of you seem to want to take the blame for this," they heard the officer bark, "which is a nice change from most of the people we get in here." He went on almost smiling. "It's clear to me that your zeal for the cause you believe in far exceeds your judgement about how to promote it. Think yourselves lucky. I have decided to let you off with a caution this time. But I warn you, if I ever find any of you up to stunts like this again, you will hit the cells so fast . . ."

They blinked out into the sunlight. Silently. Who would speak first? It was Agnes, but only to Peter and Simon.

"Listen, there's a travel agent's just down the road. Let's go in, the three of us, and get down on our knees and beg, plead, grovel, for a one-way ticket to anywhere for a passenger by the name of Mrs Sara Openshaw."

"We will invoke the words of J. F. Kennedy," said Peter. "We will do any thing, pay any price . . ."

"Look, I am sorry I got you into that mess. I really am sorry. What the policeman said was right. Our zeal exceeded our judge-ment. All right Agnes, take that sledgehammer out of your eyes. *My* zeal exceeded *my* judgement. Can you forgive me . . . please?" Sara looked imploringly into their eyes, especially into Simon's. He had to forgive.

"Come on, let's go and have a coffee, we need it," Simon was positive. Over coffee, they held a post-mortem.

"What we should have done was to keep it to street theatre between ourselves. We should not have involved shoppers. Then we wouldn't have offended anyone. We would have made the point without falling into the hands of the local constabulary," Sara's contrition was changing. Now she was smiling. "Well, OK, hindsight is a wonderful thing . . ."

The local paper was delivered to the counter. Sara picked it up.

"Look at this!" she exploded. "It's fantastic. Look at the front page headline: 'Local clergyman held for alleged bullying – resists arrest'. And the picture – you, Simon, being led away by the coppers. And look at the big story. It explains what we were doing. This is great, great!" Sara was jumping, dancing, floating . . . Simon's reaction was rather different.

"What do you mean great? It's all right for you. But what about me? What am I going to tell my congregation? How can I explain this to them. Look at me – being led away like a convict."

"Oh Simon, you'll explain it somehow I'm sure. The point is we got the issue into the paper. This means that thousands, tens of thousands, will see it and read how our government and others are bullying the poor. Never mind that we were arrested, it was all worthwhile folks, all worthwhile."

"Simon, may I have your full permission to strangle this woman? God would surely understand," Agnes said quietly, "Sara, you are utterly incorrigible. Short of strangulation, you should only be let out on licence."

Nods from the others. As they finished their coffee they debated whether to strangle or laugh. Laughter won.

As they went their separate ways. Simon took the view that at least his cat would not see the picture. And he found that going unaccountably through his head was a Laurel and Hardy tune about a nice mess "you've gotten me into." That woman! "And yet everything she does only makes me feel more for her," he told the cat.

Later that evening, recovering after a glass or two of fairtrade wine, Sara went on-line and found good news. Sne and Mbali, the two orphans who had driven her into action on that programme she came within a second of turning off on New Year's Day, they were now at school and had somewhere to live. That one second – it had decided the course of her year, the campaign, meeting Simon.

It was Sne and Mbali who had got her into this – and I wouldn't change a thing, she thought . . . except . . . God, she had been devastated to see Simon marched off like that. How she loved that man. What would he think of her now?

8

Election

A hustings meeting for all the candidates had been organised at election time by the town's churches for years. A church was considered a neutral place for a meeting. Sunday evening, May 1st, was chosen for the hustings for the 2005 General Election a few days later.

While election meetings are generally poorly attended, the all-candidate meeting tended to be the exception, drawing people from the churches and with no church connections. Voters knew it was an opportunity to weigh up the candidates in one go. People could ask about anything. The Make Poverty History committee was determined to get in at least one question about MPH as the campaign had then become known between them. And the campaign was going well. Nationally over 500 groups were now part of it – almost ten times more than the fifty-eight groups that were behind it at the launch. And locally the word was spreading, not least thanks to the ASBO stunt.

So it was a wide cross-section of the public that entered the venue, the Methodist church hall, and were invited to write down a question for consideration. And to sign it with their name. Sara went for trade: "Do the candidates believe in free trade or fair trade?" she wrote down. Not exactly a trap, but close to it.

But as people piled in, and as all the seats were taken and folk began sitting on window ledges, her hopes of getting her question chosen began to sink. While the room was full and the candidates and their agents were milling around, there was no sign of the chairman, the town's mayor. And a good-humoured crowd began to get restless.

"That mayor, he's always late, let's have a collection and buy him a watch!" someone shouted. A mock collection was then held, and the mayor's eventual arrival was greeted with a mixture of jeers and laughter. And that set the tone for the evening. The by-then frisky audience felt free to say what they thought, and to heckle if they so wished.

So the five candidates – Labour, Conservative, LibDem, Green and Independent – answered questions on health, education, crime, the economy, all to some good-natured bantering from the audience. And Sara quietly despaired. Until the chairman suddenly announced: "Would Sara Openshaw now put her question?"

It was the Conservative candidate's turn to go first. He believed, he said, in free trade not fair trade. Free trade would benefit everyone, a world without borders would lead to a world without poverty. Distortions to trade should not be allowed, controls should be abolished.

"So the big corporations can screw who they like can they, no controls!" shouted a heckler.

"The corporations are quite capable of controlling themselves," replied the candidate to a certain amount of raucous laughter. The Labour candidate went next.

"I imagine this question comes from a supporter of Make Poverty History. Now I know that some people have reservations about the government's policy over Iraq [jeers], but I think you must admit that the government has been magnificent on Make Poverty History. The Prime Minister and the Chancellor, what a lead they have given! I know them both well, and I can tell you that both are as committed to your cause as anyone here this evening. They are doing a fantastic job. What vision they have. Indeed I would go so far as to say that when an account of the campaign is written, these two glorious people will be given the highest pride of place. They will be universally recognised as being among the greatest people of our age."

"Pass me the sick bag," moaned someone at the back.

"He hasn't even mentioned trade," said Sara to Agnes sitting alongside her.

"Tells us he knows nothing about trade."

The LibDem candidate was next. She believed in fair trade, free trade and trade justice . . . "and in motherhood and apple pie," continued a heckler. But Sara noticed that she was wearing an MPH armband and had at least some knowledge of the issues.

Then the Green candidate. He believed in only a minimum of trade, because of the environmental cost of transporting goods around the world. But his arguments were badly organised and poorly presented. He ended with a reference to developing countries needing a "leg up".

And that was picked up by the Independent candidate.

"We are here today," he began.

"And gone tomorrow," drawled a heckler. The candidate was thrown.

"Let me start again. At this moment in time, we live in a world where all this giving a leg up to help people stand on their own two feet is bringing our country to its knees. At the end of the day, and in a manner of speaking, I repeat . . . why is everyone laughing?"

"Mr Chairman, could you clarify please," shouted one, "is this a hustings meeting or an early heat of the most cliché-ridden speech competition?"

"Please, let the candidate speak," said the chair.

"Manners maketh man. And man is betrayed by his manners," was the retort.

"Perhaps the questioner would like to say what she supports – free trade or fair trade," said the chair when all the candidates had finished.

"Thank you. I don't think there is such a thing as free trade," Sara responded. "Someone pays, and in practice, it's the poor.

Research shows that trade liberalisation, free trade, has cost countries in sub-Saharan Africa over 270 billion US dollars in the past twenty years. Free trade pits the weak against the strong, the peasant against the corporation. World trade rules need changing if the poor are to have a chance."

Simon, standing at the side as he had helped to organise the meeting, clapped for his first and only time of the evening. He looked far across the busy room at Sara. Their eyes met, they smiled.

"You asked the best question," Simon managed to get a word with her after the meeting. "You exposed how little they know."

"And you're not the slightest bit biased are you?" she laughed.

"Emphatically not!" And five days later, on election day, the Openshaws sat down after their evening meal and considered who to vote for.

Both had torn up their Labour Party membership cards when it became clear that Iraq had no weapons of mass destruction. And that Britain had gone to war on a false prospectus. And while Blair and Brown had said much about MPH, mused Sara, action was yet to be seen.

A WDM briefing on where the three main parties stand on development issues had awarded 6 out of 10 to the LibDems, 4 out of 10 to Labour and 2 out of 10 to the Conservatives.

"A toss up, I'd say, between the LibDems and the Greens," Sara thought out loud. "The LibDem candidate seems OK, but this is a party that has traditionally supported free trade, open markets. Liberal, well the liberalisation of trade, has become a dirty word. They are hardly different from the Conservatives on this. And the Greens, they are the nearest to what I believe in, I guess, but maybe not very distinct from the Tories with their anti-European Unionism."

"And if the Greens won . . ." William responded, "I'm fantasising. As they don't believe in having a leader, who would be Prime Minister? A committee, not a person? Would we be ruled by committee?" And Sara thought that had some attractions.

"Let's walk to the polling booth and decide on the way," said William.

After arranging for a neighbour to look after the girls they took the short walk to the polling booth at the school their girls attended, but still hadn't decided when they arrived.

"I could spoil my ballot paper. Write 'Make Poverty History' on it," said Sara. "But no. I'll vote for the least worst option." William nodded. They talked about other things on the way home.

As for Simon, he was away on POTI, post-ordination training, and as he had not registered for a postal vote, he didn't vote at all.

*   *   *

"World Debt Day is on May 16th. Let's use it to publicise the debt scandal."

The attention of the MPH committee, meeting soon after the election, was on future events and Sara as usual was not short of ideas. "How about if one of us is chained to a railing or to a post in the shopping centre, to symbolise the way that millions the world over are enslaved by foreign debt, effectively chained and bound because of debt? We'll hand out a leaflet to explain what we're doing. I'll do a press release, get a photographer along, get . . ."

"Sara, darling, how long is your memory?" wondered Agnes. "A fraction of a millimetre perhaps? Have you forgotten already the mess you got us into with your ASBO stunt?"

"Yes, but this is different. It would just be one of us chained up. And we would only be handing out leaflets." Silence. Sara felt she owed them something.

"Tell you what," she went on, "I will offer to be the one who's chained up." The mood of the meeting brightened. Sara in chains, what an idea!

"Now you're talking. Thought you'd never offer," Agnes smiled.

"And how about using the event to symbolise the tomatoes that farmers in Africa cannot sell in their local markets because of cheap imports of tomatoes from Europe?" said Peter, suddenly very enthusiastic. "Let's buy some tomatoes that are past their sell-by, going off in other words, and pelt them at our willing volunteer in her chains." An idea greeted with acclaim, although certainly not by Simon. As he struggled for words, Sara beat him to it.

"That's nothing to do with debt, Peter. No. Many things I will do for this cause but I am not standing there in chains with rotten tomatoes dripping all over me."

"No tomatoes, Sara's right," said Simon, at last finding his voice and talking as if Sara could ever be wrong in his view. "And let's learn from last time and tell the police what we are doing. I will do that. It would be best to keep them informed." All agreed.

"OK, let's talk about Edinburgh and the march," said Sara. "This is going to be a great day. And a day to bring families. My girls are coming, let's encourage as many as we can to bring all their families. Should we book a coach or is the train possible?"

A few days before World Debt Day, and the chaining up of the willing volunteer, Sara took a call from Frank Nosten, editor of the local paper.

"Sara, do you think you could drop by my office for a chat sometime in the next day or so? There's something I'd like to talk over with you."

"Er, yes, of course, but . . ."

"When can you come in? Could you manage Friday, one o'clock?"

What could he want to talk about? wondered Sara. Had she made a dreadful error, confused a billion with a million in a press release perhaps. Her relationship with local editor Frank had so far been entirely by e-mail and telephone. They had never met. Why did he want to see her now? The reason amazed her.

Housed in an old Victorian building, the office of the local paper had worn carpets, peeling wallpaper, few staff, but shiny modern computers.

"Good to meet at last Sara, to put a face to the name after all those press releases, stories, letters you've sent," began Frank. "You know, you've given us some good copy. Loved your ASBO stunt. So first of all, I want to say thank you. Coffee?"

Sara felt too nervous to respond with the usual, 'yes as long as it's fairtrade', but one sip was enough to convince her that it certainly wasn't Machu Picchu.

"I expect you're wondering why I asked you to drop by," Frank went on.

"Well, er, yes."

"It's just that I wonder if by any chance you're planning to be at the G8 meeting at Gleneagles in Scotland this July? Will you be going up for it?"

"Well no, not to Gleneagles, not to the summit. We're hiring a coach probably, to take a party to Edinburgh on the Saturday before the summit, for a big Make Poverty History march, to let the leaders know how we feel about this."

"So you will be in Scotland," Frank went on. What is he getting at, what's in his mind? Sara could not make it out.

"But you're coming back the same day?"

"We're coming back the same day Frank, yes."

"That's a pity. You see, I am looking for someone who can report from the summit for us. You're local, you write well, you know the issues, well you've convinced me you do. Sometimes I haven't much idea what you're going on about, and for all I know you haven't either, but what matters to me is that you write as if you know what you're on about," Frank laughed. He assured her that it was meant as a compliment.

While Sara was grappling to understand where this was all leading, Frank went on.

"Sara, I'll spelt it out. And I feel a bit embarrassed about this. We're a small, local paper, we haven't much cash. We can't afford to send a reporter to Gleneagles. We can't even afford to pay the expenses of anyone we ask to go. But if we know someone we trust who happened to be there, we would take a story from them each day and pay them our . . . well, admittedly low rates for the stories."

Sara was reeling. He wanted her to write stories for the paper from the Gleneagles summit. But, but . . .

"But, I will not happen to be there Frank. I'm not a journalist for a start. They would never let me in."

"Sara, we can help you get accredited to cover the summit. No problem there. I've been looking at the G8 media website. You need to download a form to apply for accreditation and send it back with a picture of yourself and with a letter from me, saying that you're covering it for us. I could give that in a moment. And the website says that there will be complimentary buses for the press going to Gleneagles regularly from Edinburgh. Could you stay on for a week? Do you have anyone you could stay with, friends, relatives?"

"Frank, could we step back for a moment. You are asking me to cover the G8 summit for you?" Sara could hardly take in what was going on.

"Exactly."

"I'm gobsmacked. Overwhelmed isn't the word. Flattered that you think I could do it. Honestly, tell me, I wouldn't want to let you down. And don't you have to be a member of a journalists' union or something?"

And Frank assured her that all that business went out long ago, and that they printed stories solely on merit from people of merit. And that he would not have asked her if he didn't think she could do it.

"Are you on? Could you get a week off work?" he asked.

Sara assured him that she could get a week off work and had a cousin in Edinburgh she could ask for a bed. But she was still reeling, and barely hearing Frank as he went on to explain that he wanted copy by e-mail each day, that he would tell her how long before she left, let her know the deadlines etc. That she was to write about what was happening, with some local colour, and not to worry about anything, he would knock it into shape.

"You'll need to take a laptop. There may be terminals there but best to be safe. We can lend you one if you like. And do you take pictures? We pay for pictures too. Again we can lend you a good digital camera so that you can e-mail pictures to us as well. Sara, this is going to be good."

"Frank, you thanked me when I arrived. I want to thank you for trusting in me like this. I will try to prove myself to you."

"You've done that already." Sara wanted to kiss him, fling her arms round him, do something to express how she felt. Her bike for the journey home was barely needed. She could have flown there.

Back home to a deserted house in the early afternoon, she rang William at work. She left a message on his answering machine. She rang Simon, another blasted answering machine. She rang Agnes, and Peter. Answering machines. So she went into the garden – and floated.

But World Debt Day was just three days ahead. Sara knew that she would then be brought down to earth by being chained to a post.

The chains to go round Sara were hired from a locksmith a few miles away in the country. The links were solid and heavy. The locksmith recommended that she did not wear them for more than two hours. They would go round her shoulders, which he would pad, and criss-cross her body without too much discomfort.

Leaflets were carefully prepared on the lines:

You see this person, a local nurse, Sara, chained up. Her chains represent the enslaving nature of the debt burden which traps poor countries and many millions of people.

Debt kills: every day, 30,000 children die because of poverty, while every day, the most impoverished countries are forced to give over £30 million in debt repayments to the rich world. This means they have less money to spend on vital services like healthcare.

People are dying because of debt, because they do not have the money for hospitals and drugs. In the last four years alone, the debt crisis has led to the deaths of more people than the brutal slave trade across the Atlantic claimed over decades.

Debt traps people in poverty, stops them from realising their potential.

Help break the chains of debt! Write to the Chancellor of the Exchequer at the address below and insist that the government cancel the debts of poor countries.

Let people live! Stop this slavery! Drop the chains of debt! SAVE
LIVES, ACT NOW.

World Debt Day happened to fall on a Monday that year. There
were few shoppers around as Agnes, Peter and Simon watched
the locksmith chain Sara to a post. As the chains went round her
body, Simon felt a pang of conscience that he had not offered and
spared her this.

"Tighter, pull the chain tighter, locksmith," urged Peter. "No,
better still, fix the lock and throw away the key."

"Peter, shut up. You didn't volunteer for this." Agnes felt
bound to come to Sara's defence. The lock was fixed on the chain
and the key duly handed to Peter, to Simon's mild irritation as he
wanted it, to make sure it was safe.

The sun came out, and with it more shoppers. Sara felt comfortable enough, the leaflets were handed out, some people stopped
to talk about the issue, and a local policeman could be seen wandering quietly around. A photographer from the paper came to take
pictures.

After an hour or so, Peter's mobile rang and he announced,
"Just got to dash off, won't be long." It was almost an hour before
he came back, wearing a different coat, Simon noticed.

"These chains are beginning to feel uncomfortable. But I guess
the two hours is nearly up," said a relieved Sara.

"Yes, we've made the point, it's been good, and you were
good to do it Sara. You got the key Peter?" asked Agnes.

"The key, oh the key," Peter fumbled in his pockets. "Oh hell,
the key! I've left it in my other coat – it was a bit heavy and I went
home to change it."

"My chains are heavy you idiot. Please Peter, go and get it."

"Well sorry, Sara, but think of how symbolic this is. Your chains
are heavy and because I haven't got the key right now, you've got
to stay chained up for a short time more. But millions have no such
luxury. No one can come along with a key and unlock them from
debt slavery so quickly. So it's good for the cause Sara, don't you
think, good for the cause." Simon could have kicked him.

"Touché, Peter, I deserve it and you're right. But please, go and get the key," said Sara.

Peter left for the key. Agnes went too, explaining that she had to get back to work. Only Simon remained, handing out the leaflets that remained and looking helplessly at the "captive" who was now bereft of her usual sparkle.

"Wish I could swap places with you. I am really sorry I didn't look after the key."

"Just talk to me Simon, I'm fed up, yes. But you know, Peter's right. Where's the key to unlock millions from debt slavery? I suppose finding that key, persuading policy makers to unlock chains, well it's what our campaign is all about."

"Are you all right madam," the policeman had wandered over. "Oh no it's not you again is it sir, I hope you're not making a nuisance of yourself?"

"No officer, no. The key to unlock these chains has been mislaid, it's coming soon." A breathless Peter rushed over with the key and with a "sorry, sorry, so sorry" the lock was turned and the chains fell off.

"I'll get them back to the locksmith," said Peter.

"I'll go home for a bath," said the dishevelled volunteer. She walked back through the town with Simon.

"Are you OK? I'm worried about you. Would you like a cup of tea or something before you go home," he asked.

"Good idea."

Over tea in a nearby café, there was an empathy between them that kept them quiet. But it was an empathy that led Simon to say, "Sara, I think we should talk."

"You're reading my mind, Simon," she smiled. "I agree. Let's talk. About things we need to talk about. Let's do it soon. But when I feel less sticky than I do now."

★　★　★

Four and half months of MPH campaigning had led to far more than Sara had ever imagined. The planning, the press releases, trade justice week, the publicity stunts . . . And now being asked to go to Gleneagles to cover what to her was the year's most important event. To be close to people who make decisions that affect the lives of millions. More had happened than she could have thought possible.

And it was all against a background of falling for a most unsuitable man. Well, any man would be unsuitable for her, with a husband and two children. She had not planned it, it had just happened. How to deal with it was the question, how best to talk about it. What could happen next? What happened next surprised her.

The day after her chaining up for longer than had been expected, Peter rang, an apologetic Peter.

"Sara, you must know how sorry I am for what happened. But I am going to make it up to you big time."

"What do you mean?"

"Can't talk on the phone. Can you come round quite late one evening, say Friday, when Charley's home?" Friday, round about dusk, she wheeled her bike up Charley and Peter's path, a glass of wine was pushed into her hand as the door opened, and Peter summoned her into the garden. Senior civil servant Charley was sitting on a bench at the end of their long garden.

"Hello Sara," she said, as they kissed on cheeks, "how are you? It's been a while. Why don't you sit here? I want to talk off-the-record, very strictly off-the-record, if you ever ascribe to me a word of what I am going to tell you, I will deny I ever said it. Understood?"

"Understood Charley, understood. Can I ask though, why are we talking out here? It's getting dark and cold. Why out here?"

"Because, my sweet, innocent Sara, for all I know the house is bugged. Take that startled look off your face. With modern technology, bugging may be a lot more widespread than you think. And I would not be at all surprised if my employers, dear old HMG, are not keeping tabs on the private doings of its senior staff."

"Good God!"

"OK, I want to let you in on something. You will not have heard from Peter, because I only told him a few days ago, that I am now working in an office which is basically keeping tabs on the Make Poverty History campaign. Oh yes, we do these things. And the first thing I want to tell you, Sara, is that the campaign really is having an impact. We are getting so many letters and e-mails about it we can barely cope. And it's changing policy. Later this month, on the 25th to be precise, EU development ministers are going to make an announcement that you are going to like. Watch out for it, mark the date. I will say no more.

"Secondly, what you may not know is that tension exists between the aid and development groups behind MPH. They are divided into the more conservative ones, who basically think HMG is doing a good job, and the more radical groups, who are more critical of government policy. The agencies you support, my dear Sara, WDM, War on Want and the like, are off-message and the government does not like it one little bit. War on Want we know in the office as 'War on HMG'. Their criticisms are sharp and they sting. What I am saying to you, I repeat, very very strictly off the record, is that the rollicking we get from the off-messagers hurts, but it can move policy. We don't like the public to believe that we – HMG – should be served with an ASBO. Yes I heard about your stunt. So without ascribing anything to me, keep your arguments sharp, be probing, see through the spin. Let's go inside and remember . . ."

"Charley, why are you telling me this?"

"I haven't told you a thing, Sara, have you forgotten already? I have shared with you because I care about the issues, because beneath the image of civil servants, beneath our stone-like exterior appearance, beneath the view that we are automats, that we run the government and twist ministers round our little fingers – well, some popular perception is sound – lie hearts that beat, that care about people and, yes, that want to see poverty made history. And as I cannot campaign, Sara, I want to encourage people like you who can."

"Thanks Charley, thanks. You know, I have never heard you say as much in all the time I've known you. You've given me a new perspective. And you have my word. I will keep the confidence."

On May 25th, development ministers from the EU's twenty-five countries met in Brussels. They announced a doubling of development aid to poor countries by 2010. A doubling of aid is what MPH had been pressing for. It was only a step, it fell short of the amount of money that would be needed to halve poverty by 2015, it would not kick in until 2010, but it was nonetheless a step that showed the campaign was working.

Sara rang Peter, who told her that he wasn't convinced the deal was all it seemed and that the aid agencies were expressing reservations. But Sara was in a mood to celebrate progress so far.

"Come round for a drink of the fairly traded stuff. I'll invite the others round too, and let's drink to some progress, and hopefully to more to come."

While they were enjoying their drink a few days later, the phone rang. "Sara, I've had the police on the phone," said Frank. Oh no, not again! What I have done now? she wondered.

"It was the G8 police vetting unit in Scotland. Checking to see if you are bona fide. Get ready for the worst, Sara. If I were you, I'd get hold of your passport quick and head to the nearest airport. It's your only hope."

"Fraaaaank!"

"Sara . . . you can collect your G8 press pass from the Caledonian Hotel on Princes Street in Edinburgh on Sunday or Monday before the summit. And you will need your passport to prove your ID. You're in Sara, you're in."

No answering machines now, they were all there and she jigged around the room and hugged them all. As for Simon, pride may be the deadliest of the seven deadly sins, the sin from which all others arise, but he had never felt more proud of anyone in his life.

9

A Talk in June

The Revd Simon Copplestone had volunteered on the MPH committee to lead a prayer group on poverty. To the rest of the committee it seemed that the assistant curate of St. Luke's had by far the lightest task of anyone.

But when the committee met on the evening of the first day of June, to report back on what they were doing, there was no competition. Sara, more than anyone, listened, fascinated, to Simon, who explained that the prayer group had led him into all sorts of action.

He had persuaded every church in the town to hang a MAKE POVERTY HISTORY banner on their wall. With the agreement of his understanding boss, Bernard, he had asked churches, not only in town but also in the surrounding areas, if he could preach about it at their main service – and also talk to their church council about it.

Simon had persuaded the Board for Social Responsibility in the diocese to put a motion on MPH to the Diocesan Synod, urging everyone in the area to campaign on the issues. He was planning an MPH service at St. Luke's for the eve of the G8 summit. In addition to the prayer group, he had started a group consisting of

Christians, Muslims and Jews. The group was looking at what the three religions were saying on justice for the poor. He had spoken to the local branch of the Mothers Union about MPH and a number of members had put their names down for the Edinburgh march.

And, he said, he had networked like never before, e-mailing every old contact he could think of, asking them to spread the message.

"Simon, that is really impressive, thank you," said Sara. But she wondered why he had not let on beforehand that he was doing all that. His English reserve, she thought.

"Agnes, how are you doing, persuading people to e-mail the government, the IMF, the World Bank and so on, to change policies which hurt the poor?"

And Agnes reported, then Howard, Nicki, Peter and, finally, Sara.

"I've spoken to a number of local organisations about MPH, the Women's Institute, the Soroptomists and Round Table. I am still working on an MPH exhibition, and I'm asking the schools and the library to take it for a while. And I have circulated all the schools to ask if I could take an assembly about it. Maybe Simon, you and I could do your school assembly together?"

"And you have said nothing about the way your press work is spreading the message," chipped in Peter. "And yes, the ASBO stunt, the debt chains, all helped. You know I reckon that most people in town have now heard about MPH. That's not bad. We've come from nowhere in five months."

"But we've got a lot to do," Agnes reminded them, saying that the next issue coming up was debt. Next week finance ministers of the G7 countries would meet, she said. "Ask everyone you know," Agnes went on, "to e-mail all seven of them, and urge they announce a substantial deal on debt."

All agreed. They went on to talk about celebrities and their role in MPH. Were they a good thing or not? Was there a danger they distracted attention from the issues? Sir Bob Geldof had announced another Live Aid concert, Live8, both in London and in other countries. This divided the committee into those who thought that, when celebrities become involved, the spotlight focuses on them rather than on the issues and that they were a distraction, and those who thought that it could only be a good thing that the message was then taken out through music to millions of young people.

"You wanted to talk, Simon," said Sara quietly as they left the meeting together.

"Yes, soon. I just have to talk with someone else first, before we talk. Can I ring you in a week or so?"

Mysterious . . . is he putting it off? she wondered. But before Simon rang, finance ministers of the G7 countries had met and there was good news – although not quite as good as it had seemed at first.

"Eighteen of the world's poorest countries will have their debts to the World Bank and the International Monetary Fund wiped out as part of a £30 billion package agreed today by the G7 leading economies," reported one newspaper on the meeting.

It went on to say that the deal would save countries such as Mozambique and Ethiopia almost £10 billion in debt payments over the next ten years and that the Treasury had stated that a further nine countries would qualify for debt relief within twelve to eighteen months, with the total number possibly rising to almost forty.

"The uniqueness of this deal is that so much would be written off almost immediately, within a few weeks of the agreement," Gordon Brown was quoted as saying. And that twenty-seven countries would qualify, "and potentially it's thirty-seven." He added that the deal would not have been possible without the pressure put on ministers by churches, campaign groups and the public.

And that was enough for Sara to throw the paper into the air and hug William with a "We're winning, we're winning, we're getting though, the campaign's working!" She rang Peter. But Peter was less enthusiastic.

"Well it looks good, Sara, but look a little deeper. For a start, take a look at the ActionAid website. They point out that many more countries need debt relief. It's good news for countries that will immediately benefit, but will do little to help millions in at least forty other countries that also need 100% debt relief."

"And it's the small print that worries me," he went on. "Look closely and you see that it runs against everything that the MPH campaign is saying about countries deciding things for themselves. The finance ministers are saying that, I quote, 'to qualify for debt relief, developing countries must tackle corruption, boost private sector development and eliminate impediments to private investment, both domestic and foreign'."

"We wouldn't argue about the need to tackle corruption, would we Peter?"

"Of course not, and it needs tackling wherever it exists, at whatever level. But let's be clear what the ministers are saying – that debt relief depends on countries opening up their markets to foreign companies, to water companies, for example. That's a corporate charter. Conditions like that contradict the notion of poor countries determining their own ways. I don't like it. It's economic colonisation. Forcing poor countries in a weak economic position to accept our way of doing things, or else. It stinks."

Sara found herself in the unusual position of wanting to defend finance ministers, mostly because she wanted to believe the MPH campaign was working.

"But Peter, I oppose conditions of course. But for all that, this deal will surely mean that more children will go to school, that money will be freed up for anti-poverty projects, for health clinics and so on. On balance, this must be a good thing."

"I'm not convinced. And there's going to be a lot of hype. I see Geldof is saying that 280 million Africans will tomorrow wake up for the first time in their lives without the burden of debt that has crippled them and their countries for so long. Yes, OK, we've come so far Sara, but we still have to work at persuading governments like ours that they need to respect the independence of other countries. I'll work on Charley."

And Sara wrote a press release, feeling that she was now, in a small way, a part of the paper.

★ ★ ★

It was an impulse that took Simon to Sara's front door late one afternoon a few days later. The door was opened by Chloe.

"Mum's on the phone. Come in. She'll be ages though. She's talking to someone about making poverty history, I guess. And she goes on about *me* talking on the phone. Do you play chess Mr Copplestone?"

"Er . . . chess?" Simon hadn't played it for years, "Well, er . . . in a fashion, I suppose."

"Have you a game while Mum's on the phone?"

"I warn you, she's good, way up the chess league at school," said younger sister May.

The pieces were duly laid out. Chloe with the white pieces led off. After only eleven moves she exclaimed triumphantly, "Check, and I think you'll find that's mate, Mr Copplestone . . . What a funny way to play chess, if I may say so. That was a really silly move you made with your Bishop. You left your King totally exposed. Wow, that's the easiest game I've had for ages."

Simon was left muttering about how good she was when Mum came off the phone to the rescue.

"Mummy, Mummy, I got Mr Copplestone checkmate in eleven moves! He's not very good, mind you, but even so . . ."

"Chloe, you shouldn't have taken advantage of Mr Copplestone like that."

"Take advantage? Mummy, I'm only nine, Mr Copplestone's old."

"Chloe don't be so rude. Mr Copplestone is not old, he happens to be younger than me."

"So-o-o . . . sorrrry, Mummy . . . Oh can I play in the inter-schools chess competition, please?"

Being told that she could and had better go and practice, Chloe left to practice.

"I'm sorry about that Simon," said Sara, killing herself laughing after Chloe had left. "You poor thing! You walked into an ambush. It was good of you to play with her."

"I did something silly with my Bishop apparently. Well, we clergy do sometimes have problems with bishops!"

Simon wanted to talk about the various issues coming up in the campaign, about the MPH service he was planning. He wanted it to be a community rather than a church occasion, and was hoping to get the MP and the mayor along and involve as many people as possible from different walks of life. And he hoped the people going to Edinburgh would come to the service. And finally he asked: "Would you like to come to the curacy house for lunch on Friday? Nothing fancy, just bread, cheese and ham."

"Thanks, that would be lovely. I finish work at 1.00. Just after that OK?"

Oh God this is it! What is he going to say, what I am going to say? Sara still hadn't resolved the issues that had been running through her mind since earlier in the year. She did not see Simon that much anyway, but always felt happy when he was around. Can't be wrong to feel that, surely? Perhaps together they could work it out.

On the patio overlooking his back garden Simon laid out the table with bread, cheese, ham salad and a jug of water. He decided it was better not to have wine. The mid-June day was sunny, not too hot and the patio would be in the shade at least for a while. He placed two chairs facing the garden around the same side of the table.

Sara wobbled up the path soon after one o'clock and he kissed her on the cheek. She seemed to be expecting it.

"Thought we'd have lunch in the garden, it's a lovely day," he said.

"Yes, lovely, great idea."

Politely they passed the bread, the cheese, the ham, the salad to each other. Simon poured the water and they began to eat, quietly for a while. It was Simon who broke the silence.

"My cat has died," he said.

"Oh Simon," Sara dropped her fork, her hand going over to his in a gesture of comfort. "How? When? Oh Simon you loved that cat."

"Bernard, my boss, ran over him, in his car."

"Your boss ran over your cat! Oh Si-i-imon," her hand moved around his body and she extended the comforting process to a hug. "Oh that's awful, how did it happen?"

"It was not Bernard's fault. He was driving round a corner and Flick just ran out in front of him. Poor Bernard didn't have a chance. He is very upset. I have been comforting him rather than the other way round. Anyway, we gave Flick a good send-off and buried him at the bottom of the garden."

"Poor Flick. Do you remember? I nearly ran over him that night I nearly . . ."

"Spilled the beans?" he ended the sentence for her.

"Spilled the beans? I nearly knocked over every pot on the oven top!" They laughed. And Sara took the opportunity to move on.

"Simon, can I ask you – do you think it's possible to be in love with two people at the same time?"

He thought carefully. He did not want to give a glib answer, or one that sounded too churchy, and felt that he had to start with the basics.

"The Greeks have four distinctive words for different types of love. But in the English language we only have one. The Greek words are Eros, which is being in love; Philos, the love between family and friends; Agape, unconditional love, putting others before yourself whether you like them or not; and finally Storge, which is the love of things and situations. That word has attracted some attention recently as J. K. Rowling was said to be thinking of calling the next Harry Potter book, the 'Pillar of Storge'. But she thought better of it."

"Well I'll improve my street cred with Chloe telling her that! But there's overlap isn't there, must be? Eros and Philos, being in love, and the love between family and friends, they're pretty close."

"Yes, very close."

"Simon, what I hear you saying is that love manifests itself in many ways. Can a form of Eros manifest itself between a man and a woman who have strong commitments elsewhere? Remember that scene in the film 'When Harry Met Sally' – no, stop smiling, not that scene – but when one of them asks: can a man and a woman ever be friends or does sex always get in the way? Could I change that slightly and ask: can a man and a woman meet, and, despite having existing commitments of love, fall for each other, really feel something deep for each other, a feeling that goes far beyond the platonic, without sex getting in the way?" Again Simon paused before answering. This was a big question, *the* big question, a question that needed an answer.

"And you would not have anyone remotely in mind?" he asked.

"Not even remotely." They laughed, the language of their bodies louder than words.

"How did it happen, Sara? I didn't plan this, and I'm sure you didn't. That cold January evening when I first looked into your eyes, my world seemed to change. This has taken us into a world that neither of us bargained for."

"And it was me who declared, wasn't it, giving the game away at that meeting in your chapel. When we met," she turned to look full into his eyes, "I thought you were very posh, although I reckon you talk less posh now. Maybe I've got used to it, or maybe a little of my rough northern accent has rubbed off."

"I envy you your accent, there is nothing rough about it. It's about as classless as you can get."

"Thanks," she responded. "But Simon, can we get back to the question – is it possible to be in love with two people at the same time?"

"I think it's a matter of recognising the boundaries. What was the reply to that question in 'When Harry Met Sally'. Was it not along the lines – yes, provided that both of them are committed to other people?"

"Yes, something like that. And, Simon, could I try out a bit of amateur theology on you? Simply, that you cannot be unfaithful to what you truly believe in. I can be a bit of a flirt at times, but I cannot be unfaithful to William, to my family who I believe in. And I have the feeling that you cannot be unfaithful to what you believe in, your God, your faith, your ministry, your commitments to your parishioners – including me!"

"Sara, that's brilliant. There's nothing much amateur about that. I agree – but then I always agree with you. You have set the boundaries. You know, one of the agencies we support is War on Want. I guess the two of us have to battle against another kind of want – want for each other. And to remember that at your marriage you vowed to forsake all others. So the answer is no, in what we might call the ultimate way of love. For me you are out of bounds – how shall I say it – beyond reach. But I think we can care for each other within a proper relationship, and good can come from it."

"The situation is that both of us are beyond reach – to each other," Sara responded. "I just hope we can feel something deep for each other, yes, love for each other, while still being faithful." They sipped their water on a lovely June day, both feeling uplifted.

"There's something else I think we should allow for, and that is human weakness," said Simon. "We are not automats. We can sit here and rationally agree that we feel love for each other, but that we are out of bounds to each other in a certain way of love. But we can only be, say 99% certain we will keep to that. To believe we are 100% foolproof would be to turn us into robots. And we are not robots. I did not offer you any wine today because I think it is best if we avoid situations where weakness might surface."

"You are so sensible Simon, thanks for that."

"Tell me, have you told William about this. Will you tell him about today?" Simon wanted to know.

"I will tell him we had lunch of course. But you know, William is so laid back, I could repeat this entire conversation to him word for word, and he would yawn. If I peppered it with: 'Oh, some cricketer or other dropped in while we were there', then he would prick up his ears. He's cricket mad. If I told him I was having an affair with some famous cricketer he would go to work and boast about it. He'd give me his cricket bat and tell me to get his autograph next time I was with him. But seriously, I would like to think I could tell him. That's it. How can we have a friendship that we can talk about, that we are not ashamed of? Have you told anyone?"

"Yes."

"Who?"

"I have told my spiritual director."

"You have a spiritual director? Simon, explain, please!" The phone rang in the house. With an "excuse me", Simon left to answer it. Sara decided to stretch her legs and take a walk down the garden, a narrow garden that had the look of belonging to someone who did not spend very much time caring for it. It was warm in the full sun, and Sara felt the heat beating down.

A spiritual director, she mused, sounds good; "I may not go to church much but I wouldn't mind one of those."

At the end of the garden lay a small toolshed. Just to the side of it, on a roughish piece of ground that had recently been disturbed, was a small wooden cross. Two bits of wood had been nailed across each other, and the name Flick appeared in the middle. Flick's burial site. Poor cat, Simon really cared about him, she thought, wandering back up to the house.

"That was someone about a baptism," said Simon, returning to the patio. "Where were we? Oh yes, my spiritual director. Do you remember me saying after our last committee meeting that I wanted to speak with someone before we talked? Well it was with my spiritual director. All clergy have spiritual directors, but they are really more like a guide than a director."

"I could do with one of those. Do people in your congregation have them too?"

"No, not as such, but they can come to me or to Bernard for guidance."

"Doesn't sound fair to me. But Simon, what did you tell your spiritual director?"

"Everything. I tried not to hide a thing."

"And what did he say?"

"It's a woman, a very senior woman in the church, one of the first women to be ordained priest just over ten years ago. Well her response was interesting. She said that I had been weak falling for you, and that I needed to recognise the dangers. But that maybe the weakness has been turned into opportunity. That being close to you has energised me, and it really has. I would not have done half as much for the MPH campaign if it was not for you. You have fired me, inspired me. What my director said was that my closeness to you, yes, the love I feel for you, has helped further the campaign, which is good. Good, because this is a campaign to end poverty, to bring about justice for the poor, to show love for your neighbour. And that although, she said, I must never forget where I stand with you – that you are a married parishioner – our friendship has a positive side."

"That's fantastic. Oh Simon, that's really lovely. Weakness turned into opportunity," she said. "I had never thought of it that way. Well I too was weak falling for you. And you have energised me as well, you really have, it's worked both ways. I was driven by those two orphans on New Year's Day, but it's you that helps to continue that drive. Yes, as you say, good is coming from it."

They sat in silence for a while. The sun had now come over the patio and was in Sara's eyes.

"I'd better go, thanks for the lunch – and guidance," she said, "but, before I go, that meeting in your chapel all those months ago . . . I've never apologised for spurting out how I felt, and for almost bringing you to the brink of disaster. I really am sorry. Forgive me?" she asked, kissing him on the cheek.

"Instantly, of course. I must admit that the little bit of hair I have, well it kind of stood on its end! Anyway, changing tack, let's go to a concert sometime. Remember the music you were playing that day I called when you were recovering? Beethoven's Ode to Joy. Happens to be one of my favourites."

"That would be great, I would love that. I'd invite you to dinner but I'm not sure how I would cope with the two men I love round the same table. This time it would be the peas, not the beans I might spill. And that would start William off on his ball bearings. Then you'd be sorry. We've always got to have peas. They remind William of his bloody ball bearings. Er, sorry. But I warn you, my husband is a ball-bearings bore."

As they walked into the house, Sara thought she heard a noise. The noise of someone moving around upstairs. "Simon, Simon, there's someone in the house."

"Oh that's Joe. He is a guest at the church's drop-in centre for the homeless. I'm a volunteer helper there. Joe is completely homeless at the moment so I've told him he can stay here while we help him to find somewhere. He would have come in and gone straight upstairs to lie down, probably a little worse for some cheap alcohol."

"Are you sure about him, Simon?" The concern in Sara's voice was not calmed by his reply.

"Not entirely. But then sometimes you have to take a risk." As she walked through the house, Sara could not help but notice cards on the mantelpiece, happy birthday cards.

"Simon, have you had a birthday?" Her tone was inquisitive.

"Yesterday."

"And you never told me?" It was now impatient.

"Well no, I had no occasion to. And anyway you might have felt obliged to send me a card or something."

"Obliged to send you a card? You know, you are a steaming great idiot! I would have wanted to send you a card. Simon, really!" It was now exasperation.

"Well, put it down to my English reserve," he pleaded.

"That always strikes me as a deadly disease. Simon, I tell you, I send so many cards I keep the world's card industry going. And I shall not be denied your birthday. I will send one later. Happy birthday anyway, happy birthday."

She kissed him on the cheek, a kiss that went far beyond a peck. They hugged each other, holding tight for quite a time.

"I'd better go, Simon, or that 1% weakness you spoke of might experience sudden, massive and exponential growth!" She rode back down the path, with a "let me know about a concert soon."

★   ★   ★

Something remarkable was going on in the press. The papers had picked up Make Poverty History in a big way. Over five hundred organisations were now behind it, including organisations that did not have any direct connection with world poverty, like the Musicians' Union and Equity. Over six million white bands had been sold. And by late June 2005 the issues were being debated like never before.

The details of aid, debt and trade justice were being poured over in the media. The arguments were analysed, scrutinised and sometimes criticised. The aid agencies were responding to the criticisms, defending the campaign, and, in Sara's eyes, positively routing the critics and the sceptics. Tony Blair was reported to be going around the capitals of the G8 countries to get agreement on a deal for the poor at the G8 summit in Gleneagles. Preparations were well advanced for Geldof's Live8 concert in Hyde Park and elsewhere. There was a feeling that something was about to happen, that so many people now cared about the issues that politicians would have to listen, a feeling that the world stood on the brink of a real breakthrough for those whose daily lot is poverty.

Sara called at the newspaper offices to see Frank, pick up a laptop and camera and check what he wanted – seven hundred words every day, longer if something out of the ordinary was going on, to be e-mailed to him by 10.00 a.m. And for Sara to make sure that her mobile was switched on and fully charged in case of queries.

Sara rang the committee to tell them that the coach for Edinburgh was now full, thirty-five people in all, including eight children. Simon for his part was preparing an eve-of-Edinburgh MPH service at St. Luke's. He had organised it as a short early evening event, hopefully to get people on their way from work, and to allow those going to Edinburgh the next morning to get an early night. The coach planned to leave at 4.30 a.m. sharp. He invited the mayor and the MP to do a reading and also Sara as the co-ordinator of the town's campaign. And he made sure to invite people from all the different churches to lead parts of the service, so that no one was left out. He also invited Peter to give an address on prospects for the summit.

While the church was not full, there was a reasonable congregation as Simon started with a prayer that Sara felt she could relate to: "Living and loving God, You are movement and change, action and energy, peace and tranquillity. We are all made in your image and likeness; we are your people. We are restless but faithful, seeking but believing, urgent but patient. We believe in a future where poverty is history. We believe in change, we believe in life, full of opportunity and hope. We commit ourselves to change, to life, to our neighbour. We commit ourselves to working towards a world where poverty is history. Amen."

Energy, opportunity, working towards a world where poverty is history, all of them rang bells for Sara. Simon had suggested that she choose any reading she liked. Sara opted for one titled "Who is my neighbour?", which she had adapted from a website on racial justice:

My neighbour is Christian, my neighbour is Jewish, my neighbour is Muslim.
My neighbour never goes near the door of any church.
My neighbour sits at the corner of the street asking for change.
My neighbour is a prisoner in an Iraqi jail.
My neighbour is a victim of a bomb blast.
My neighbour is an earthquake victim.
My neighbour is the victim of the famine in Niger, in Malawi, in Zambia.
My neighbour is the starving woman and child in Sudan, shielding their faces from a desert storm.
My neighbour is dying of HIVAIDS in a hundred countries.
My neighbours are the children, one of whom in every three seconds of this service, has died of poverty."

After a hymn had been sung, Agnes followed with prayers: "We pray that all of us may cry out against the injustice of poverty and live our lives as a loving example of global community. We pray for the world's leaders that they may take this opportunity to make a real difference to the lives of those who live in poverty.

"We pray for our local community, that we may live out our principles of fairness and equality at home and in our own town. We pray for ourselves, that we may have the strength and courage to continue the quest for change, long after it has faded from the public eye. And we pray especially for those who are travelling from all over the country to the march in Edinburgh tomorrow. We pray that the plight of the poor will move the eight leaders at Gleneagles into action. We pray for Sara who will be in Gleneagles to report on the summit for our local newspaper."

"Oh God, am I up to this," thought Sara, fighting a tear. "Can I be up there, away from my family, from Simon, can I do it? Oh God help me!" It was then Peter's turn.

"Next week there will be a unique opportunity for world leaders to show they care about the poor. Thousands of us will be in Edinburgh tomorrow to tell them – please build on what you have achieved so far this year. Don't rest on your laurels, that's always uncomfortable, but build. So what's at stake next week?"

And Peter went on to outline the issues involved, how Africa and climate change would be central to the discussions. He reminded them that Make Poverty History is urging more and better aid, 100% debt relief and trade justice for developing countries, and that the government's position was still some distance away from campaigners.

"On aid, progress appeared to have been made in late May when European Union countries agreed to double their aid by 2010. But they need to go further. More is needed if aid is to make its contribution towards halving world poverty by 2015 – one of the millennium development goals. And more aid alone is not enough to beat poverty. Aid should focus on needs – and genuinely benefit the poor and support developing countries' and communities' own plans and paths out of poverty."

Peter explained that on debt relief there was limited progress at the G8 Finance Ministers meeting in June; that eighteen countries would benefit under the deal, but that this needed to be extended to cover many more.

"And I share with you a concern – that to qualify for debt relief, recipients have to show they have liberalised their economies in a way that satisfies Western countries. This includes trade liberalisation, opening their markets to imports. But trade liberalisation, free trade, is failing the poor. A new report by Christian Aid tells of how democratic institutions in Ghana have been subverted by the demands of doctrinaire free-market policies – of how the IMF, backed by the World Bank, overturned a law to protect poor farmers. In Jamaica the report says that increasing numbers of women have been driven to prostitution and drug smuggling by a continuing round of liberalisation that has wrecked their employment opportunities." British government policy, he went on, was still strongly based on liberalising principles.

"This is not good enough. It is not free trade, but trade justice, changing the rules of trade, that will help the poor. Gleneagles will come up with a package on aid and debt but it will be unacceptable if it is conditional on countries having to undertake trade reforms. Again, if leaders have nothing of any substance to say about combating climate change, then the benefit of more aid and debt relief could be wiped out.

"To the eight leaders we say," he concluded, "listen to the cries of the poor. Deal with their real needs, the world is watching you. If you want to be judged as statesmen, do not fail the poor next week. To the eight leaders we say – make poverty history." Sara wanted to clap, but no, you don't clap in church.

"I wanted to clap Peter," she told Simon on the church doorstep after the service, "but remembered in time that it wasn't the done thing to clap in church."

"What a pity you remembered! Thank you for what you said. You could have heard the proverbial pin drop. See you in the morning."

10

Edinburgh: 2nd July

There is a calm about 4.30 on an early July morning that is not always appreciated by those who have just had a night's sleep curtailed. A long day lay ahead for the bleary-eyed people who mounted the coach to Edinburgh, Sara, William, Chloe, May, and all the members of the MPH committee among them. Peter had someone with him wearing dark glasses and very obviously a wig, someone who Sara did not recognise. Her list read "Peter and friend". Maybe a work colleague, she thought.

The party had a seven-hour journey there and another one back in the evening. But people came because they wanted to be there, to tell their children "I was there" on a day that could advance the cause of making poverty history. And everyone was wearing white, as requested, as it was hoped to ring the centre of Edinburgh with a human white band, the symbol of the campaign.

Sara, complete with suitcase for the week, noticed that Simon was carrying an overnight bag. But at 4.30 a.m. you don't ask why. For two hours or so, most people slept as the coach sped up the M1. Chloe, sitting next to May, was soon playing chess with herself on a travel set. A stop for breakfast was followed by some shuffling around, with Sara next to Agnes.

"Agnes, can I ask you something? The first time we spoke about MPH six months ago, almost to the day, I sensed you were not happy about aid. And I would love to know why?"

"You know Sara, one of the hardest things in the world is to help someone. I see that in my job as a social worker. The recipient can easily resent it because she or he is in a position of inequality. Someone comes to help, comes to give, but the recipient cannot give back, does not have the resources to give back. The simple giver–receiver relationship does not do justice to the receiver. It does not do justice to the complexity for Africa. You know there's an old Chinese proverb: 'Why do you hate me? I've never helped you.' I'm sorry if I reacted negatively. Does this makes sense, Sara? Aid is better if it's two-way. And British people have so much to receive from African people as well as to give to them."

"Thank you, it does make sense. And Agnes you have given the MPH campaign so much. You have provided something that's unique. And by the way, thank you for praying for me last evening. If there is a God, I'd like him on my side!"

More shuffling around was going on with Chloe trying to see if she could interest anyone in a game of chess. Excuses abounded, until finally she alighted on Simon, sitting near the front of the bus with Jean, the 81-year old anti-apartheid activist who had been at the Mandela meeting in Trafalgar Square.

"Mr Copplestone, could I teach you the Réti Opening and the Sicilian Defence?" asked Chloe.

"Er, the what?"

"Do you like the Réti Opening, my dear?" asked Jean, while the curate struggled for words. "That's one of my favourites. Will you have a game?"

"Really, really? Oh cool, cool! At last, someone on this bus who's cool." Simon gave up his seat for Chloe and for the rest of the journey she sat with Jean, the games keenly contested, and with Jean teaching the budding chess star the Danish Gambit, the Dutch Defense, the Max Lange Attack and much more.

Simon walked down the bus and sat with May, until Agnes came over with a "Sit here by Sara, will you? I want to ask Peter about something he said last night."

He needed no bidding and they sat together, barely exchanging a word. Their friendship, their relationship, no longer needed words. Sara's curiosity eventually won through.

"I see you've an overnight bag. Are you planning to stay over?"

"Er, yes, did I not say? My English reserve again I suppose. Yes, I have the weekend off. There are loads of things going on today after the march, and tomorrow there is an alternative summit. I thought that would be worth going to. So I'll come back on the train on Sunday afternoon."

"You and your English reserve, Simon!" said Sara quietly, smiling. "If I may use churchy language, I reckon your English reserve should go to hell because that's where it belongs!"

"I like that," he laughed, "I'll preach on that sometime." Another stop, more shuffling about. Sara went over to where Peter was sitting with the woman in dark glasses.

"Aren't you going to introduce me?" Sara enquired.

"Yes, this is Judith."

"Judith!" At that moment "Judith" whipped off her glasses to reveal – Charley.

"It's me, you fool," she said. "I am in disguise because I have reservations about a high-ranking civil servant prancing around Edinburgh about a matter of government policy. But I'm damned if I was going to miss the fun. Today, I am Judith."

The coach arrived in Edinburgh as planned, near enough to midday. They got off the coach, amid an armada of coaches from all over the country, also bicycles, tandems and rickshaws. And with literally thousands of people around.

"Please listen everyone," said Sara, "You all have maps, the march starts in The Meadows, and I suggest we walk down together. We may get separated. There are two open-air stages in the Meadows and we may choose, after the march, to go to different ones. But please can we meet back here at 6.30 sharp? Where we are now is marked with a cross on the map and the route from The Meadows is marked with a red line. My mobile number and Agnes's number are on this map should you have any problems. And, before we go off, I want to take a picture of everyone – for the paper!"

They walked to The Meadows alongside people overwhelmingly dressed in white to form the human white band around the city. Some were dressed as clowns and puppets. Campaigning groups had let their imaginations run riot. They witnessed a WDM G8 Monster, controlled by corporate fat cats, racing through the crowds in pursuit of a terrified globe. The police had been expecting 100,000 people. But it was clear that many more had come to show leaders that they cared. And that people wanted them to take action to make poverty history. When they reached The Meadows the line of people waiting to start the march stretched back for what seemed like miles.

So the Openshaws wandered over to one of the stages, Simon having disappeared with a "see you later, better go and find a hotel." They watched as a Zambian, Mulima Kufekisa, took to the stage alongside celebrities such as Jonathan Dimbleby and Billy Bragg.

"It's like the welly queue at Glastonbury, times a hundred," said Billy Bragg.

"I've seen for myself," said Mulima Kufekisa, "how more and better aid and debt cancellation has changed people's futures from one of despair to one of hope. The G8 leaders have the means to stop 30,000 children dying every day and giving them the chance of an education – now they need to show the will to do so."

They listened as actor Pete Postlethwaite quoted Gandhi, "'First they ignore you, then they laugh at you, then they fight you and then you win' . . . We're here to win. We have to win. And we won't be ignored." His message to the G8 leaders was: "Give us action not words. We've had enough. Our objective here today is crystal clear, to make poverty history," he said to a roaring crowd.

"Please can we go and join the queue, or we'll never start," pleaded May. On the way to the start they picked up hand banners with the different messages: "Trade Justice, not free trade", "Cut the strings from aid", "Cancel the debt", and simply "Make Poverty History".

And so they joined the queue and stood in the sun, hardly budging. They didn't know it then, but not 100,000 but 225,000 people were there, and the stewards were overwhelmed. Music was filling the air, drums were playing, whistles blowing. And people were singing chants such as "What do we want? – Trade justice! When do we want it? – Now!" And they slowly inched forward. Having joined the queue soon after 1.00 they had still not started at 3.00, although they were then almost under starter's orders.

Then at exactly three o'clock, a flare signalled the beginning of the one-minute silence that it had been agreed would happen at precisely that time. Total silence followed, except for the whirring of police helicopters above the human white band. Everyone stood there, motionless. White balloons were released and moved noiselessly up into the sky. Sara thought about the twenty children who would had died in that minute of silence and cried as she had done on New Year's Day. But tried to hide it.

At the end of the minute's silence, a wave of sound came towards them from every direction. The roar was huge. A few minutes later the Openshaws were over the line and had started the march, a two-mile circular walk. Up a broad path towards the city centre they walked, with people around them blowing whistles, clowns performing, people singing, people happy. They walked into The Mound and could see the marchers in front of them turning the corner into Princes Street.

"This is cool, all these outfits," said Chloe. They turned left into Princes Street, the city's main shopping street, pedestrianised for the day, and looked up at the castle to see a huge Make Poverty History banner on the wall. Glancing back along the street Sara got a sense of how many people were there. As they turned left into Lothian Road, Sara noticed the Caledonian Hotel on the corner.

"That's where I pick up my G8 pass from," she said with a skip.

"Do you think you'll remember where it is?" William was being mischievous.

"Wish you were staying up with me," she said, putting her arms around him. "I'm abandoning you, aren't I? Leaving you to look after the girls. Will you be ok?"

"We'll be fine, especially as I've got the week off. And the girls are dying to read your stories every day. Try to get a coded message to them in what you write."

"Darling, I'm a rookie . . . if I write anything it will be a miracle. Did I tell you that Simon is staying over, going back tomorrow? So there will be two empty seats on the coach going home. Maybe the kids could stretch out and get some sleep."

"That's good about Simon, nice that someone's staying to keep you company. Where is he, by the way, where are the others? We haven't seen any of them."

"In this crowd, it's not surprising. I'll ring Simon's mobile." She rang Simon. And Simon hadn't even started the march yet.

"I'll ring you later," she laughed. So they wound their way back into The Meadows, sat down on the grass for a picnic and watched as huge letters spelling out the words "Make Poverty History" were raised into the air by cranes to form a massive billboard on a side of the field. And underneath, thousands of people had added messages for the G8 leaders.

They watched more performers, listened to Bianca Jagger and sat in the sun till just after six. By then others from the coach party had started to appear, including Agnes and Jean.

"Nelson Mandela in Trafalgar Square and now this," said Jean to Sara. "Thank you!" And so they walked back to the coach to swap stories about who they had seen and heard. Agnes seemed to speak for them all.

"That was an amazing day, the atmosphere was just fantastic," she said, giving Sara a big hug. And Sara remembered in time to pick up her luggage for the week. Giving the girls and William big tearful hugs, she watch the coach drive away. As it did so she felt for a moment utterly alone. She rang Simon. He had nearly finished the march.

"Look Simon, there's a meeting starting soon in the Assembly Hall. Gordon Brown's speaking, also someone from Ghana and the director of Christian Aid. Could we meet there in, say twenty minutes? You've got your map haven't you? It's clearly marked."

And so they met, in little more than twenty minutes, as it happened. They met and kissed on cheeks.

"What happened to you today?"

"Well I had to sort out a hotel for the night. That was tricky as they are pretty full! But in the end I managed to get a good deal from the lastminute.com people for a hotel in Princes Street. Very central."

"Simon, if your English reserve wasn't such a drag on your life, if I'd known you were staying over, I could have asked my cousin Maureen to find you a bed. I think I told you that I am staying with her."

"Oh no! I could not have imposed myself like that!"

"Simon . . ."

They walked into a packed meeting and heard Christian Aid director Daleep Mukarji urge Gordon Brown to use his influence to ensure that rich countries support trade justice and stop forcing free trade on Africa. He said that the benefits of debt cancellation and more aid would be undermined if poor countries were forced to open their markets and cut support to vulnerable producers. When Gordon Brown spoke, he said it was partly down to the efforts of campaigners that the government had decided to act on debt relief.

"Let me say it is because of your efforts and your demand that the rich countries meet their obligations to the poor, that I can tell you now that, this year, eighteen of the poorest countries of the world will, for the first time, have 100% of their debts written off."

The Chancellor then pledged that Britain would unilaterally write off its share of debt payments, and try to persuade the rest of the G8 that for these countries too the burden of unpayable debt should be cancelled. Aware that the audience wanted to hear about trade justice, he went on:

"It is because of your plea that fundamental to justice is trade justice that finance ministers also agreed only three weeks ago to demand the right for poorest countries themselves to decide their own trade reforms, rather than be directed from outside, and demanded for the first time a timetable for the end of export subsidies. You are right to demand trade justice. We accept it is our duty to answer your call for action."

"Sounds good," Sara whispered to Simon, "or he is just saying what we all want to hear. Will he keep to it?" Someone who stood up to heckle was jostled out of the hall.

Revd Dr Aboagye-Mensah, president of the Methodist Church in Ghana, said that like most countries in Africa, "Ghana does not have the strength to compete with countries that are so much more economically developed than ours, It is, to use a biblical analogy, like David facing Goliath with all the power, strength that Goliath brought against David."

"I like that," Simon smiled.

"Thought you would. Tell me, are you hungry? I know I am. Shall we go and have a bite to eat?"

"That would be lovely." But, he was aware of a verse from his beloved bit in the middle of the Bible flashing through his mind: 'Never dine with another man's wife, or revel with her at wine.' Well, I am going to eat with Sara, but not really dine, and yes, no wine. Leaving the hall they walked up towards Edinburgh's Royal Mile, a street packed with restaurants of all shapes and sizes.

"Some good-looking women in Edinburgh, Simon, perhaps you should come and live here . . ."

"Stop teasing! But yes, I had noticed. But none better-looking than the one I'm with." She squeezed his hand and they opted for a middle-of-the-range Italian restaurant which had a short queue at the door. The place was packed, the tables were fairly close together, the atmosphere was comfortable, not intimate. Simon felt it was an eating rather than a dining place. But why did he hear himself asking Sara "Would you like some wine?"

"I don't think I will," she replied, aware of her need not to let any senses be dulled, "maybe later. For now, I'm so thirsty, I could kill a large jug of water." They asked for the water, munched at some bread and looked at the menu.

"I will have a salad niçoise and a cannelloni, please," said Sara when their turn arrived.

"And I will have the same, thank you," said Simon.

"Were you really about to choose the same as me? Or did you switch when you heard what I'd ordered?" To which Simon replied, a little hurt, that yes, he had meant to order a salad niçoise and a cannelloni and no, he did not change his mind. They talked about the day. Both were buoyed up by what had happened, feeling that things now stood on the brink, that something important could happen next week at Gleneagles, something positive for the poor.

"And how do you feel now about next week, being at Gleneagles?" Simon wanted to know.

"Terrified. Well terrified on bad days, very, very apprehensive on good days. I just don't know if I'm up to it, Simon. For God's sake, I'm a nurse not a journalist."

"Sara, you will be fine, you're a nurse but you write better than most journalists."

"Thanks – just keep on telling me." The food arrived. It was good and they ate slowly, enjoying the flavours, talking little. When they had finished the cannelloni, the waiter came round with a pudding menu.

"I don't think I want a pudding," said Sara, "I'm full. That was delicious."

"Well I see they have Monti Bianco on the menu. I remember having that in Rome. You don't see it much in Britain. It's kind of creamy, nutty, lovely."

"Sounds like a hundred calories in every mouthful. How about having one with two spoons? And perhaps a glass of wine with it?" Sara felt it was now OK.

Their heads were almost touching as they tucked into the Monti Bianco.

"This takes me back to university days. You know Simon, I was wrong, this is 200 calories in every mouthful. It tastes gorgeous.

And after all that walking today, great." They ordered coffee, fairtrade. And Sara was feeling very relaxed.

"Simon, can I ask you something? You know when I first came to your house, on that fateful evening, you went off to get some wine and l looked at your books. I couldn't help noticing a copy of 'The Joy of Sex'. And I was kind of . . . a little bit curious," she was smiling and Simon laughed.

"Well, this might surprise you but I was thinking of preaching about it, about the joy of sex," he said quietly, without embarrass-ment. "Why not. Sex is one of life's great gifts – in the context of a stable relationship of course. So why not say so? From the pul-pit, yes. The snag is that misunderstandings may arise. So, coward that I am, I decided not to."

"That's fascinating. You would have certainly packed them in. But then I suppose that you, as an unmarried curate, might hardly be considered a leading authority on the subject?"

"Good point, but I like to explore the little known, the neglected, to go to areas that are overlooked. That's why I like the bit in the middle of the Bible. That's why the relationship between us is on such fascinatingly different ground. It will be really good to know if we can be really close to each other while recognising the boundaries. There may well be surprises along the way, twists and turns we cannot foresee."

"Oh, so I am just part of an experiment am I?" Sara's eyes had widened but were still smiling, "You picked me up for an exper-iment, to see how a little theory you have might work out. And when the experiment's over, you'll discard me, toss me away like driftwood. Well Simon, this could be the end of a beautiful – if purely experimental – relationship. I am a used woman. What does the future hold for one such as I . . ."

"Sara . . . stop it. The Fringe doesn't start till later in the month. And you are teasing again. I did not mean that and you know it. I mean that now it has happened, our relationship, it will be inter-esting to see how it works out."

"Simon, when you're in a hole, stop digging." They smiled and drained the fairtrade coffee.

"That was lovely," said Simon, deciding that it was now his turn. Could she take it as well as give it?

"Do you mind if I light up a cigarette?" he enquired, matter-of-factly. Sara's eyes did not so much widen as bulge. She's fallen for it, thought Simon. And Sara was off.

"Simon, Simon," she said slowly and painfully, "you're not a smoker are you? You've never told me that. That's awful. Simon, do you realise the damage that smoking does to your health? Have you any idea of the heart disease, the respiratory disease, the lung cancer it causes? What does it say on cigarette packets, Simon: Smoking kills. And how. It cuts people down in the prime of their lives And do you realise that if you smoke, everyone around you has to smoke, because they breathe in your smoke?"

"Sara, will you stop . . ."

"No I will not stop. Do you realise that smoking is one of the major public health disasters of today? That smoking is the leading preventable cause of death, killing five million people a year, with disease and death rapidly shifting to poor countries? That at current levels of tobacco use, smoking is expected to kill about 10 million people a year by 2020, with two-thirds of those deaths in developing countries?"

"Sara, please, let me . . ." But the reading of the Tobacco Riot Act continued unabated.

"Do you know what King James – yes, him of the Bible – said about smoking? 'Loathsome to the eye, hateful to the nose, harmful to the brain,' he called it. You do realise, surely, that faced with declining sales in Western countries, because people are giving up the disgusting habit, the tobacco industry has switched its attention to developing countries where there are often no health warnings on packets? That cigarette makers put higher tar and nicotine contents in the cigarettes they sell in poor countries so as to get people addicted faster and to keep them addicted? Do you realise that the industry is trying to get people smoking, poor people, and that people have been persuaded to buy fags rather than food, to the detriment of their nutrition?"

"Sara, please can I get a word in?"

"No Simon, no. How can you say that you believe in making poverty history when you support with your purchases an industry which is the most irresponsible in the world, that worsens poverty, that makes a product that kills people when used as the manufacturer directs. But, hang on a minute. . . .I cannot believe this," Sara's voice shot up, "I have fallen for a smoker. How could I have fallen for someone who uses these vile, smelly sticks. I . . . am . . . furious. Furious with myself, but I am mad with you, Simon, mad!."

With that, she stood bolt upright, threw her serviette on the table, and if looks could have killed, Simon's life would have come to a sudden end. People at the surrounding tables downed knives, forks and spoons, stopped eating, stopped talking, to wonder – wonder what on earth was going on.

With a "You can go off people you know . . . I'm going to the loo," she stomped off. Except that Sara was too mad to read door signs. So she charged through the first door she came to. It was the kitchen. She opened another one. It was the broom cupboard. She stepped on a broom head. The handle flew up and hit her on the forehead. Finally, she made it to the loo, but marched into the wrong side. A cry of "Lady, not in here please" rang out. Back at the table, Sara sat with her head in her hands, looking down.

"Sara, will you please listen to me . . ."

"No Simon, I will not listen to you. You could have nothing to say to me that could remotely interest me. This explains 'The Joy of Sex'. I suppose you are the sort of person who smokes after they have had sex, burning the bed sheets, the bed, burning down the building, killing everyone . . ."

"Sara, for a start, rumours of my death have been greatly exaggerated. Thank you, I have always wanted to say that . . ."

"And there's something else I want to tell you . . . ." She was preparing for another charge.

"NO SARA, SHUT UP AND LISTEN!" he was shouting. The food froze in the mouths of the now statue-like surrounding diners. Sara was stunned into silence.

"Sara, I am not a smoker, I never have been a smoker. I have no plans to become a smoker," he said, now very quietly. "It was a tease. You tease me so much, I was getting a little of my own back. I never thought you would take it so seriously. I did not realise that you are president, chief executive officer and chair of the board of directors of the anti-smoking mafia, all rolled into one. I am sorry you got upset, I really am. You are just about the last person in the world I would want to upset. I tried to stop you but couldn't."

Silence descended. People around them started chewing their food again. A sheepish hint of a smile came to Sara's eyes.

"You missed out, er company secretary – of the mafia."

"Of course – sorry."

"That was a strong tease you know, Simon. And why didn't you stop me? You should have just sat on me, not let me go on like that . . ."

"I couldn't stop you – you have no idea how fired up you were, how passionate . . . You're lovely when you're livid by the way. But you are right, I should have just come round . . . and sat on you."

"Oh Simon, fancy me going on like that. Can you forgive me?"

"I've forgiven you. It was my fault anyway."

"What must everyone have thought?"

"They must have thought we were auditioning for The Fringe, or that this was the cabaret. I should have passed the hat and had a collection."

"Simon . . . let's pay the bill and go."

"Oh, and by the way Sara, did you see that notice? We were in the no-smoking part of the restaurant," he said as they left.

"I'll murder you for this!"

★　★　★

They walked down North Bridge towards Princes Street, Simon carrying Sara's luggage. On Princes Street, Sara would catch a number thirty bus to her cousin Maureen's and Simon would bed down for the night in his lastminute hotel. As they walked, their hands met and stayed together. On Sara's mind was just the question: what will he think of me? I should have known he wasn't a smoker. He doesn't smell of smoke.

"Simon, can you really forgive me for that?" She released her hand from his to put both her arms around him and to put her head on his shoulder.

"You'd better forgive me too. I sparked you off. You have a much lighter touch when it comes to teasing than I have. I love you teasing me. It was stupid of me. Can we forget it?" She nodded a smile, her arms staying around him.

"But just tell me this – did you really go into the wrong loo back there?"

"It's not funny." Her arms came away.

"It happened to me once – and worse. I was in Church House in Westminster for a conference, first time I had been there. The toilets were signposted down into the basement. I rushed down, mistook the signs and was so desperate I didn't notice there were no urinals, only cubicles. I had been in one for a few seconds when two women came in, clearly women priests. I stood there frozen, and then more and more came in. I was stuck. I just couldn't leave. It was about twenty minutes before all seemed quiet; I made a dash to the door and nearly knocked over a startled woman coming in. And I thought, will she ring the police and tell them there's been a pervert in the women's loo? And in Church House, too." By this time, Sara was rolling with laughter over the pavement.

"Oh dear, that's the best after-dinner liqueur ever. Oh dear . . ." She felt light-headed and began to sing: "Oh dear, what can the matter be, the Reverend Copplestone's stuck in the lavatory. He was there, that naughty young curaty, nobody knew he was there."

"Sara, shut up or you will be arrested for being drunk and disorderly. They will lock you up. You couldn't go to Gleneagles, and I would have to write a press release for the paper about you."

"Well, the way you write a press release, my dear Simon, no one would ever read it. It would be down with the "Would Like to Meet" folk again. That reminds me – you remember that ad: 'Man, early 30s, WLTM leggy, busty blonde for companion-ship only . . .' Go on, tell me, was it you?"

"Might have been."

"Oh Simon, so it was you, otherwise you would have denied it! Did you get one? How's the 'companionship' going," she asked, tickling him in the ribs.

"No Sara, it was not me. I cannot hide anything from you can I?" Her arms were round him again and they walked down over a railway bridge on a warm and still July evening, light, even through it was almost ten.

"You know," he said, "I reckon that if every smoker in the world could hear you speak about smoking, they would give it up tomorrow. Perhaps you should start a company and train people to go out the world over and tell everyone, the way you tell it. That would be fantastic." Her arms came away again.

"Simon, first of all you hoax me in that restaurant, now you're trying to turn me into a transnational corporation. Is this your very nice way of saying thank you and good-bye and have a nice life?"

Simon decided not to rise to that one, but went on: "But if you have a good idea, how can you scale it up? Without becoming a transnational?"

"It's a fair question but I am not going into it now, at 10 o'clock when I have been up, and so have you, since four this morning. You must come and have lunch with me, soon after I get back." They reached Princes Street and stood there. Sara's bus stop lay to the right, Simon's hotel to the left. Moments of silence followed. They were broken by Sara.

"You know, I just love being with you Simon, talking with you – give or take a wicked tease. Can I come with you to your hotel?" she asked quietly, her eyes deep into his.

"I don't think that would be a good idea."

"Would it count in another country?"

"It would count in another country."

"I lost my temper in the restaurant, Simon. I want to make it up to you."

"Sara, this is not easy. We have had a lovely meal – and want to go on; but you know we can't. Let's just say that my certificate of insanity will be with you in the morning, but we can't."

"Oh I could kick you," she said, putting her arms round him again. "Why did I have to fall for someone so sensible? I say these things because I trust you, because I feel completely safe with you. I knew what you would say."

"Sara, do not trust me, not completely. Remember that 1% weakness we spoke of? I am not a robot."

"Ah that 1%. It's a bit too clever if you ask me," she responded. Simon smiled and asked: "Shall I see you tomorrow, the alternative summit in the Assembly Hall?"

"Yes and Maureen says she'll come. See you there about one-ish?"

"I'll come to the bus stop with you. Better still, can I get the bus and see you to Maureen's?"

"No, I am not a five-year old. And kiss me goodnight here, not at the bus stop, please. We've eaten Italian, so two smackers on each cheek." The required smackers were followed by a long, lingering hug.

"Oh and by the way you've got a bruise on your forehead – the broom handle I guess. How will you explain that to Maureen?"

"I will tell her that I bumped into a gorgeous, gorgeous man – but not for nearly long enough." So Sara waited for the number 30 bus on the street she had walked down earlier in the day with William, Chloe and May. They would not be home yet, she thought, many of those who had been there would not be home. She had had a lovely evening, give or take losing her temper and a bump on her head. She watched him as he walked down the street, wanted to run after him, but knew that he was . . . beyond reach.

11

Edinburgh: 3/4 July

Sara slept well but woke early. That flirting in Edinburgh last evening, she told herself, that was silly. She had wanted to do it, and half of her wanted Simon to respond, to take her to his hotel and make love to her. But the other half of her said that she was playing with fire. And that both of them could get badly hurt.

Over breakfast, she told cousin Maureen how she had got that bump on her forehead. But Maureen had the look of someone who did not quite believe what she was hearing.

"I'd like to collect my pass for the G8 today from the Caledonian Hotel at the far end of Princes Street. We walked past it yesterday. Can we pick it up on the way to the Assembly Hall? I remember you saying that you'd like to come with me."

But they strolled first to a local paper shop to buy Sunday papers and to see the coverage of yesterday's march. Not far from Sara's mind was that looming first deadline, that she had to write 700 words for Frank by 10 a.m. Monday on the events of yesterday and maybe of today. But to her annoyance it was the Live8 concert in Hyde Park, rather than the rally in Edinburgh, that had received more space.

"Bloody Geldof!" she muttered.

"What do you mean, bloody Geldof. I thought you campaigners called him Saint Bob?"

"Let's say that I have mixed feelings about him. He's spread the message out to more people, that's true. But does the glitz, the hype, deflect the message? I'm still thinking it over. And I'm jealous he got more coverage than we did."

Nonetheless the coverage of the march was positive. "They came by trains and planes and buses and bikes," read the *Observer* story, ". . . an adventurous 75-year-old grandmother even pedalled more than 500 miles to Scotland's capital on a rickshaw . . . . And they came from Spain, Poland, the Netherlands and the US, as well as every corner of Britain."

"Among them were politicians, church leaders, actors, singers, comedians, as well as ordinary people from three-month-old babies to great-grandmothers," it went on.

"Their message was emblazoned across their T-shirts, foreheads and the thousands of banners being waved in the summer breeze: 'Drop the Debt', 'Trade not Aid' and, of course, 'Make Poverty History' . . .

"For three hours, the city had been like a carnival . . . the great cacophony of noise and energy was courtesy of African drums, deafening klaxons, shrill whistles, trumpets and shouts and cheers.

"But at 3pm, it gave way to a moment of silence and reflection, to think of those who have died of poverty, which was observed perfectly . . ."

And yes, we were there! Sara's heart leapt. "We were there!" She wanted to ring William, but decided to do it later so as not to wake him.

The alternatives event, entitled "Corporate Dream – Global Nightmare", started at 11.00. But first Sara was anxious to get that pass. Edinburgh's Caledonian Hotel is an imposing, swish place, and she walked along thick pile carpets through a long corridor and up some stairs to a large room where the passes were being handed out. She found a desk marked M–O, had remembered to bring her passport, and danced back down the corridors to give Maureen a hug.

"I've got it, I'm legal," she said, immediately putting the pass around her neck, there for it to stay. On the other corner of the road she noticed St John's Church, with a sign "Make Poverty History Service, 10.30 today."

Simon had said something about going to that, she remembered. Wonder if he's there? And Simon was there, praying for an end to poverty, but still wondering about the events of yesterday and especially the quite amazing evening. So many mixed emotions were going through his head, he found it difficult to sort them all out. His comforting thought was that at least he would see Sara again today.

Well over a thousand people were in the Assembly Hall when Sara and Maureen arrived. The conference was billed as "The G8 counter-conference", to look at the alternatives to the G8 and its policies. A session called "Challenging Privatisation" was followed by "Challenging Global Trade Rules". One of the speakers was Walden Bello from the Philippines, the director of a think-tank called Focus on the Global South. Bello was blunt about the World Trade Organization.

"The WTO is an opaque, undemocratic and non-transparent organisation driven by a free-trade ideology . . . to generate greater poverty and inequality. The WTO is simply a representative of American state and corporate interests. Its development has been closely linked to the changing needs of the United States. The problem we face is a determined effort to impose a neo-liberal trading order by an organisation that is dominated by the trading superpowers."

Bello felt the WTO should close down, that it was incapable of being reformed, that the poor would be better off without it. And he added a word on debt: "When the leaders talk of wiping out $25 billion of debt, remember they found $30 billion for the Iraq war at the drop of a hat."

It was around one o'clock when Sara turned round to see Simon entering the hall. He was limping.

"Simon, come and meet Maureen," she shouted over to him, "you're limping."

"Yes, my right foot's hurting like mad. Don't know why."

"I'll take a look at it later if you like," she smiled. "Oh Simon, before I forget, I want a quote from you to include in my first story for the paper. Just a sentence or two. Your feelings about yesterday. Could you e-mail it to me by nine in the morning, please?"

He nodded. Trying to keep up with Sara was something he'd come to live with. They sat listening to Meena Raman, chair of Friends of the Earth International, and Green Party MEP Caroline Lucas talk about climate change – a topic that, in Sara's view, was the missing link in the MPH campaign.

"Cup of tea, ladies?" asked Simon. "I need to go soon to catch a train back to London." The three of them trooped out of the hall for a cuppa, with Simon clearly in some pain.

"What have you done to yourself? You were OK when you left me," asked Sara.

Simon shook his head, they drank the tea and talked about what they had heard. Simon looked at his watch and Maureen said: "They've just started showing part of the film 'The Corporation', and Joel Bakan, who wrote it, is speaking."

"Maureen, you go ahead, I just want to look at Simon's foot before he goes," said the nurse. So they went out of the building to some steps. People were coming and going, and there was little space or privacy. But Simon limped to an empty step and was instructed to take off his right shoe and sock. Sara's hands slid easily and gently around his foot as she asked "How does that feel?"

"Heaven. Pure, pure bliss. Play me 'The Ode to Joy', hand me a glass of champagne, and . . ."

"Simon, stop it. I am trying to find out what's wrong with your foot. Does that hurt?"

"Ow!" he jumped, "that hurts."

"Well I don't know how you've done it – what were you doing last night after you left me? – but you've strained that foot and need to rest it. So no dancing up and down the corridor on the train journey home! Rest it."

"Yes, nurse. And, for the record, after I left you last night I went straight to bed."

"Hmmm . . . very suspicious if you ask me. Must have something to do with all the walking I suppose. Anyway, rest it. And there's something I want to ask you. I feel a bit embarrassed asking you this . . . where do I start? Look, I am not a very good person, you've seen that. In the space of just one hour last evening, I lost my temper in a restaurant, sang lewd songs in the street and tried to seduce a clergyman. But, well, I feel very apprehensive about this week and I wonder, please, even though I am not even sure there is a God, I wonder if I could ask you to pray for me?"

"Looks pretty bad Sara. Sometimes even God must want to throw the book."

"O shut up, I'll kick your good foot in a minute. Then you'll be sorry. Please Simon."

"Sara, of course I will," his hand went to hers. "I think you have a wrong impression of the Church. We have a lot in common with the medical profession. We are a hospital for sinners, not a museum for saints. People do not come to St. Luke's once a week to polish their halos. And we need to pray for each other.

"I will pray that you have the strength to do what you need to do this week, and for the discernment to see through the arguments, to see the truth and to write it. I will pray for you every day, several times a day – I give you my word." Sara flung her arms around his neck and weepily hung on tight.

"Wish you were staying on," she managed.

"You will be in my thoughts so much, I promise you. And I look forward to reading your piece every day."

"You'd better go and get that train," Sara bucked up. "Let's have lunch again soon. You must come to me next. We'll fix it when I get back . . . don't forget that concert . . . Oh, and by the way, I haven't had that certificate yet, you know the one . . ."

"I've sent it to the G8 for approval." His touch is lightening she thought as she watched him go towards to the station, that limp apparently rather better. Now feeling utterly alone, Sara rejoined Maureen in the hall.

"What an interesting relationship you two have," smiled Maureen, "I was fascinated. The body language! It went far beyond, well, just friends?"

"Tell you later. Let's listen to Joel Bakan."

Bakan, a law professor at the University of British Columbia, spoke of the power of transnational corporations and in particular about Coca-Cola and the effects of its operation in India on local water supplies.

Coca-Cola's bottling plants draw vast quantities of water from the ground, he alleged, leaving people living and working around these plants with little water for drinking or agriculture. Coca-Cola draws as much as 500,000 litres of water a day for their plant at Plachimada in the state of Kerala, he said, and their activities also bring up sludge contaminated with toxic metals like cadmium and lead, which pollute the land and water around the plants. As a result, farmers have lost their livelihoods, and women have to walk long distances in search of drinkable water.

"That's it," thought Sara, "I am never buying that again." So another product was added to her boycott list: Nestlé, Mcdonald's, KFC, Esso, Shell – it was lengthening all the time. The afternoon ended in laughter with a performance by the Yes Men, a humorous group of impersonators. And Sara went back to Maureen's to begin writing her first story of the week, and be ready to send it by ten the next morning.

"One amazing day in Edinburgh," she entitled it. "Almost a quarter of a million people came to Edinburgh on Saturday, thirty-five of them from our town (see picture). They came to tell the world's eight most powerful leaders: stop just talking about poverty and take action at your summit to do something." And so the story went on. She ended by saying "Throughout this week, I shall be reporting for the paper on what is happening at the G8 summit. And I hope to report real progress . . . I hope to be able to tell us that this week was a real breakthrough in the campaign to Make Poverty History." And she e-mailed it just before ten the next morning and breathed a huge sigh of relief.

And that morning, that day, was another day in Edinburgh. A number of things seemed to be happening. For a start, there would be clowns on the street, it had been billed as a Fun Day. But there was talk of protesters doing something rather less funny.

Maureen had suggested that Sara should take the morning off to visit the Dean Gallery, part of the Scottish Museum of Modern Art. "There is something there I think you would be interested in seeing," she said. After taking the bus into the centre, where a strong police presence was evident, they walked along a path to the gallery. Maureen led the way to a room with just one exhibit – a huge cast iron statue of a sort of human which filled the whole room, from floor to ceiling.

"Wow," said Sara. "I know why you wanted me to see this. It depicts power, so much power, such huge power. The power of rich countries to trample on poor countries, of huge corporations to abuse power. I'd like just to stand here for a while and take it in."

They visited other rooms in the gallery and walked back towards Princes Street. Sirens were then wailing and police cars and vans began rushing past them. Oh-ho, there's trouble somewhere! thought Sara. As they walked on they came to a solid line of parked police vehicles and beyond them about a hundred people detained in a small area. But there were no banners and no one seemed to know what it was all about. They walked on to Princes Street. Now the clowns were out, colourful, but with a serious message. One protester handed her a leaflet which read: "During the G8 summit, as Tony Blair beds down in the Gleneagles Hotel, owned by drinks company Diageo, is he aware that his host is accused of forcing products into the African market, undermining labour rights and lobbying for free trade? Well, yes."

And someone with him was singing a Gilbert and Sullivan ditty, to appropriate words: "Diageo is the very model of the modern neo-Liberal, new-Labour company party."

More police cars, police on horseback were now rushing north of Princes Street, and there were more protesters with banners. They watched, hardly believing that this was taking place in the middle of Edinburgh. They watched a scene of chaos. People were running everywhere, some were knocked over, some arrested.

Then the action moved, this time to Princes Street itself, and the fun really started, and was to go on until late in the evening. Lines of protesters faced lines of police. Then, suddenly, the lines moved, and police came up behind them and the two women were trapped, like hundreds of others. Blocked in between police, protesters and police, and with no way to escape.

"We're trapped, we cannot get out," said Maureen. Sara thought back to May Day and Oxford Circus in London several years ago when police had detained people for six hours. Oh no, surely not that, she thought. Other journalists were also there on the street, plus photographers galore.

"Maybe we can cut though one of the big stores with a back entrance," said Maureen. But the stores had all closed their doors. Mothers were screaming, children were pleading with police to let them go. But to no avail.

"Tell you what – we can go into the gardens and sit in there for a while," suggested Maureen.

"Just a mo, I want to talk with some of the protesters. This will be part of my story for tomorrow."

"What are you protesting about?" she asked one of them.

"About the G8," he replied.

"But what are you trying to achieve? There are no leaders here in Edinburgh."

"No, but they are meeting up the road at Gleneagles in a few days time." So the two women sat in the gardens on the side of Princes Street, Sara checking her notes.

"You know this protest is OK but it's nothing like the Make Poverty History march. Or perhaps I'm biased." Suddenly, with no warning, from the far end of the gardens, a line of riot police came charging towards them, shouting "move, move!"

"God, this is terrifying!" exclaimed Maureen as the women sprang up and were pushed towards the other end of the gardens, Sara almost losing her notebook in the rush. Finally they found themselves a yard from a concrete wall, with someone shouting "stop, please, you will crush us." Before they reached Sara and Maureen, the police did stop, just. But about ten yards away from them, a woman screamed and collapsed in pain.

"You've crushed her, you fools," Sara heard herself shouting, "you've crushed her. Get an ambulance quick."

The urgency compelled action and an ambulance was soon there. The injured woman was lifted into the back of it and taken to hospital. Sara rang the hospital later and was told that the woman had three cracked ribs. She also found out that the woman had just been out shopping and was caught in the middle of it all. At least the charge of the riot police seemed to clear the blockage, and the two women escaped from Princes Street.

"God, that was a bit over the top. What was it all about anyway?" asked Maureen.

Sara tried asking a policeman but he was tight-lipped. She felt shaken, but had not really been frightened by it. And it was good for the story. But as they walked north of Princes Street, there was more trouble, this time in Rose Street, a narrow cobbled street, full of bars and cafes. Some of the cobbles were being ripped up and hurled at the police.

"You know, this is getting nasty, I think we should get out of here and go back home," said Maureen. Sara took some pictures and agreed – "good idea."

The riots were the story of the day. Over one hundred arrests were made and over twenty people had been hurt. Late in the evening, Sara wrote her story.

"Crushed. It nearly happened to me. Crushed by riot police in the middle of Edinburgh on a sunny afternoon when I was sitting enjoying the city's gardens. A woman only yards away was not so lucky . . .

"Heavy-handed is the only word to describe the police action . . .

"Lines of police faced lines of protesters . . .

On a street renowned for its classy shops, it was not the tills that rang out but the shouts of protesters, of police . . ."

She continued carefully, beginning each paragraph with the initials of Chloe and May so as to spell out their names. And to see if they would notice. She e-mailed it to Frank, hoping he would not change it. And a neighbour of Maureen's called in later to tell them that at 9.30 that evening lines of riot police and protesters were still facing each other on Princes Street.

12

G8 Gleneagles: 5/6 July

Princes Street was back to normal the following morning. Buses were running, people walking to work, shops open, hardly a policeman or protester in sight, as Sara walked along it to the Sheraton Hotel to catch the complimentary bus to Gleneagles. She thought about the march, the family, Simon, yesterday. But today would take her to new territory. The G8 summit started tomorrow. Today there would be briefings plus speculation about what leaders would achieve. Sara needed to set the scene for the paper.

With the countryside becoming more stunning with each mile of the journey, Sara made a mental note that the family must come to Scotland for a holiday. It took almost an hour and a half before they reached the Gleneagles media security tent. Passes were carefully scrutinised and journalists then allowed through to the media working area, an area with huge tents. It was a good half mile away from the hotel where the leaders would meet. A place you could go only if you had a special pass. And there were police everywhere.

So Sara found her bearings, discovered some lockers, and had a drink and a snack. No one was there to take any money. All the food and non-alcoholic drink were free, she was told. She could apparently sit there from early in the morning till late at night, and stuff herself silly. She tried relating this invitation to self-indulgence to the poverty under discussion that week. She remembered her remark about the pudding in the restaurant on Saturday being 200 calories in every mouthful. Stupid, senseless, she thought, when half the world does not have enough. What was the responsible approach to food for people in Western countries, she pondered, in a world of poverty?

Journalists were invited to pick up a complimentary media bag. The bag was heavy. Sara found out why. It included a full bottle of Scotch plus a large tin of Scottish shortbread biscuits. I'll keep the biscuits for the family and give the Scotch to Maureen, she thought.

In the vast working press area, Sara found a spot for her laptop and read e-mails. And she read about Gleneagles, a luxury former British Railways hotel surrounded by three top-class golf courses, it was said. It even had its own railway station – to bring guests straight there. To Sara, it seemed a strange venue for a meeting on poverty. It was to here that the leaders of Britain, the US, France, Germany, Italy, Canada and Japan would be helicoptered tomorrow and taken out again on Friday. President Putin of Russia would be there but was said to distrust helicopters because of their poor safety record in his country. Too many crashed for comfort. Mr Putin would come by road.

In addition to journalists in the press room, Sara found there were many representatives of the MPH agencies. This made her feel at home. She was a journalist for a week, but a campaigner nonetheless. And she found herself in possession of a large and growing number of press releases about what the agencies hoped would come out of the summit. And this was her story for the day – the hopes and aspirations for the summit of organisations that represented many millions of people.

An MPH press release urged the G8 "not fail the world's poor." It said the summit should build on achievements so far and "deliver on demands of trade justice, total debt cancellation and more and better aid." It urged Blair and the other leaders to "demonstrate true leadership".

A press release headed "Children for Change", caught her eye. It said that seventeen young people from all over the world had come to Gleneagles for a C8 – a children's version of the G8 summit. They wanted leaders to ensure no more poverty, free quality education for all, health and a healthy environment for all.

Tomorrow . . . the leaders would not arrive until mid-afternoon, and it would be the evening before their first meeting. But campaigners were planning a march around the heavily guarded perimeter fence of the hotel. The march would start in the nearby village of Auchterarder, but such was the tight security that to get from the G8 press centre to the village was apparently going to be difficult. Best choose, she was told, between Auchterarder and the press centre. Sara chose Auchterarder, but as the G8 buses did not go through the village, she was told by an aid agency worker to get a G8 alternatives bus from Edinburgh. This had been announced at the alternative meeting on Sunday and Sara had made a note of the starting point, just in case.

The following morning, just before seven, Maureen shouted up the stairs: "There are problems. Protesters are everywhere, roads to Gleneagles blocked, Stirling is cut off. Chaos reigns. Police are advising people not to travel to Gleneagles for the next few hours due to serious public disorder. What will you do?"

"Get there, NOW," said Sara, shifting out of bed and out of the house like lightning with a "better get a bus quick." And with Maureen thrusting a bun and a bottle of water into her hand, she bolted for the G8 alternatives bus.

The bus was a double-decker of the type used on suburban routes, except that this one seemed to have been retired some time ago. Sara paid £5, had the back of her hand stamped in lieu of a ticket, and found a place on top. In contrast to the air-conditioned luxury of the press bus, the ride was bumpy, slow and seemed to be taking a very roundabout route. But she noticed numerous roadblocks, diversions and police everywhere. The people around her were great and the double-decker was soon filled with happy, noisy singing.

But then disaster struck as far as Sara was concerned. Someone a few seats behind her lit up a cigarette. The smoke drifted her way. She tucked her head in her coat and tried to block it out. And someone said to the smoker: "Look, if you smoke, we all have to smoke." And he put it out.

"Thank goodness for that," said Sara to a young African sitting next to her. "Smoking is really bad for your health."

"Yes, and in more ways than one," smiled the woman. "I was on a minibus in Kenya a few weeks ago, twelve of us crammed in, and a man lit up, even though there were no-smoking signs. We pleaded with him to put it out but he wouldn't. Tempers got heated and a very large guy threatened to beat him up. We calmed him down and the smoker stubbed it out. But I remember thinking at the time – this is further proof that smoking can be dangerous to someone's health!"

A rumour flew round the bus that the police had cancelled the march on the grounds of public safety. There was disbelief. What right had the police to do that? Only about 5,000 people were expected. But some coaches with protesters on their way to Gleneagles had been turned back, they heard on a radio. Could that happen to them wondered a dismayed Sara. "I should have gone on the press coach!" she told herself.

At around midday they stopped at a service area. She bought a sandwich and heard that London had been awarded the 2012 Games. On and on they crawled before reaching the outskirts of Perth, which Sara knew lay to the north of Gleneagles. Then the bus swung round to go south and was stopped by police. Two policemen mounted the bus and silently inspected everyone. But the march was on, they said, and it was under police escort that the bus finally crawled into the village of Auchterarder.

"Even G. W. Bush couldn't do better than have a police escort," said the African woman. At 1.30 they finally arrived, five and a half hours after leaving Edinburgh, little more than fifty miles away.

They walked up the main street which was full of Make Poverty History banners on buildings and MPH window stickers in people's houses.

The march was due to start in Auchterarder's park at the top of the village. But first there was music and speeches. The Rinky

Dink sound system was playing, lots of people were dancing. The Infernal Noise Brigade was on the other side of the park. George Galloway was speaking on a stage. The atmosphere was good, local people were waving and cheering the crowd. The marchers lined up and started off, led by police with no numbers on their shoulders. Sinister, thought Sara, why no numbers? Not a question she cared to ask them.

The march walked slowly up to the Gleneagles hotel fence, people carrying a wide range of banners: "Stop the War", "Trade Justice", "Drop the Debt". Some were singing: "They say drop the bomb, we say drop the debt". Sara talked with a woman carrying a Trade Justice banner who told her: "I want Blair and the other G8 leaders to drop their corporate-led, neo-liberal agenda, and to change their policies so that the world's poor benefit."

Local people were looking on, some with picnic tables and chairs in the garden to watch the proceedings in comfort. "You know, this is the most exciting thing that has happened in Auchterarder for years," said an elderly woman to Sara as the march paused by her gate.

"Well that's great to hear. Because all this must have disrupted your day," she responded.

"It will be worth it if those bloody folk in that swanky place up the road listen," said the woman. At just after three o'clock the walkers reached the Gleneagles hotel fence. It was raining. Six solid lines of yellow-jacketed police stood behind the tall metal fence, with police on horses behind them. George Galloway rattled the fence, the police taking no action.

The marchers then turned right, as if round the top of a horseshoe. To their left, over a large field, Sara could see the press security tent, some 500 yards away. And between them and the tent was a line of about 15 mounted police. But there was only a low wire preventing people from going into the field. And while most of the marchers kept to the road and the prescribed route, several hundred people decided to go over the field and towards the mounted police and the press tent. Although still nowhere near the hotel.

While some protesters were turned back by the police, others got through and made it to the tent. Chinook helicopters circled overhead and one landed noisily. Some of the protesters sat down in the field surrounded by police who had rushed over. And other reinforcements in yellow tried to stop more people from entering the field. A BBC TV camera crew took off across the field to take pictures.

Sara spoke with one man who had been turned back. "Well I got bored on the march," he said, "it was going nowhere, just round in a timid circle. Then some of us made the break and the atmosphere changed and we became quite excited, but I'm quite scared about what's going to happen."

Soon it all calmed down. There were few arrests, the advertised closing rally did not seem to happen, and at six the march was over. Sara badly wanted to get back to the press tent to see what was happening, to check on the latest news. And also to go to a 'Taste of Scotland' evening in the press area. The country's first minister Jack McConnell had invited journalists to attend.

While the march was over, however, the road from the village to the G8 media area had been closed by the police as a security precaution. This is what Auchterarder's three taxi companies told Sara. And they added that the road might be closed for another two hours yet – their cars were not venturing out anyway until all the marchers had left the village. Furthermore, the police would not allow anyone to walk to the media centre.

Stranded in the village, Sara stood at the side of the road wondering what to do, whether to hitch a lift from someone who might be willing to take her there, perhaps by a roundabout way. There was a church over the road with a large Make Poverty History banner draped across the tower. She thought of Simon, how she had asked him to pray for her. On impulse, she stood in the church porch and dialled his mobile.

"Hi Simon, it's me, Sara. Guess where I am? In a church. I'm applying to become a nun . . . I haven't got the ideal profile you say . . .? Well no . . . but I know something about them, I know why they are called nuns . . . You know that and it's crude . . .?

Sorrrry. I sound a bit high? That's because I am very high up Simon, I'm stuck in a highland village called Auchterarder; and I can't get back to Gleneagles because the road's shut. Are you praying hard enough for me? . . . Prayer doesn't work like that . . . oh, you can't get staff! . . . It's lovely to talk to you Simon, how's your foot?"

She wandered into the church. A church minister came over and said "welcome". He told her that he had been a minister in Northern Ireland for many years and had witnessed many disturbances. He thought he had left that behind when he came to Auchterarder . . . but now he wasn't so sure, he joked.

A banner at the back of the church caught Sara's eye. "Love is social justice. Social justice is love," it said. She wrote it down in her notebook. Someone came into the church with a large camera on his shoulder. Seeing Sara's press badge, he said, in a broken accent: "Excuse me. Can you tell me how I get back to the media area?"

"I am trying to work that out myself," she said. "Where are you from?"

"I am from Ukraine" he said, holding out his hand, "I am a cameraman for a television station. My name is Joe – for short."

"I'm Sara," she smiled. "Joe, we have two options. We can either wait until the road is open, maybe not for two hours yet, and then a taxi will take us. Or maybe we could get a lift with someone who would take us there sooner, perhaps by a longer route. Tell you what – let's try that, shall we?" They stood at the side of the road, Sara's thumb outreached. Several cars whizzed by without stopping. But an old Land Rover pulled over.

"Thank you," she said. "We have a problem. The road to the media area at Gleneagles is closed and we wondered if perhaps you know a longer way round, and could take us there?"

"Get in," he said.

"Really? Oh thank you. I'm Sara, this is Joe. He's from Ukraine."

With Sara in the front seat, and Joe in the back, the car pulled away, travelling very, very slowly, the driver noticing her press badge but not saying a word for a mile or so, before asking – "so you're a journalist then?"

"Well, yes, sort of," she said, waving her badge.

"I hate journalists!" said the driver, "Hate them. When my brother got into a spot of bother with the police a few years ago, the journalists got it all wrong. All wrong. I hate journalists!"

"I'm sorry to hear that. Well actually, I am not really a journalist, I'm a nurse," said Sara, a little edgily.

"Oh you're a nurse now. I tell you I hate journalists and you become a nurse. Another false journalist's story if you ask me." The tone was unpleasant and malicious. Suddenly he speeded up.

"You know what?" he went on, screeching round a corner, almost on two wheels. "I will take you to the media centre . . . perhaps . . . by a very roundabout route." Alarm bells did not so much ring in Sara's head as utterly explode.

"Look, this was a mistake," she said, on the verge of panic. "Would you put us down here, *please*?"

"No. I will not put you down here. I am taking you a round-about route, just like you asked."

Oh God! We've been kidnapped! she thought, freezing shivers running down her spine. "You fool," she told herself, "I tell the girls never under any circumstances whatsoever to get into a car with a stranger and here I am doing just that . . . At least Joe's with me." Joe was in the back, smiling, immune to what was going on.

"This area is very beautiful," said Joe. As Sara sat there, numb, the car turned off the road and went up a steep narrow lane. Then the driver suddenly announced: "I've changed my mind. I will not take you to the media centre. Instead I am going to boot you out at the top of the hill."

Anywhere, anywhere, she thought, although God knows where we are. The car stopped. Sara could not get out quick enough. Joe got out with a "thank you, thank you. Are we near the media centre here?"

"Only five miles down the road, mate," said the driver, adding as an afterthought: "I hate journalists. Got my own back on one, anyway. Bye . . . nurse." With that, he drove off.

Sara was shaking, shocked but relieved, and had managed to take a hard look at the number plate, to remember it and ring the police. She sat down on the damp grass, badly wanting William or Simon to be there to give her a hug. She thought of asking Joe for a hug – but no, she thought, he seems OK, but I cannot risk another stranger, definitely not on top of a bleak Scottish hill.

"This area is so beautiful," said Joe, "and that driver was exciting." At least Joe's happy, she thought, deciding not to tell him what had happened.

Sara rang one of the taxi companies. Thank goodness for mobiles, she thought. The road to the media centre was reopening soon, she was told, but where was she? And that took some unravelling. Sara remembered the road the driver had taken out of the village, and that the turn had come after about four miles. And she was on the top of a hill. To Sara's great relief, she heard down the phone: "I think I know where you are. Stay there. Be with you in about ten minutes."

Just before eight o'clock, her phone rang. It was Chloe. Sara tried hard not to cry.

"Mummy, Mummy, thank you so much. We read the paper and we saw our names. Not at first, Daddy saw them first. How are you Mummy?"

"I'm all right now," she said. "I'm crying because it's so lovely to hear your voice."

"Hello Mummy," said May . . . and then she spoke to William.

"You sound weepy", he said.

"I'm OK," she didn't want to burden him with details. "I'm off to the press centre for a 'Taste of Scotland' evening with the first minister."

"Oh it's all right for some! You name dropper! Enjoy it, talk to you tomorrow," he said. She heard a taxi wind slowly up the hill. The driver got out with a "what on earth happened to you two?" Sara told him.

"Oh God, you were unlucky. He's a well-known local nutter, the guy who owns that old Land Rover. Bears grudges against everyone, been banned for dangerous driving. You must tell the police."

They arrived at the press centre soon after eight. The first minister had gone; the 'Taste of Scotland' evening was over. Well I've my own taste of Scotland, thought Sara, and on the top of that hill, the midges had had a good taste of her.

She made a bee-line for the dining area, had an ample meal, courtesy of God knows who – probably the taxpayer, probably herself, she mused. And then the coach, the lovely coach back home – well, to Maureen's. On the way, she wrote the day's story in her head. She would include what happened with that maniac, but only in a paragraph at the end. Would not do to make it too "I, I, me, me", or show what an idiot I am, she thought.

13

London and Gleneagles: 7/8 July

It wasn't that Charley was going bald. Far from it. It was just that her hair was sort of thinning out. And she was beginning to get sensitive about it. Charley emphatically did not want a wig – she had a very obvious wig that she had worn in Edinburgh as a means of disguise, but that was a fun wig. No, for normal use she wanted a solution that was far more discreet, far more – Charley.

She had heard of a hair expert-cum-wigmaker between Edgware Road and Paddington station. Someone who could do something with thinning hair, who could arrange things so that hair looked the way it used to look, without it being too obvious. So Charley arranged an appointment for 9.00 a.m. on Thursday, 7th July, before work.

She got off the mainline train at Euston, as usual, but instead of taking her normal tube to Westminster, Charley walked the short distance to Euston Square to catch a Circle Line tube to Paddington. And then sat in the packed second carriage of train number 216. Should she get off at Edgware Road, she pondered, or stay on it until Paddington? She examined the A-Z and Paddington looked just a little closer. She stayed on. It was the worst decision that Charley ever made.

The train had just pulled away from Edgware Road station, when suddenly there was a large flash of light and an explosion further down the carriage, which was then pitched into darkness. Charley took the blast on her face and screamed – as did everyone.

Pain seared through her face and hair and she pulled out a handkerchief for comfort. But she could see nothing, only hear screams such as she had never heard before. She felt her legs and arms, they were still intact, but her clothes were ripped and she felt blood running off her hair and down her face.

It seemed like hours before anyone came to their rescue. Charley, like the other survivors, was taken to a nearby hotel and then to a hospital. She heard later that seven people had died on that train, some of them in the same carriage that she had been in.

★ ★ ★

Exhausted from the day before, Sara struggled out of bed to finalise her story. Just after nine, she e-mailed it to Frank and left to catch the press coach. On the coach, Frank rang.

"Like your story, Sara, but you've got it the wrong way round. It should begin with what happened to *you*, the human interest angle. Then I can lead off with 'Highland nutter kidnaps our reporter'."

"Do you have to, Frank?"

"I do, and I'd like a few more details. We're right on deadline, so can you send me a couple of extra paras right away?"

"Frank, I am sorry but I'm on the coach and won't be there for another half an hour."

"In that case, you'd better tell me and I will feed it in." She did, and Frank ended with "have you heard?"

"Heard what?"

"About the bombs. Four have exploded in the middle of London. Not clear yet how many casualties but they seem to be mounting. Take care." Who do I know who is likely to be in London today, she wondered. Not William, Simon, Agnes . . . but, of course, Charley and Peter. She rang Charley's mobile, the line was dead, Peter's mobile the same. Why, why, she puzzled. And Sara thought she had better ring William and tell him about yesterday, or he would be shocked by the 'nutter' story in the paper.

Large screens in each corner in the room were a feature of the G8 press area. As Sara walked in it was clear that few people were working, nearly all were crowded round the screens. Suicide bombers had attacked three trains and a bus, she heard. Casualties were growing by the minute. And mobile phone networks were down all across London.

A feeling of helplessness coupled with desperation to know if Charley and Peter were safe came over her. She rang William who thought it most unlikely that either would be anywhere near the bombed sites. But he promised to ring Peter at the university and come back to her. And Sara told him about yesterday.

The G8 summit was thrown into chaos. This was the main day, the only full day. News came that Blair would fly back to London. The G8 meetings were on hold. William rang back.

"Peter's worried. Charley has not arrived at work yet. He's ringing the hospitals and will let me know. I will ring you when I hear anything. What it's like there?"

"Awful. This is just cruel, for everyone." Sara watched as Tony Blair's helicopter took to the sky on the first leg of his journey to London. It was announced that Jack Straw would be coming up to take his place and that the meeting would resume. But why not Gordon Brown, she wondered, if they're going to be talking seriously about aid and debt?

Something else was happening in the press room. Desks of foreign journalists were emptying. A Brazilian, scurrying away, told her: "My editor's ordered me to London to cover the bombings." Which means less coverage for the G8 and poverty, she realised.

Her phone rang. It was William. Charley was on the underground train that had been bombed at Edgware Road. She had minor facial and head injuries, was badly shaken but nothing worse; would be detained in hospital overnight and probably go home tomorrow.

She rang Peter. No reply from either of his phones. Poor Charley, but a lot of people had fared much worse. The number of confirmed deaths had risen to over forty. Press releases were now appearing, linking the summit and the bombs. Steve Tibbett, head of policy at ActionAid UK, said: "The attacks on London have shocked and horrified everyone here in Gleneagles, but we are hopeful that despite these tragic events the focus will stay on Africa and fighting global injustice."

Press briefings continued to be held in tents across the road from the main press areas, and on the verge of the golf courses. Most were given by the campaign agencies, but some were by leaders, not just of the G8 countries. Leaders of several developing countries, including Algeria, Brazil, China, Ethiopia, India, Ghana, Mexico, Nigeria, Senegal, South Africa and Tanzania were also at Gleneagles. Some of them came to tell the press of their hopes for progress at the meeting.

Waiting for a meeting to start, Sara wandered past some TV cameras in the hope of a glimpse of a golf course. After she'd taken a few steps, a policeman suddenly jumped out from behind a bush and shouted: "What are you doing here? This is a restricted area. Get back there."

She got back there. Police from all over the country had been drafted to Gleneagles. Enough to have a cop behind every bush, she thought.

From the hotel itself, there was no word of anything happening. At around six o'clock, Sara sat down for a coffee at a table with two people wearing more than one badge around their necks. This usually meant that the wearer was allowed into the hotel itself. They turned out to be two of the summit's simultaneous interpreters, translating one language into another instantaneously.

"Have you done much interpreting today"? Sara enquired.

"We haven't done anything today. Nothing has restarted yet," said one. The other nodded. Hell, thought Sara, it's turned six o'clock and according to the interpreters nothing had happened. And they should know.

Word came that Blair was on his way back from London and that there would be an evening meeting. The bombs had wrecked the schedule. So it all hinges on tomorrow, she thought. Or did it? She heard that the summit communiqué had already been drafted and that leaders would in any case have discussed it only superficially and agreed to sign up. But where does that leave the idea of the world's eight most powerful leaders listening to people, responding to concerns and showing leadership? she wondered.

In the lead-up to the G8, almost half a million MPH supporters had e-mailed Blair about ending poverty. Over 8 million people in Britain had bought MPH wristbands and nearly a quarter of a million people had marched in Edinburgh. Was all this demonstration of support for making poverty history lost on the leaders? It was beginning to look that way.

So Sara wrote her story for Frank, telling how the bombs had affected the summit, giving the reactions of people at Gleneagles. She rang Peter again, and this time there was a reply. He was with Charley at the hospital. Her face and hair had burns but they were not serious. She would, however, need a wig.

"I just thank God, she's alive," he said tearfully.

"Do give Charley my love and say I will call to see her very soon."

Almost fifty people were by then known to have died in London. For it to have happened any time, any day, any place was tragic, but for it to happen today only made it worse, mused Sara. We've another challenge now, not to let this deflect attention from the poor.

Friday July 8th was the last day of the G8. As Sara got out of bed, she knew that she had the luxury of not having to write anything today as the local paper was not published on Saturday. She could write her story on Sunday for Monday's paper.

In the press area the news was that leaders had met last evening, would meet again this morning and end the summit by lunchtime. Their communiqué was being finalised.

Press briefings continued. At a briefing by Friends of the Earth and Tearfund came a warning that any progress made on development at the summit would be undermined by failure to commit to urgent action to address the causes and effects of climate change. Climate change was already having a devastating impact on many African countries and communities, worsening already critical water crises, putting millions more at risk of hunger, increasing the spread of malaria and other diseases, and increasing the frequency and severity of floods and droughts.

At around lunchtime, the eight leaders were shown on television on the steps of the Gleneagles hotel signing their agreed communiqué. And it was announced that Tony Blair would give a press conference at 2.15 p.m. Sara arrived at 1.30 to get a seat near the front. She managed the third row, sitting next to an American journalist.

"Do you think Bush will follow after Blair and give a press conference?" she asked.

"Oh no, Bush would never do that!" said the American, "He would need the questions in advance, a list of everyone who would attend, their mothers' maiden names, their hat sizes, etc., etc . . . No, he couldn't do it."

They waited and waited, the doors and windows shut for security reasons, the atmosphere stifling. At 2.50, the Prime Minister finally arrived, surrounded by men in suits, dark suits. Sara was not one inch a Blair fan, the Iraq war had seen to that. But she felt nonetheless that for a man who had flown to Singapore earlier in the week to back the Games bid, and who had returned to London yesterday to oversee the government's response to the bombs, he was looking pretty good.

Documents running to some seventy pages were then handed to journalists: the communiqué and supporting papers. Sara, like everyone else there, barely had time to read the large print, let alone the small.

"I believe we have made very substantial progress," said Mr Blair. They had not gone as far as some would have liked, he added. "It isn't the end of poverty in Africa but it is the hope that it can be ended. It is the definitive expression of our collective will to act in the face of death and disease and conflict that is preventable."

A $50 billion aid increase for developing countries had been agreed, he claimed. Leaders had also agreed that agricultural export subsidies should be scrapped, although no date had been fixed.

"There are commitments here which are hugely significant. I'd like to congratulate the Make Poverty History campaign," he said.

Questions followed, fairly tame questions, thought Sara, nobody challenging very hard, maybe because of yesterday's bombs, maybe because no one had the time to read the documents and were unaware of any pitfalls. As the press conference was ending, the aid and development agencies began distributing press releases with their verdict on the summit. And the verdicts were damning and unanimous.

"G8 turn their backs on the world's poor," said a War on Want release. "The G8 have today betrayed 1.1 billion people living in poverty."

"This will not make poverty history," ran a Christian Aid release. "It is a vastly disappointing result. Millions of campaigners all over the world have been led to the top of the mountain and now we are being frog marched down again. This is a sad day for poor people of Africa and all over the world." On debt, there was no real progress, it said, and on trade, no new deal.

"The G8 did not deliver the commitments on aid, debt and trade that WDM and the other members of Make Poverty History had been campaigning for," said a WDM news release. "The final communiqué is an insult to the hundreds of thousands of campaigners who listened in good faith to the world leaders' claim that they were willing to seriously address poverty in Africa."

An Oxfam release asked what the $50 billion extra aid – which would not start till 2010 – would actually mean. Aid would then be $130 billion a year, it said. But "if the $50 billion had kicked in immediately," it went on, "it could have lifted 300 million out of poverty in the next five years . . . the United Nations is clear that by 2010 we need $180 billion each year if we are to reach the Millennium Development Goals."

Sara looked at the G8 communiqué. The leaders said that a "substantial increase in official development assistance is required

in order to achieve the Millennium Development Goals by 2015."
Yet those same leaders were not offering such an increase. No
leadership there at all, she thought.

On debt, the G8 communiqué said that the debts owed by eligible indebted countries would be cancelled "as set out in our
Finance Ministers meeting on 11 June".

"On debt, the summit brings nothing new," said an ActionAid
release. "The announcement by G8 Finance Ministers in June
was good news for the 18 countries that will have their debts cancelled, but addressed only 10% of the problem and fell far short
of the full debt cancellation desperately needed by more than
60 countries. This leaves many spending more on debt repayments than on education or healthcare. And if you check the
small print, it largely uses money from existing aid budgets."

The Jubilee Debt Campaign pointed out that the G8 debt deal
is not 100% debt cancellation as it only applies to some of the
debt. So no advance there it seemed.

"The summit has failed to deliver justice for Africa. Make Poverty History campaigners have succeeded in putting poverty and
Africa at the centre of the G8 agenda, but there is still a yawning
gulf between expectations raised and policy promises delivered,"
said ActionAid.

"G8 leaders failed to end the scandal of forced trade liberalisation," it went on. "G8 leaders have at last recognised that poor
countries should be free to determine their own economic policies, but have given no indication that this will apply to debt
relief. Women such as Sabina Nicholas, a nurse in Tanzania who
had her water cut off following a privatisation project forced
through via debt relief, will continue to suffer."

A nurse in Tanzania, thought Sara, doing the same job as her,
but with no water in her home. Sara could scarcely imagine it.
The press releases kept on coming.

"All dressed up and nowhere to go," ran the headline of a
WWF release on climate change. It described the summit as a
missed opportunity to make the world's top eight economies agree
to an effective agenda on climate change.

A few minutes after Blair and his entourage had left, another press conference started. This time it was Bob Geldof, Bono and Kumi Naidoo of South Africa, chair of the Global Call to Action against Poverty, of which MPH was the UK arm.

"The people have roared, the G8 has responded with a whisper," was Naidoo's verdict on the summit's outcome. Sara watched as Geldof turned to Kumi Naidoo and branded his criticism a "disgrace". To the dismay of other poverty campaigners, Geldof had nothing but praise for the G8's announcement. He said that 10 million lives would be saved as a result of the deal. And he awarded the leaders ten out of ten for their pledges on aid, and eight out of ten for debt relief. "Mission accomplished," said Geldof.

"Geldof has done a disservice to the hundreds of thousands of people who marched in Edinburgh at the weekend," said a WDM press release in response. "His comments do not reflect the collective conclusions of the development campaigns who make up Make Poverty History. Mr Geldof has become too close to the decision makers to take an objective view of what has been achieved at this summit."

And John Hilary of War on Want said: "Bob Geldof may be content with crumbs from the table of his rich political friends. But we did not come to Gleneagles as beggars. We came to demand justice for the world's poor. We have no problem with Geldof celebrating the 10 million lives he feels will be saved as a result of this deal. But what about the other two billion people driven into poverty by the policies of the G8? Did the leaders of the rich world have nothing for them?"

There was at least a bright spot in the summit communiqué on fair trade. "We welcome the growing market for fairtrade goods and their positive effect in supporting livelihoods and increasing public awareness of the positive role of trade in development," it read.

Yes, thought Sara, trade can play a positive role in development. But only if the rules are changed. And there was nothing about that in the communiqué.

It was around five o'clock when the press conferences were over. Time to get on that coach for the last time, she thought, and get back to Maureen's, to take her out for a meal and say thanks and sorry for being a guest who's never been there. Those seventy pages – she needed to read every word and make up her own mind before she wrote anything. She would do it on the train home in the morning.

One day, she would come back to Gleneagles and Auchterarder with her family, she told herself, when there were no leaders, no protesters, no cops behind bushes, no deadlines. They would walk the hills and cycle the lanes, taste the real Scotland – and let the midges taste them. And she would think back to a week of drama, both amazing and tragic, a week of missed opportunities for the poor.

As the coach drove away from the press area, Sara realised that she had thought less about Simon in the last few days than at any time for months. She wanted to speak with him about the sign in that church: "Love is social justice. Social justice is love." She was starting to think out what it could mean. And grappling with the idea that it could throw new light on her relationship with him.

14

Post-Gleneagles

The phone rang, somewhere between Edinburgh and Newcastle on the Saturday morning train taking Sara home. It was Frank.

"Sara, the papers are full of G8 news this morning. We don't come out till Monday, so what I want from you is not a news story, but what we call an Op Ed piece. An opinion piece for the editorial pages. I'd like you to analyse what happened and give your opinion of what the summit achieved and did not achieve. Where does it all go from here? And make it as strong as you need to."

"Thanks Frank, would love to do that. I am right now reading over seventy pages of government documents that were handed to us yesterday afternoon. I can tell you there are so many holes you could make fishing nets with them. They say more about what did not happen than the government could ever have realised."

As the train rattled south, Sara continued reading, the whole lot, every word. And what a collection of papers. In addition to the G8 communiqué, there was the "Chair's Summary" of the summit, "The Gleneagles Plan of Action", papers on "What an Agreement at Gleneagles Means", a paper on Africa, on trade, on the millennium development goals, on climate change, on the

Middle East peace process, oil, Iraq and more. Simon's certificate of insanity was the only document missing.

And the fault lines – the gap between what Tony Blair was claiming and what had actually happened – were becoming clear. The agencies were right, she realised. If anything, it was worse than they said. She took out her laptop and began to write . . .

The G8: Half-truths, Half-lies – and Worse
by Sara Openshaw

Eight of the world's most powerful leaders came to Scotland last week to talk about Africa, poverty and climate change. They claimed much – but delivered little.

Police forces from fourteen areas of Britain were on hand to keep order. The summit cost a lot. But for all the good they have done, leaders may as well have stayed at home and reduced poverty by putting the money into village water wells instead. For leaders missed a unique opportunity to give a lead in making poverty history. Their own documents give the game away.

"We came to Gleneagles to work to combat poverty," says the "Chair's summary" of the meeting. More aid would help, but the documents reveal no additional aid that was not already in the pipeline.

"Aid for developing countries," says one document, "will increase, according to the OECD, by around $50 billion a year by 2010." The clause "according to the OECD" – the rich country club, the Organisation for Economic Co-operation and Development – is significant. Aid from the G8 countries and other donors was predicted, before the summit began, to increase by $51 billion a year: from $79 billion in 2004 to around $130 billion in 2010. The leaders of Western countries deserve credit for these increases, but as they stepped into Gleneagles hotel they left leadership at the door. Their summit added nothing. They confirmed the aid that was in the pipeline. They did not increase it.

"A substantial increase in official development assistance is required in order to achieve the Millennium Development Goals by 2015," said the leaders. These goals include the halving of poverty. But this "substantial increase" was not given.

The United Nations estimates that $180 billion a year is needed by 2010 if the goals are to be reached. An additional $100 billion a year, not $50 billion, is therefore called for.

Leadership would have seen two things. It would have seen the eight leaders going beyond existing commitments and announcing an increase in aid to $180 billion a year; and it would have seen them announce that the additional aid will start immediately, rather than in five years time.

There is also a sting in the tail. The extra aid will be for countries "which have strong national development plans and which are committed to good governance, democracy and transparency."

Their next sentence contradicts this: "We agreed that poor countries must decide and lead their own development strategies and economic policies." Countries judged to have weak development plans will presumably not qualify.

On debt relief, again no progress, again half-truths. Step forward the Chancellor of the Exchequer. In a speech a few days before the summit, Gordon Brown said: "Eighteen of the poorest countries of the world will for the first time have 100% of their debts written off." Yet the G8 communiqué says that the debts owed by eligible indebted countries will be cancelled "as set out in our Finance Ministers' meeting on 11 June." But this only cancels half the total debts of these eighteen countries. It's a long way short of 100%.

And there are strings. To qualify for debt relief, developing countries must "tackle corruption, boost private sector development" and "eliminate impediments to private investment, both domestic and foreign." So debt relief depends on opening up markets to foreign companies. Such a condition contradicts the notion of poor countries deciding their own plans.

What is clear is that Bob Geldof – someone who has done much to alert the world to Africa's poverty – got it spectacularly wrong this time, with his high marks out of ten. Geldof gave a signal of approval to Western governments. When you receive such high marks, why do more? That way encourages complacency. But the poor will die if we are complacent. For the sake of the poor I would urge governments: ignore such views.

On trade, again the leaders achieved nothing by being at Gleneagles. A commitment to abolish agricultural export subsidies had already been made.

Leaders also failed to make the connection between poverty and climate change. More aid and debt relief would help the poor, but would be undermined by climate change. This is already having a devastating impact on many African countries and communities, increasing the frequency and severity of floods and droughts, affecting agriculture and food output, leading to even worse hunger.

Leaders failed to tell us that climate change could put the halving of poverty by 2015 beyond reach. Tony Blair said at the end of the summit: "There are commitments here which are hugely significant." That is at best a half-truth. And a half-truth can be a half-lie. The commitments that leaders could have made to end poverty, they simply did not make.

That extra aid that was promised – Oxfam says that had the increase kicked in immediately, "it could have lifted 300 million out of poverty in the next five years." And Oxfam is right to point out that "neither the necessary sense of urgency nor the historic potential of Gleneagles was grasped by the G8."

What a travesty of a response by leaders – to recognise a need and say we will meet it in five years time. Today we know how to make poverty history. We know what needs to be done. Poverty goes on because those with power to end it are not giving it priority. That is the scandal.

The government has misled us. But then of course it's part of government spin to put a good gloss on events. PR, spin, whatever name it goes by, should be called what it is: organised lying, organised conning. It is a black art that has no place in a democratic society. It distorts the truth. And now, it hurts the poor.

The London bombs were tragic, but fighting terrorism should not deflect priority away from the need to end poverty.

Where do we go from here? In September the General Assembly of the United Nations meets in New York to review progress of the millennium development goals. The opportunity for leadership should not then be missed.

Western countries must agree in New York to give the extra $50 billion of aid a year immediately, and pledge a further $50 billion – the amount that's needed to halve poverty by 2015.

The government must rise above the deceit of half-truths, half-lies. Rather it should face the truth – that it can help make poverty history if it chooses. The poor are waiting. And as leaders delay, the poor are dying.

★ ★ ★

On Monday the Op Ed appeared, little changed from Sara's text. And in the days following . . . there were letters.

Sir,
Sara Openshaw's article was a disgrace. How dare she criticise our prime minister Mr. Blair like that? Does she have no respect? I write as a lifelong Tory voter until the last election, when I had begun to see Mr Blair as the true heir of our greatest ever prime minister, Mrs Margaret Thatcher.

Sir,
Thank God for your reporter! She has cut through the fog of official deceit and told it as it is. She took the trouble to read the documents. And unlike most of the journalists at the G8, she did not fall for the government's spin.

Sir,
Your reporter on the G8 is perhaps a little unfair. Give credit where it's due! Mr Blair is personally committed to ending poverty, and the government has increased aid and debt relief – not by as much as it should maybe, but politics is the art of the possible, and the government did what was possible.

Sir,
Sara Openshaw's account of the G8 summit, and of Mr Blair's alleged duplicity, brought to mind another Prime Minister, Harold

Wilson. He was committed to ending poverty. Mr Wilson helped to form War on Want in 1953, he wrote a book about poverty and started the Ministry of Overseas Development in 1964. Our aid was then a great deal higher than now. But Mr Wilson was knocked off course by events. Poverty lost priority with him. I fear the same is happening with Mr. Blair.

Sir,
I am inspired by Sara Openshaw's article to ask readers if they would join me in a campaign to eliminate spin from public life.

Sir.
Openshaw has sure opened . . . a can of worms.

A few days later, Frank rang. "Sara, your Op Ed has caused quite a stir. It's brought just about the biggest response we've ever had to an international issue. The letters we printed were a fair sample of those that came in and I can tell you there were more. And you may like to know that other papers in our group noticed your piece and asked me if they could reprint it. That means you will be paid by them as well as by us. Well done. Come round for a drink soon, will you?"

But it wasn't the letters, it wasn't the money, that most thrilled Sara. It was receiving the shortest letter she had ever received in her life. A note through the door, in handwriting she recognised, read simply: "Sara – well done! Spot on. C."

To have Charley's approval, someone who knew how things in government worked, this meant more to Sara than anything. It was the pickup she needed to get back to normal life – family, work, planning the next stage of the MPH campaign. And invit-ing Simon to lunch. But first to visit Charley.

Charley was looking as good as could be expected, thought Sara, for someone who had been through such an ordeal. She spilled it all out to Sara, explaining why she had been near Edgware Road that day. Vanity, vanity, all is vanity, said Charley, adding that she felt humbled and lucky to be alive. And went on to say that she'd had a pastoral visit from that "nice young curate at Luke's."

"He's a dear, isn't he?" said Charley. "And he's as batty as you about Make Poverty History. And when your name was mentioned, his eyes lit up. You know, I reckon that you two are quite fond of each other. Bit of scandal here, Sara? You can tell your old friend!" Sara managed to fend the query off, and Charley went on to say that she liked her Opinion piece in the paper . . . but . . .

"The media mafia in HMG will be furious with you. You know that letter in the paper saying that you were perhaps a little unfair . . . that would have come from one of them, under a pseudonym of course. Most journalists we have under control. We drip them a drop of Krug now and then, and they don't say nasty things about the PM and ministers or we'd cut them out of the loop. You're a problem Sara – we don't control you." They laughed. Charley wanted to know if Sara planned any more forays into journalism.

"No. Gleneagles was special, and it was fantastic to be there. But I think I prefer doing something myself rather than report what others are doing. So I doubt it."

"Well, don't knock it," was Charley's response. "A shrewd analysis of what policy makers are doing can change policy. One of the letters in response to your piece mentioned Harold Wilson. He's said to have changed a key aspect of government economic policy while reading *The Economist* on a train journey from Liverpool to Manchester. It's just that if you were planning more, our heavies would need to have a quiet word with the chairman of the group that includes our local paper. A knighthood, even a life peerage in the offing perhaps . . . wouldn't do to let any of his papers rock the boat too much . . . the merest hint . . . no fingerprints."

"This is control freakery gone mad Charley . . . any of it on the record?"

"All of it a million miles off the record," responded Charley, going on to talk about bugging, saying that she was being paranoid when they talked in the garden back in May. And that no, she did not think she was being bugged by her employer – but would not be at all surprised if she was.

Cycling back home, Sara was left wondering about the spin, the control freakery, what it said about a free press, which was supposed be a pillar of democratic society. About how government ministers complained about people not turning out to vote at an election, when it was ministers with their spin who were undermining the very basis of a democratic society.

★   ★   ★

"Didn't you do well!" said the nice young curate when they met a few days later and hugged each other tight at Sara's. "I said that you would be OK. I read you every day, I was so proud. And that Opinion piece – wow!"

"Again, you're not the slightest bit biased are you, Simon?"

They laughed, and talked about Gleneagles, Edinburgh, the campaign and where it went from here. They agreed the UN summit in New York in September was crucial. Leaders had to be persuaded to increase their aid to the level that was needed, and to deliver it immediately.

Sara suggested that they organise a march round town before the end of July, to show people how important this was. And that she would ask everyone on their list to write to Mr Blair and urge him to act at the UN summit.

"Good idea. And several people have told me they have already written to Tony Blair enclosing a copy of your article."

"Will it be the Tower for me?" asked Sara. And she remembered that sign in the church at Auchterarder.

"Simon, in the church at Auchterarder I noticed a banner. It said: 'Love is social justice. Social justice is love'. It got me thinking. Is working for social justice, which is what MPH is about, is it a way of showing love to people . . . no, let me finish . . . and does it put the relationship between you and me into perspective? We met through the MPH campaign and we believe in it. If we, in a tiny way, are trying to show love, however inadequately, to 800 million people who live in poverty, does that not put our own relationship in perspective? Does it not make it rather irrelevant, compared with the big picture, and keep it in check?"

"Sorry I interrupted. Yes . . . yes, but with reservations on the last part. Another word for love is *caritas* which means care – for community, for all communities. My brother, my sister is everyone, no matter where they live. It is the responsibility of all of us, as individuals and governments to work for social justice. If we love others we will want to do that. Love your neighbour as yourself – want for your neighbour what you want for yourself – this is one of the great Christian commandments.

"So yes, love is social justice because you show love when you work for social justice. And social justice is love, love in action."

"You know Simon, you take me back to University days and remind me of a quote that was quite famous at the time, one of Che Guevara's: that the true revolutionary is guided by feelings of love."

"Guided by love, I like that. But Sara, the reservation I have with what you said before is that . . . well, I agree that working for a cause which is higher, far higher than we are, keeps our role, the relationship between us, in perspective. But it does not make it irrelevant. No friendship is irrelevant. All of us have unique gifts, unique talents. And when people combine their talents in a friendship, the result can be much greater than the sum of the parts. If our relationship, even though we know it has grey areas, inspires us to work for the cause that brought us together, well then it is very relevant. And yes, if working to make poverty history helps to stop us doing anything silly with each other . . . good." Silence followed. Sara had expected a good answer and wasn't disappointed.

"You're a star Simon, you shine light on things," she said, reaching out to hold his hand. "You know, I don't think I said sorry for Princes Street. You could so easily have . . . but, you're a good man."

"No," he shook his head, "I'm not good."

"Oh come off it, of course you are. Look at how you responded to me in Princes Street! And how many people have you murdered in the last week?"

"Very funny, but, for a start, I tend to have thoughts I shouldn't have."

"Thoughts! Surely thoughts don't count do they?"

"Er . . . yes, they count."

"Oh hell! There's no hope for any of us then." Simon laughed and insisted that yes, there is hope. But Sara wanted to know more of Simon's thoughts.

"Do you ever imagine . . . that . . . you're making love to me?"

"No, I have avoided that – just."

"Oh, what a shame! I was going to ask you what I was like . . . er, sorry . . . there I go again. But that certificate you promised me – where is it?"

"I gather the G8 threw it out. They didn't want to add to your seventy pages of documents," he said.

"I'm glad they got something right." They laughed together, at ease with each other, silent for a while.

"Talking of thoughts," Sara picked up the conversation, "I want to share one with you. The day you came for coffee when I was recovering after collapsing, you told me about the women in your life. By your own admission, four inappropriate women. But it hit me that I was inappropriate woman number five, and that in some ways I'm the most inappropriate of them all. And this bothers me. I care enough about you that I don't want to continue your run of . . . well . . . inappropriate women." Silence followed. Simon did not want to give a quick, glib response, but struggled beyond the cliché.

"I appreciate your concern. I suppose it shows that love is blind. It's just that, well, I cannot see you as inappropriate. You've fired me, you've energised me – inappropriate, no, not if it stays in the context we've agreed. I had to smile, reading your opinion piece, that you had used the phrase "beyond reach". I just wondered if you were referring to our relationship, to the way it is between us?"

"Yes, it was deliberate," laughed Sara. "I'm glad you noticed. Simon, it would be very inappropriate if we wanted to bring . . .

what you might call the ultimate expression of a relationship . . . within reach. Rather, we just, both of us, need to hold on to seeing things in the way we're agreed: love beyond reach."

"But you know, when I say that," Sara again, "I feel, well fine, that's the theory, but it's more complex, isn't it? On the Sunday morning, after that lovely evening in Edinburgh, I just wondered if perhaps we might be playing with fire . . . that we are, how should I say, loitering on the fringe of adultery. And I suppose, well, I suppose my flirting doesn't help."

"Well, talking of theories," Simon responded, "I have one about your flirting. Don't look surprised. It is that you flirt from a very assured base, even to see how far you can push things. I just have a feeling that, had I said to you on Princes Street , yes, come back to my hotel, that I would not have seen you for dust in the direction of the bus and Maureen's." Sara laughed, roared.

"Well I don't know about the dust! But you're right, I guess."

"On the more substantive point," Simon went on, "are we playing with fire? Well it's that 1% weakness I talked about that could kindle it. But I don't think we are, because we are both aware of the dangers, aware of the background to our relationship, the MPH campaign, aware of our commitments, aware that we are beyond reach of each other."

Sara looked at him, wide-eyed, put an arm around his neck and said: "You are my guru, Simon." And he kissed her lips, gently, tenderly, briefly, for the first time.

"I don't think you should do that," she said quietly, "it might . . . kindle the fire?"

"Sorry."

"Don't say you're sorry. Love doesn't say sorry. So it once said in a Hollywood film."

"I think that's wrong don't you? I would say instead that love . . . makes it possible to say sorry." Silence. Sara needed time to think about that one.

"The Reverend Copplestone takes on Hollywood – and wins by an Oscar! That's good Simon. Thank you. I love that!" They talked about the march to highlight the MDGs. Realistically this could not be held before the end of the month, with the last Saturday in July the obvious choice, even though some people would be on holiday.

"Sorry, but I'm afraid I will miss it," said Simon, "I'm taking about a dozen young people from church to Taizé in France that week, as I did last year."

"What's Taizé?" she asked, "I've not heard of that." Simon gave a potted history, explaining that Taizé was a small village in Burgundy, where a young man called Roger Schulz, the son of a Swiss pastor, had bought a house in 1940. He wanted to form a community that people from different churches could belong to and reconcile their differences. When friends learned he was living there, Schulz was asked to shield refugees, mostly Jews, who were fleeing from occupied France, not many miles away. The Gestapo got wind of what he was doing and, in 1942, he had to flee for his life.

"He returned to Taizé when France was liberated in the autumn of 1944," said Simon, "and on Easter Day 1949, six Christians made a commitment to live a community life as brothers. Their numbers grew. And in the late 1950s small groups of mostly young people began coming to Taizé to take a look. For the brothers at Taizé were doing something completely different.

"The number of visitors kept on growing, until the tiny village church was unable to hold them all. A new church was built further along the village and news of Taizé's work continued to spread. People began coming from Africa, Asia and Latin America as well as from Europe. Today around 5,000 mostly young people come every week in the summer, to camp in tents or sleep in dormitories and share in the community's life. There are now over a hundred brothers, from Catholic, Anglican, Lutheran and other backgrounds, from more than twenty-five countries. Its songs have become famous; they're now sung throughout the world.

"It's a very special place and the young people love it. And it is strong on social justice issues. Some of the brothers live away from France in the slums of poor countries, living proof that love is social justice, social justice is love."

"Sounds great. We go to France soon after you get back I guess. We've booked a gîte in the southwest for two weeks. But William's getting worried he might miss some cricket – you know the Ashes start in a day or two?"

"Yes, and around the time you get back I may be going to Niger in West Africa. St. Luke's helps to support a church worker there, Sue, who happens to be a nurse. And Sue has invited me to spend a week or so there, to get a glimpse of their life."

"Simon, that's fantastic, it will take you right to the coalface, as it were, of poverty. But Simon, I won't see you for weeks . . . give me a big hug . . . and you'd better come in for your jabs and anti-malarial tablets in good time."

Sara wrote a newsletter to MPH supporters:

"Make Poverty History has put poverty firmly on the political agenda but we still have a great deal to do. We must now urge leaders to raise their sights and not be satisfied with any policies that fall short of ending the scandal of a child dying of poverty every three seconds.

We need specifically to urge that governments use the UN Millennium Summit in September to increase aid and to deliver it quickly. Please come to a march around the churches on Saturday 30th July, starting at 10.00 a.m. at St. Luke's – and write to Tony Blair to urge action at the Millennium Summit.

Yours etc.

Sara

NB: Like me, you're probably tired and need a break from campaigning. This year has been hectic, but please come to this last event before summer . . . and take August off – richly deserved."

Before the march, a few of the aid agencies began to row back a little from their G8 analysis. They now said that the outcome was mixed, not as bad as they had at first declared. Sara realised what was happening – that these agencies were fearful of disillusioning their supporters, even jeopardising their incomes, by announcing that the G8 had achieved nothing, after all their efforts. But she wondered if this were not a case of aid agency spin with an eye to funds.

Then the Ashes started. And William was glued to his other passion after ball bearings. Cricket. But Australia won the first Test by 230 runs, and William drooped around the house like a lost soul. There was no inkling then of what was to come.

The MPH march took place, and was well attended for late July. A photographer came and took pictures, and Sara thought: "That's it for a few weeks. For seven months, I have just about kept to my resolve to do something every day about MPH. Tomorrow it's WOMAD."

The annual World of Music, Arts and Dance festival, held by the river in Reading, was an event the Openshaws went to every year, often with Sara's sister Laura and her family. So they met just before noon on a bright sunny morning, and bought a programme.

"Sara, look what's on," said Laura. "Must be just for you: At 1.30 on the One World Platform, Make Poverty History, football match/escape artist."

"I thought I was having a break, but this I have to see," she replied. The football match was street theatre, superbly done. One team wore thick American-style padded outfits and looked enormous compared with the poorly dressed weak-looking side, which carried weights on their legs. The referee – with WTO in large letters on his back – was hugely biased in favour of the stronger side. The result was a foregone conclusion. Then came a sketch in which a man tried to get out of a straitjacket. He wriggled and wrestled, he strained and stretched – to no avail. Not until another actor came to help did he escape. Brilliant, thought Sara, we must do something like that, and we haven't organised a multicultural carnival yet.

A few days later the second Test started and this one was a cliffhanger. Hardly a sensible word passed William's lips and he seemed to have gone totally deaf. Requests such as "tea", "coffee", "me"? went unheard. So Sara opted for the shock tactic.

"Oh and by the way, William, I'm having an affair with Tony Blair and Richard Brans . . ."

"Got him! Good old Freddy, good old Freddy. Another one down," William was positively hyper. "Come on England, come on . . ."

"Nothing serious, just three-in-a-bed romps. We're off to the Virgin Islands at the weekend, the three of us, to perform in public. Tickets are selling well I hear . . ."

"You know, I think we have 'em now, we can win this one and level the series . . . What do you say dear, something about virgins and romps? Steady on love. The Aussies are no virgins, and it certainly won't be a romp. Tough cookies, those guys." Then Chloe and May became interested in cricket.

"Freddy Flintoff looks a bit like the Reverend Copplestone," said Chloe. At which Sara suddenly became a cricket fan.

Their holiday started just days after England had won the Test by two runs, with William moaning: "I'm going to miss the third Test. Must remember to take a radio. Good job we're back before the fourth one starts."

Before they left, Sara received a cheque from the paper. It was for more than she expected, and made her recall the conversation with Charley – and to wonder whether maybe there was a case for doing more journalism.

Simon, meanwhile, had returned from Taizé, gone to visit his parents in Cornwall and was preparing for Niger. Since he had agreed to go there, Niger had been hit by famine and Simon sensed that he was in for a shock. And Sara was still away when he went to the doctor's, held out his arm to nurse for the jabs and started taking the anti-malarials.

15

Niger

Simon had read all he could about the country he was visiting. He read about a country some four times the size of Britain. About Niger's culture, its economy, about how it was the world's second poorest country. How 90% of its twelve million people were employed in agriculture, that 60% of the population lived on less than a dollar a day, that only one in six adults was literate, that life expectancy was a mere forty-five years . . . And he read about the drought and plague of locusts that had destroyed much of last year's harvest in some areas, and was now taking its grim toll of life.

This is poverty as its worst, he thought. Sitting on the flight to Niger's capital Niamey, on the last day of August, Simon continued reading press cuttings. Sara had called him her star. But it was Sara's thoroughness in immersing herself in the issues, in reading and analysing those G8 documents the way she had that had stirred him. Sara was his inspiration.

And so he read of how aid agencies around the world had seen the crisis in Niger coming. How they had appealed for assistance in November last year. Of how the Niger government, under instructions from the International Monetary Fund and European Union, had at first refused to distribute free food to those most in need – for they had ruled that nothing should be done to interfere with the free play of market forces.

He read of how the United Nations calculated that only one-third of the money needed for famine relief in Niger had been pledged by the rich nations. Of how the desert in Niger had spread because of the drought, taking over food-growing land. He read of how land that once grew food for local people was now growing watermelons for French supermarkets. And he wondered . . .

He read of a woman who had lived on nothing but water for two weeks. Of how two-thirds of the men in some villages had left in search of work elsewhere. Of how people in one village were starving while there was food in nearby markets – the villagers had no money to buy the food they needed.

Simon read of how families that had only small amounts of food served girls and women last, and the elderly last of all. Of how children were eating weeds to stay alive, how their mothers would boil weeds with salt and spices. He read of how the relief organisations were trying to deliver food to some three million people in a vast, landlocked country.

Simon's plane landed late at night. Sue worked as a nurse in a church-run hospital some six hours drive northeast of Niamey. Simon was told that a hotel in Niamey had been booked for him for an overnight stay, and that a car would meet him at the airport, take him to the hotel and pick him up at ten the next morning.

The humidity that greeted the assistant curate as he stepped off the plane in Niger was like nothing he had ever experienced, enough to make him feel dizzy. A visit to a biscuit factory in the UK was the nearest . . . but hardly compared.

The following morning the hotel breakfast buffet table was laden with a greater variety of fruit than Simon had ever seen, or knew the names of. What irony! he thought. Such abundance in a country where people are starving! The coffee came with six cubes of sugar in the saucer. After breakfast, he walked the humid streets of a city bustling with life. He noticed a man on the pavement selling lawnmowers. And the stall next to him was selling televisions from Japan and refrigerators from Germany. The food markets seemed to betray the very idea of shortages. He saw green beans, onions, cowpeas, rice, millet, sorghum, tomatoes, exotic fruits, piled high – for people with money.

He also saw beggars, a lot of beggars, and street kids, a lot of them, poverty in the midst of plenty. He walked back to his hotel and a car was soon taking him east. The road was pitted, the journey slow and uncomfortable. It was impossible not to notice dead cattle and donkeys in the fields, dead from lack of fodder. Bleached bones and wrinkled hides were all around. Vultures regularly swooped down to pick at what they could.

The driver stopped for a lunch break. Soon the car was surrounded by children, One girl, about twelve years old, said to Simon in broken French, "Please give me some food. I have eaten nothing for days." He had not prepared himself for this. The packet of digestive biscuits that he had with him was divided between the children. It seemed such an inadequate response. He should have brought more food, he told himself.

The car bumped along and Simon fell asleep. He awoke just as the vehicle was passing through a town and soon after turned into the hospital compound. It was almost dusk. Sue, fifty-ish, small, slim, wiry, came to greet him.

"You must be Simon," she said. "Welcome, and thank you for the love you have shown in coming all this way to see our work, to stay with us and get to know us better. We really appreciate it." Love, thought Simon, another insight.

"Thank you for your welcome. This is my first visit to Africa. And I bring you warm greetings from all at St. Luke's."

"And would you give your congregation a huge thank you from me and everyone here? Your support enables us to do so much more."

So Sue outlined the position, her life, her work, the additional problems the drought was causing, the lack of medicines, the essential drugs they needed and, above all, the lack of food.

"I hope you're ready for what you will see," she went on. "It's going to shock you. You will see suffering that should not be happening. But you will see hope in the midst of suffering, people refusing to be beaten in the face of huge adversity. What we are trying to do is help those families that are most severely affected, whose food reserves have either run out or are about to run out. In some villages the famine is the most severe since the "great famine" of 1984, so they tell us.

"Many pastoralists have been badly hit by the death of their animals. With no fodder for the livestock, animals have died or been sold at greatly reduced prices. So pastoralists are deprived of their most immediate source of livelihood, and all too easily descend into poverty. They lose their dignity and are forced to go to the city and beg for money."

And Sue was right. Simon was shocked by what he saw. In the course of the next week he saw babies lying, silent and impossibly thin, in their mother's arms, the worst cases with tubes taped to mouth and nose, eyes wide in desperation. Babies between life and death.

It was not just what he saw, it was the smell of poverty that got to him. Poverty is so sanitised back home, he thought. If only people could smell it, taste it, they would work to end it, he was sure.

Simon met families who had trekked for over ten miles to where they had heard food might be distributed. And he watched as food aid was handed out. But there was never enough. He saw food run out while people were still in the queue. Aid workers told Simon that rich countries had failed to fund appeals early enough to pre-empt the crisis. He watched children weighed and measured in the hospital, many in a weak state, some classed as "moderately" malnourished, meaning they could still avoid slipping into such a fragile state that their immune system was destroyed.

Sue took him to a primary school one day and the children he saw seemed happy enough, he told Sue.

"Yes, but you are seeing the survivors, the healthier children. The sick ones don't come, many of the poorest don't come." The children were keen to touch him and peer into his bag, curious about what he was carrying. They walked into a classroom. There were just a few benches around the side for the children who got there first. Otherwise they sat on the floor. Sue introduced Simon, and then asked them: "Would anyone like to tell me: what has been the happiest day of your life?"

The hand of a boy of about eight shot up. "The happiest day of my life," he said, "was the day I started school." As they walked back to the compound, Sue explained that the boy had sisters who did not go to school, like many other girls in the country. That boy counted himself among the lucky ones.

Early nights were the pattern of life in the compound and Simon took the opportunity to pray, to read and to think. To think about Sara inevitably. And to wonder: "How does what I'm seeing relate to the MPH campaign in Britain? Would more aid, debt relief and trade justice help the people I am seeing?"

More aid was certainly needed, he thought. Simon had brought with him a copy of an Oxfam report which said that Niger receives US$12 per person per year in aid. By contrast, each Iraqi receives on average US$91 per year in aid – over seven times as much, it said. If Niger had received the same levels of aid as Iraq, this crisis might never have happened.

Trade – well, the people Simon met did not have much to trade. But he was aware nonetheless of some important links to trade. Some of Niger's farmers grew cotton for export on their small family farms. But the price they received had fallen sharply because the United States paid its cotton farmers large subsidies. This had created a cotton glut that had lowered world prices. The West African cotton producers had gone to the World Trade Organization in search of justice.

But for most farmers in Niger, it was livestock that mattered. And cattle farmers and herders had been hit by the beef that had come from Europe and the United States. Simon had with him a copy of an aid agency report called "Brussels' blind spot", which looked at the lack of coherence between poverty eradication and the European Union's other policies.

The report said that farmers in EU countries had produced more beef than could be eaten in the EU or exported on normal commercial terms. Helped by generous support from the EU's Common Agricultural Policy, a beef 'mountain' had resulted.

And some of the beef had been 'dumped, sold below the cost of production, in West Africa. It told of how this dumped beef competed on unfair terms with locally produced beef and severely damaged farmers' incomes. The prices that Niger's farmers received for their cattle had dropped by over 50%, plunging many into poverty. They were unable to compete. The EU policy was not consistent with its obligations to the poor, said the report.

Uranium was Niger's main export and its price had fallen over the last six years by almost a third. This meant it had less money to pay off its foreign debt. Niger was one of the most profoundly indebted countries in Africa. Debt relief would help. And Niger would qualify for debt relief under the G7 Finance Ministers deal announced in June. The question was, when would it start? And when would the poor see any benefit?

What about climate change? Was that making things worse? Almost certainly, yes. Simon had also brought with him a copy of a report called "Africa: Up in Smoke?" prepared by over twenty development and environmental agencies. It said that efforts to alleviate poverty in Africa would fail unless urgent action were taken to stop climate change. But where was the urgency? he wondered.

Early mornings were his best time of the day. Simon often rose at dawn and went for a walk. "The first morning of creation, who could act rationally on such a day?" That went through his mind most mornings, although he could never recall the source. But every morning was the first morning of creation, every morning new. And every morning there was African music in the air, music that seemed to blend with creation. But he was also aware that as glamorous as it seemed to him, a visitor, every morning was the beginning of a hard day for many of the people he would meet.

"Simon, you've not eaten very much since you came here," Sue said to him the day before he was due to leave Niger. "Look at you. You must have a lost a stone in weight – in a week. Would you like a chicken for dinner tonight?"

"It's just that I have not felt like eating with all these hungry people around. But chicken would be lovely, thanks," he said, but without enthusiasm.

"Come with me and choose one then," she said. As they walked towards the town, Simon wondered why he had to come and choose a chicken that he didn't feel like eating. He expected to be taken to a shop and to choose a cellophane-wrapped chicken with a bar code. Instead they went to an open-air market where a few skinny, very skinny, chickens were running around.

"Well, which one would you like?" asked Sue. Simon's heart sank. So this is what Sue meant. He was being asked to be an instant executioner, to choose a bird that would die for his dinner, one he did not fancy anyway.

"You want me to choose one?" he asked in disbelief.

"Well you did say you'd like a chicken, didn't you," was Sue's brisk response. Simon closed his eyes – and pointed.

"That one, you'd like that one." Whereupon Sue picked up a bird and carried it back to the compound, squawking all the way. Simon did not say a word, neither did he eat much of it later. He wasn't hungry. And the thought of eating a bird that he had chosen to die, a bird that was running around a few hours earlier – it was enough to make him vegetarian.

But picking at the food the way he did that evening gave Simon the opportunity to say something about Sara.

"I am sorry, I am not doing this justice, not eating properly. I have a good friend, Sara, who is a nurse in my home town. She will sort me out," he said. "Sara is fantastically committed to the Make Poverty History campaign. She has energised us all."

"Simon, remember that it does not solve anyone's problems if you don't eat. And from one nurse to another, give Sara my love, and tell her – keep on. The answer to the poverty you have seen here is many, many sided. Why don't you join me doing my rounds on your last day here?" He nodded, and went to his room to read.

He picked up the report on climate change that he had started reading: "Africa: Up in Smoke?" Climate change was disrupting vital rains, bringing more droughts and floods and this was devastating the livelihoods of many Africans. These are overwhelmingly the poorest people, the report said. Unable to afford irrigation, their crops depend on the rain. Livelihoods built for generations on particular patterns of farming may become unviable. And with the report came a warning about the effects of climate change on the poor from the UN's Food and Agriculture Organization. Climate change could increase the number of hungry people "by reducing the area of land available for farming in developing countries," said the FAO.

In many developing countries, warned the FAO, "production losses due to climate change may drastically increase the number of undernourished people, severely hindering progress in combating poverty and food insecurity." The severest impact could be in sub-Saharan African countries, it said.

The problems that Simon was seeing, Niger's severe drought, all seemed to him to be part of the pattern of more extreme weather that could prove the real scourge of the people he had met. All this pointed to the need to tackle climate change in a serious manner. The report called for new and deeper emission cuts in rich countries to a level that would halt global warming. It suggested that these needed to go well beyond the modest Kyoto Protocol targets for reducing greenhouse gas emissions.

Ironically, it rained, rained heavily, on some of the days that Simon was in Niger, including the last day of his visit. It was a good day to stay in the compound and accompany Sue as she walked and talked with mothers, holding sick and withered children.

"Hold this baby, Simon. He's close to death," said Sue. "There is nothing more we can do for the poor mite. His mother knows this and I have told her that you are a priest. And she would like you to hold him and pray for him."

Simon took the baby boy in his arms without a word. He could feel a tiny, very tiny, weak pulse. Then suddenly, nothing. The boy's life had come to an end, killed by poverty. Simon gave the baby back to his mother. And wept. The baby, he thought, alive one second, a grim statistic the next.

★ ★ ★

On the opening day of the UN's summit to review the Millennium Development Goals, the day that Simon was also returning home, Sara had a short article in the local paper:

Some people thought my article in July on the outcome of the G8 summit was too strong, unfair to the government. In fact, it was not strong enough. Two months later, it's worse. I have been shocked by the speed at which promises have been broken.

Documents obtained by the World Development Movement show that four of the IMF's European directors are trying to overturn the G8's debt deal. Germany and Italy have announced that they might not be able to meet the commitments they made, due to "budgetary constraints".

Leaked documents from the World Bank show that the G8 has not granted 100% debt relief to eighteen countries, but has promised enough money only to write off their repayments for the next three years.

And Gordon Brown has dropped a bombshell. He's admitted that the aid package the G8 leaders had promised includes the numbers for debt relief. So let's be clear. The extra money they had promised for aid and the extra money they had promised for debt relief were one and the same. This is dreadful deceit on Mr Brown's part.

This week, governments at the UN's General Assembly in New York will review a promise they made five years ago – to halve the number of hungry people by 2015. There is enough food in the world for everyone to lead a healthy and productive life. But millions of people go to bed hungry every night. More funds are urgently needed. Governments know what to do. This week, we will be watching to see if they do it.

As for Simon, he looked positively emaciated when Sara called to see him a few days after he had arrived home.

"Simon, what have you done to yourself? You've lost so much weight! Welcome back, it's lovely to see you. Missed you," she said, kissing him on the cheek and hugging him tight. And Simon told her about the poverty he had seen, how it related to MPH . . . and he ended with the baby boy who had died in his arms.

"I remember you telling me, earlier in the year, that when you watched those orphans in 'The Vicar of Dibley', that they had moved the issue of people who live in poverty from your head to your heart. Well I had to go to Niger for that to happen to me. Yes, I have been committed to making poverty history, but until I held that tiny boy and he died in my arms, it was all in my head. Now, the whole thing has shifted, from my head to my heart. Now it's something I care about at a much deeper level." While Sara was listening, something was troubling her.

"Simon, I'm worried about you. You look so thin."

"I just don't feel like eating," he responded.

"Please Simon, you must. Tell you what, why don't you join us for a meal on Saturday evening. Risk the peas?"

"Thanks, that's very kind but I can't. I help at the churches drop-in centre for the homeless on Saturday evenings."

"You give up your Saturday evenings?"

"Well it's no big deal. We serve soup and sandwiches. I do the soup. They call me Simon the soup."

"Simon the soup," she was smiling, "I command you to eat some of your own soup and more . . . Anyway, the UN summit ends tomorrow. And it's not looking good."

"I am going to be furious if they do nothing after what I've seen in Niger . . ." They did nothing. The summit ended the following day, a disaster, worse than Gleneagles. The reports said it all.

"The Millennium Development Goals, designed to rescue people from poverty and bring hope of a better life for all, now themselves stand in need of rescue," read one report.

"The summit did nothing to advance the goals," said another. "Leaders were supposed to review progress towards meeting the goals. You would have thought that a review would consist of leaders sitting down and asking: what progress is being made towards meeting the goals? Why are we behind? What do we need to do now to reach them? What action do we need to take? But leaders failed to do that. The goals need more funds if they are to be achieved. That is the bottom line. But leaders did not pledge one pound, one euro, one dollar more."

"Leaders squandered the momentum for tackling global poverty," Charles Abugre, Christian Aid's head of policy was quoted as saying. He described the tone of the summit as "bleak and depressing. It is hard to believe that the cry for justice issued by anti-poverty campaigners across the world earlier this year has fallen on such deaf ears. Never was there such a chance to improve the lives of millions; never was there such a mean-spirited and self-interested response from the rich and powerful."

Hilary Benn, the UK's international development minister, saw it differently. He criticised those who were writing off the summit as a failure, saying: "This summit has helped to make 2005 an extraordinary year for development, and significant progress has been made to reach agreement on issues of huge importance."

That is a disgraceful statement, thought Sara, it just flies in the face of the facts, a serious misjudgement.

Simon rang her. "I am livid. I am really mad about this, such apathy in the face of such poverty. Such meanness, such . . ."

"Simon, calm it. Does your faith allow you to get angry like this?"

"Yes, it does, if it's righteous anger. If people are suffering an injustice, then it's right to feel angry. And Sara, I've made a decision. I am going to fast, I am going on hunger strike in protest, to draw attention to what is going on. I will sit by the church gate, a lot of people pass there, with a sign saying that I am doing this to protest at the failure of governments to take action to end poverty."

"Simon, is this wise?"

"Yes, I shall drink water but not eat. I have to make a statement about this. I heard of a woman in Niger who had nothing but water for two weeks. If she can do it, Sara, so can I, and for longer."

"Simon, listen to me. People can live without food for quite a while. But you have barely eaten, it seems to me, for over two weeks. You are weak. You are in a poor position to start a fast. You have already lost some of your fat and muscle. If you don't eat anything now then your body, instead of digesting food, will start to digest itself. Please listen. I know what I'm talking about."

"I respect your medical knowledge and expertise of course. But I am doing it Sara, I am fasting. I feel that I must show solidarity with those who are dying from lack of food, and protest about those in power who turn away. And you are not going to stop me."

16

Fast

Simon began his fast after church on Sunday evening. It was September 17th. He had run off some handouts earlier about why he was doing the fast. And he made a banner to sit by: JUSTICE FOR THE POOR, NOW. MAKE POVERTY HISTORY.

He decided that he would sit by the church gate during the day and sleep on the floor just inside the church overnight. The church had a kitchen, and water from the cold tap was all he needed to drink. The modern and adjacent church hall had a shower that he could use every morning. He took a plentiful supply of clothes, a sleeping bag, waterproofs, toiletries, an i-pod, a radio and a lot to read. He was aware that he could go home for more clothes and books, but wanted to do that as little as possible. But he also was aware of how much 'stuff' he had to help him. And he compared it to the people he had met in Niger. People who had little if any 'stuff'.

"If people knew how awful poverty really is, if they could see it, smell it, it would be stopped – today. I have just witnessed it for myself in Niger. But governments do know. They have no excuses. They claim to act, but don't. They must act to end poverty – now," read Simon's handouts. They went on to say that he was fasting because governments at the UN summit had failed to do anything to end the scandal.

Monday morning – and commuters rushing for their trains went past, some with a smile, some taking a handout, a few stopping for a brief chat. Then later the shoppers came and had more time. A number stopped for longer chats. Bernard, his boss, and several regulars from St. Luke's congregation dropped by. Some came with drinks and food, which were politely declined. And some of them sat with him for a while. At the end of the first morning Simon was feeling it was worthwhile, that he was beginning to get through to people about what was going on.

Then, at just after one, Simon's heart missed a beat. Sara had cycled to the church after work.

"How are you?" she asked, pecking him on the cheek.

"Early days yet, but I am fine. It's funny, I do not really feel hungry. I have a kind of dull ache, but it's not hunger like you feel when you are waiting for a meal. I know that a meal is out of bounds for a while."

"You are not feeling hungry, Simon, because your taste buds have dried up. How long do you plan to do this for?"

"Well, I have heard that a person can live on water for 30 days. I have not fixed an end-date. I will stay here as long as it seems right. But for least two weeks."

"Simon, people vary, and lack of food can do different things to people. I am going to come and see you every day after work, and I want you to promise that you will tell me if there is any change in the way you feel. You need watching."

A parishioner came by, and stayed. Simon drew back from giving Sara the hug he so badly wanted to give her.

So the fast went on. A reporter from the local paper came to interview him. Also someone from a local radio station. The following day, a television crew arrived. This was news, it was different, they told him. But Simon was nonetheless sitting there alone for much of the time. He prayed a lot, and had plenty of time to think.

His mind went to the question that Sara had asked – are we loitering on the fringe of adultery? He realised he had not answered that. Did it need answering? he wondered. The answer was surely no. And yet . . . and yet, he thought, is there a danger that we are? Are we closer to the fringe than we thought?

Fringe . . . Simon's mind wandered to that magical evening with Sara in Edinburgh, and the jokes about the Fringe. That had been fun, but the notion of loitering on the fringe of adultery was dangerously serious. He had cautioned Sara not to trust him completely, to be aware of weakness. And anyway, next year, he would have completed four years at St. Luke's. That was the time when a curate traditionally moves on. But where would he go? Close by, or hundreds of miles away? He had no idea. Should he tell Sara, he wondered? No, better to wait and see.

By the end of the first week of his fast, Simon was feeling weak, physically very weak. But a little bolshie, nonetheless. He remembered telling Sue how Sara would sort him out.

"But no," he thought, "Sara will not sort me out. I will sort myself out. Until now she has mesmerised me. I have been a total fan, everything she did, everything she said, was beyond question. No longer. I still feel love for her, but I have broken free. And after Niger I now feel more secure about my relationship with her, that any danger has diminished, that I have it more in proportion." But he could not wait to see her each day and told her so.

"You know, when you eat nothing, when there is no food inside you, it's as if there is more room in you for other things. Other things become more important . . . like you coming to see me every day. Your senses change."

But after a week and a half into the fast, Sara was noticing a distinct deterioration in his condition. His face was looking haggard, his movements were listless, his speech not as clear.

"Simon, darling," she said to him quietly, "I admire enormously what you're doing, we all do, but I think it's time for you to end it. Prolonged lack of food can damage the brain, permanently damage it. No one wants that to happen. Please listen."

"I will consider it," he said.

But he wasn't going to end it. Weak though he may be, he felt he was achieving something by going on. He even felt a sense of power. People were bringing him national daily newspapers. The papers were reporting what he was doing. He was on national television. The church papers were reporting it. The message was spreading, his statement was having an impact. People were applauding his action. The fast was working. Why should he give up, he asked himself?

One of the parishioners had told him that he was showing love for the poor, love in action. Maybe. But then he thought of a song written some years ago: "Don't give when it suits you and call it true love."

Mixed motives were one thing, but Simon was aware that his mind was playing tricks, that he was not thinking straight, that he was having some very out-of-character dreams. One night he dreamt of Sara. He dreamt of the 1% weakness he had suggested they build into their relationship. That if he could see Sara every day for a year, and the 1% weakness factor applied, then they would make love 3.65 times during the year. He dreamt he woke up, wondering why he wasn't seeing her every day. Then he did wake up. And felt guilty.

A parishioner had told him the day before that she had given up feeling guilty for Lent. When Simon had asked how it worked out, she said that at least this was one decision she did not feel guilty about. But Simon thought that he should feel guilty, that it was right to feel guilty.

"I must stop this relationship," he told himself. "What did Sara vow when she got married? To forsake all others. She must forsake me. I will tell her so. I will tell her to stop loving me and I will stop loving her. Full stop. End of story. God Save the Queen. Nothing will save this relationship."

But when Sara cycled up to him the next day, all Simon could think of was that, because of the fast, he was able to see her every day. He felt torn. Despite his intentions, he knew that he could not be certain about the outcome of their relationship. He remembered saying in Edinburgh that there might be surprises along the way, twists and turns that neither of them could foresee. For now, he told Sara about his dream.

"It's like the average couple who have – what is it? – 2.2 children," she responded. "I have 2 children, I cannot wait to see what the 0.2 will be like. As for the 0.65 of love making . . . Simon, do you normally have dreams like this?" Weakly he shook his head.

"Simon, it's now nearly two weeks. You have made your point. You have done brilliantly. You have attracted media attention well beyond this town about the duplicity of our government. You have brought the matter before millions of people, for all we know. You have made them think, you have raised awareness. Simon I don't know much of the Bible but I seem to recall that the man you worship in this building behind us said from the Cross: 'It is finished.' Surely, what you have done, you have now completed, finished." Simon smiled, very weakly.

"Yes, but Jesus said that when he was about to die. I am not fasting to death, Sara, that is not my intention, I promise you." That at least reassured her, but she wasn't giving up.

"Simon, you can reach a point when the body is deteriorating, and you are too weak to realise it. Will you give up tomorrow, Sunday, two weeks after you started?"

"I will think about it." But on Sunday evening, October 2nd, he was still there by the gate. "How can I give up, how can I just walk away when some of the people I met in Niger couldn't just walk away. If I am in solidarity with them I have to go on," he reasoned. But then he thought of what Sue had said to him in Niger, that it did not solve anyone's problems if he did not eat. And he felt torn.

With no energy, nothing inside him, he felt he was torturing himself. The fast that started well had turned into becoming very painful. Sleep became the best option and he drifted off whenever he could. Alarmed parishioners were waking him up, fearful that he might even be close to death. Physically he was so weak he could hardly move. And on the following night, Simon found it was all he could do to drag himself into the church.

On her visit next day, Sara decided to try a different tactic, a gift that had come in the papers.

"Simon, there is good news from Niger, it was in the papers this morning. The rains have been good, the farmers are producing bumper crops. Some of the people you met will now live not die.

Simon please, will you celebrate with them – and end your fast now?"

"That's good news about Niger . . . I'll think about it." For Sara that was no longer enough. She cycled straight to the vicarage, praying that Bernard was in.

"Bernard, you've got to come and talk to Simon. He's weaker than he thinks. And I think he's in danger of going on with the fast because he is too weak to decide to end it. His mind is not functioning properly, that's my concern. Will you come with me now?" They went together. Bernard sat down beside the half-awake, half- asleep curate.

"Simon, you are a peaceful man. I know that. But what you are doing has ceased to be peaceful to your body. You risk damaging your body. There's a verse from the Apocrypha that you love: that if a man is mean to himself, 'to whom will he be generous'. Be generous to yourself, end your fast now."

"Thank you. I will think about it." They could not get any further with him. But Simon was feeling too weak to make a decision. And too weak to move.

Sara could not rest, could not go to bed. She barely thought of anything, anyone else that evening but Simon. Normally in bed just after eleven, she was still up at midnight. It was decision time. She made up a flask with a water-based solution, packed with nutrients, and told William, "I am taking this to Simon. I've a dreadful feeling that something awful is going to happen to him."

"Are you sure? Take the car – and your mobile," he said.

"Mobile yes, car no; I can cycle there in five minutes." Five minutes later, in sight of St. Luke's, she could see him, still by the gate. Simon must have been too weak to get himself into church, she thought. Worse, two large dogs were around him. One was sniffing his face, the other trying to chew his trousers. She shooed them away, and knelt down beside him. He was muttering, sounding delirious. She tapped him gently on the cheek.

"Simon, Simon." He opened his eyes, and there was something about them that worried her, that told her he was ill, very ill.

"Simon, I don't like the look of your eyes," she said.

"I adore the sight of yours," he drawled, barely audibly. "Why have you come now?"

"Because you need help. And because I love you. That's why. I just can't bear to see you decline like this. You understand that, surely . . . Simon, I want you to drink some of this, now. It's a water-based solution packed full of nutrients. It will give you what you need to begin your recovery. And if you don't drink it, I am going to ring for an ambulance – it's that serious."

"Please don't do that," he said. Silence followed. Sara felt that at least he was thinking about it. The wind was howling around them, it started to drizzle. And the dogs came back.

"Simon, you must move into the church." But he couldn't move. He could not get up. Sara managed to get his right arm around her shoulder and to half-drag him into church. He made such a light parcel after his fast that it was hardly difficult. She propped him against a wall inside the church and held the flask before his eyes.

"I am not leaving here, I am not leaving you, until you drink some," she said. Silence again. Then Simon smiled, very very weakly.

"So if I don't drink any, you would never leave me? You would always be with me."

"Yes, but there's a problem, you would be dead," she smiled back. The flask hung in front of him.

"I've made the point haven't I? I am sorry I have caused you such worry, dragged you out of bed at this time." Sara's heart leapt. Simon tried to hold the flask but his grasp was too weak. Very gently, Sara poured several drops into Simon's mouth. His fast was over.

"I wasn't in bed, anyway, I was too worried about you. We must take this slowly, a few drops at a time." And he drank again. Then started to fall asleep.

Sara realised she could not leave him, that he would need small doses throughout the night, that he did not have the strength to feed himself. He needed nursing. She rang William to explain that she had to stay.

After feeding him more of the solution, she laid him down, and laid down herself next to him. The irony . . . she thought. Lying beside a man she loved, but fully clothed, on the floor at the back of a church. The man had turned patient. Until dawn she stayed, feeding him the solution regularly. She rang Bernard and told him the fast was over, but that Simon would need checking over at the hospital, and that she would call for an ambulance.

But before the ambulance arrived, Simon reached to try to hold the flask himself and take the final drops. Sara told him that he needed checking and that she would come with him and work out a recovery diet with the doctors.

"Sara, thank you. You've saved my life," he said, and, with the little strength he had, put his arms around Sara and hugged her.

It was October 5th. Simon had eaten nothing for sixteen days, and barely anything for five weeks.

*　*　*

"Vicar Praises Nurse," ran the headline in the local paper, two days later.

"The Reverend Bernard Hastin, vicar of St. Luke's, today praised a local nurse for her role in saving the life of his curate, the Reverend Simon Copplestone.

Only recently back from a visit to poverty-stricken Niger, Mr Copplestone, 34, had been fasting outside St. Luke's for over two weeks to draw attention to world poverty. He believes that governments are not doing enough to make poverty history.

"The nurse, Sara Openshaw, a Make Poverty History campaigner, who reported on July's G8 summit for this paper, went to the aid of the curate in the early hours of Wednesday morning. He was then in a perilously weak state and being attacked by dogs.

"'Nurse Openshaw persuaded Simon to end the fast and stayed throughout the night to feed him,' said Mr. Hastin. 'Had she not taken the action she did, there is no knowing what would have happened.' He said that Mr Copplestone was staying at the Vicarage with him and his wife Mary until he had fully recovered.

"Contacted about her role, Mrs Openshaw, 39, mother of two, said 'it was the least I could do'. St. Luke's will hold a special 'welcome back Simon' service this Sunday morning."

Just before the Openshaws left home on Saturday morning for their weekly shop, a huge bouquet of flowers was delivered, with a card that read simply: "To Sara – love Simon." At the shops they bumped into Agnes.

"Come here you. Let me give you a big hug." And Sara almost needed treatment for crushed ribs.

"I felt so embarrassed when the paper's reporter rang and asked me to comment. What could I say? I tell you, I would far rather report on what someone else is doing rather than have someone report on what I'm doing. And the paper exaggerated it all. It wasn't that dramatic."

"Anyway, as you've read, tomorrow we're having a special 'welcome back Simon' service. That should be good."

"You know I would quite like to come to that," Sara responded. "But I can't, can I? Simon needs space right now. I wouldn't want him to see me."

"Of course you can come, silly. Look, why not come with me. We will arrive at the last minute and sit at the back, on the side. Simon won't see you there. Sara, you have been such a central part of all this, it would be lovely if you were there."

★　★　★

"Some of us come back from visits to faraway places and show our friends pretty pictures, animals, mountains, beaches and so on." Bernard was speaking to a packed church at the start of the service the following morning. Sara was squeezed in next to Agnes on the back row, a number of people she recognised having smiled and nodded as she walked in.

"Simon, you came back from Niger and you did not say much at all. Instead you gave up food and sat outside for over two weeks, having hardly eaten for three weeks before that. Your actions spoke far louder than any words. A lot of people talk about over-coming poverty, but you acted. We are all enormously proud of what you did." Simon, still weak, responded.

"Thank you, Bernard. And may I thank the many, many people here today who came to talk with me when I was by the gate; for spending time with me, for offering me something to eat and drink. You will understand that I had to decline. And thank you, all of you, for holding me in your prayers. I am recovering well, and from today, I am back to work. Light duties, very light, Bernard says."

"I want to put on record, as I don't think she will be here, my special thanks to nurse Sara Openshaw. The best definition of a saint that I know is . . . someone who is in the right place at the right time. And by that definition, Sara is a saint. When a couple of stray dogs apparently fancied a late supper the other evening, Sara picked me up and half-carried me into church. She may well have saved my life.

"Visiting Niger has changed my life. When a baby dies in your arms, you can never be the same again. I am a changed person – you will be delighted to know."

The pin-drop silence was broken by relieved laughter. And soon after that, by warm, prolonged applause. And the service started. Sara noticed that one of hymns included the line: "He turns our weaknesses into his opportunities", and remembered Simon saying that over lunch.

During the final hymn, she whispered to Agnes: "I am going to nip out before the end. Simon doesn't think I'm here and he might be embarrassed to find I was."

As Sara opened the church door, the organ paused between verses. The door creaked noisily; the congregation was facing the other way, Only two people were facing the door, Bernard and Simon, who were at the far end of the centre aisle. And while Bernard's head was in the hymn book, Simon looked up and, even at that distance, Sara could see the look of astonishment on his face. Rumbled, she smiled faintly and gave him the very tiniest of waves, then closed the door, and floated down the path. He was alive.

17

Assembly

"Mummy, Mr Copplestone took assembly this morning," said Chloe after school a few days later. "Cool. He told us about Africa. Made us laugh telling us how he had to choose a chicken for dinner that was running around. Not Anna though, she's vegetarian, she cried."

School assembly! It brought Sara up short. She remembered that the primary school head had asked her to lead an assembly on a Make Poverty History theme. Sometime in October before half-term.

Sara rang round the MPH committee. They would need to help her to sort something out. And they needed to meet anyway, for Simon to report back from the front-line, both Niger and the church gate. And ringing round the committee would give her a chance to speak with Simon.

"Why didn't you tell me you were coming on Sunday?" asked Simon. "I would have asked you to stand up and we would have given you a round of applause."

"That's exactly why I didn't tell you I was coming. How are you? You were looking a great deal better on Sunday than this time last week. And in good form at the school assembly, my spies tell me. And talking of the assembly . . ." A meeting was organised. Sara wanted Simon to agree to talk to as many local organisations as possible about his experience, and to help with the assembly.

But before the meeting, she wondered: what did Simon mean when he said that he would never be the same again, that he was a changed person? Well clearly his experience in Niger had changed him. The poverty issue was now in his heart. How would this change their relationship, would it be weaker or stronger? Was it time it weakened anyway?

"How do we explain MPH to seven-to-ten-year olds?" was Sara's opening question after the committee had welcomed back Simon and listened to his story. Sara remembered asking Peter much that same question back in January.

Some two hundred children would be at the assembly, she told them. Some could be highly influential one day. A future prime minister could be there for all they knew – so they had to get it right. They decided role-play would be good, something that involved as many of the children as possible. With the Millennium Development Goals so timely and important, they opted to focus on these. They worked out a script.

Sara asked the school's head if she could have a rehearsal the day before. And asked too for sixteen volunteers. Sara took a large globe to school with her, also a MAKE POVERTY HISTORY banner to hang on the wall, and sashes on the MDG issues: Poverty and hunger, Education, Girls dying, Children, Dying mothers, Disease, Environment, Partnership. And also four country headbands.

Four children were chosen to represent countries, and eight to wear the sashes and read the goals. Another four were chosen for a follow-on discussion. Sara would lead, and Simon would tell them about the boy in the school in Niger.

"Don't let on that you know us. Don't wave or do anything silly to embarrass us, will you?" Chloe had cautioned Sara over breakfast on the morning of the assembly. And May had nodded agreement.

Sara watched as the children came in, they just kept on coming. Simon began with a prayer, then it was Sara's turn.

"Thank you very much for asking me to come to your assembly, which today is going to be about the need to end poverty in the world, to make it history. When we talk about making something history, what do we mean?" Silence. A hand eventually went up slowly.

"Would it be to make it something that happened in the past?" enquired a small voice under the hand.

"Yes, that's exactly it," said Sara. "Thank you. History is something that happened in the past. That's what we need to make poverty – we need to make it history. Poverty means not having enough food to eat, not going to school, being in poor health. Making poverty history would mean that everyone has enough food, and every boy and girl goes to school. And that's why it's important to achieve what are called the Millennium Development Goals. What is a goal? Yes?"

"Something you aim to score, like in football. I scored a goal on Saturday," said another, to a ripple of laughter.

"Fantastic, well done you. You scored a goal. Now it's the world that needs to score. The Millennium Development Goals were agreed by the leaders of every country in the world. That's about 190 – wow, about one country for every one of you here this morning! They agreed the goals in 2000, at the start of this millennium. They are intended to be achieved by 2015. They are about ending poverty. The readers are going to tell us what the eight goals are. But first, here are some people from around the world."

Reader 1 (wearing Bolivian headband): "I'm from Bolivia. In my country thousands of children do not have a school to go to."

Reader 2: "I'm from Ethiopia. In my country, hundreds of villages have no clean drinking water."

Reader 3: "I'm from Indonesia. In my country thousands of acres of forest are being destroyed every year."

Reader 4: "I'm from Tanzania. In my country two million people are in need of help, because they do not have enough food."

"Thank you," said Sara, "and now the goals."

Reader 5: "Goal number one is to halve the number of people who live on less than a dollar a day, that's about 70p, and halve the number of people who suffer from hunger."

Reader 6: "Goal two, to make sure that all children start and finish primary school."

Reader 7: "Goal three. Make sure that as many girls as boys go to school."

Reader 8: "Goal four. Cut by two-thirds the number of children who die before they are five-years-old. A child under five dies every three seconds."

Reader 9: "Goal 5. Cut by three-quarters the number of women who die when they are having babies."

Reader 10: "Goal 6. Stop terrible diseases from spreading and make them less common."

Reader 11: "Goal 7. Halve the number of people without safe and clean drinking water. Improve the lives of 100 million people who live in slums, the poorer areas of cities."

Reader 12: "Goal 8. All the nations to work together to help poorer nations receive a fairer share of the world's wealth."

"Thank you," said Sara, "all of you, for reading those so clearly. Now, the next please."

Reader 13: "Did you know that about a billion people don't have enough food to eat, that's one in every six people in the world?"

Reader 14: And that more than a billion people don't have safe drinking water?"

Reader 15: "Yes, and over 100 million children don't go to school?"

Reader 16: "And that our part of the world eats half of the world's food?"

Reader 13: "You know something – Governments, people in power – they have really messed up our world."

Reader 14: "What do you mean – 'They'? What about you? What are you doing?"

Reader 15: "Oh, come on! You can't blame the state of the world on me! What can I do; I'm only one person."

Reader 16: "'I'm only one person'. If we all said that, nothing would ever happen!"

Reader 13: "So, what can I do? What can you do? What can we do?"

Reader 14: "Loads of things! The world leaders have said they will work to achieve these eight goals to halve world poverty by 2015. We could help to make that happen."

Reader 15: "How can we do that?"

Reader 16: "We can write to government ministers to ask them what they are doing. Ask them how much Britain's aid budget needs to be increased to help achieve the goals."

Reader 13: "Changing the way we live can help to lift people out of poverty too. Did you know that the earth's climate is changing, making life harder for poor people, more difficult to grow food? And that climate change is caused by emissions of gases from our houses and our cars?"

Reader 14: "So what can I do?"

Reader 15: "Try to use less electricity at home. Switch off lights when you leave your room, don't leave the TV on standby. Get the family to cycle, walk or take the bus instead of the car. Ask your mum and dad to slow down. Did you know that a car driven slowly uses less petrol than a car driven fast?"

Reader 16: "And you could buy fair-traded chocolate so that the people who produce the cocoa that makes the chocolate are paid fairly."

Reader 13: "Will all this really make a difference?"

Reader 14: "Yes, especially if you tell your friends and get them to join in."

Reader 15: "I suppose, if we tried, we could make a difference."

Reader 16: "That's the challenge!"

"Yes, that's the challenge," said Sara. "Thank you all so much. Mr Copplestone would now like to say something about one of the goals: about going to school."

"Thank you. In this country we take going to school for granted. A few weeks ago, I was in Africa as you know . . ." And he told them about the boy who said that the happiest day of his life was the day he started school.

Sara picked it up. "So, let's dare to imagine a world where everyone goes to school, where hunger has no chance to show its face, where everyone has enough food. Let's make poverty history. Ending poverty is the challenge and the great opportunity of our time. And yes, we can all help to do it. So let's make poverty history. All shout! . . . I didn't hear that . . . Again: LET'S MAKE POVERTY HISTORY!"

Simon ended the assembly with a prayer: "We pray for world leaders, that they may have a hunger for justice. We pray for all who are suffering around the world. We pray for ourselves, that we will care enough to build a fairer world. Jesus said, 'I have come to bring Good News to the poor'. We are called to bring good news to the poor, to share what we have with those who have less."

The children left, Sara took down the banner, the school's head thanked them profusely. Sara just hoped that some of what the children had heard would remain with them, even that seeds may have been planted that would make a difference.

★   ★   ★

And talking of changing lives . . . They had politely turned down the head's request that they stay for coffee. Not that they didn't need it. But they needed it with each other.

"Coffee, Simon?" she asked as they left the school.

"That would be lovely." It was two weeks since Simon had ended his fast. And it was the first time they had been alone since then. They stood in the hall of Sara's house and hugged without a word. Sara fixed the coffee, and they sipped it, looking down the garden, again without a word. Words were superfluous.

"I thought I'd lost you," Sara finally broke the silence. "You really had me worried – that your solidarity with the poor would leave you solid in the ground. You must promise me that you will never, ever, do that again."

"Well, not this week," he kidded.

"*Simon*! Tell me, you said in church – and you didn't know I was there – that Niger has changed your life, that you will never be the same again. Tell me more." And Simon knew what Sara was getting at.

"Sara, I have been totally in thrall to you. If you had told me to jump off the end of the pier, I would have asked you what was the best time to do it! I feel I have broken just a little of that, that I am more my own person, more independent perhaps. But that doesn't mean that our friendship is weaker. How could it not be strengthened by what you did? It's changed . . . but it is not weaker. No, it's at a much deeper level."

Sara sighed, a deep sigh of relief. She never wanted Simon to be in thrall to her anyway. And yet she wondered . . . A deeper level – but a little ambiguous nonetheless.

"And what about that concert? I am still waiting!" she said.

"Well other things have been going on. Life, for example. Life, you know, the things that happen to you when you are making other plans – it happened to me. I will look for a concert, I promise."

"You'd better. And Peter would like us to go with him to a meeting at the university about the trade in armaments at the end of the month. He feels the MPH campaign is not taking on board how some of the very poorest countries are also the ones where there is armed conflict, countries where Britain is selling armaments."

★   ★   ★

The meeting was organised by the Campaign Against Arms Trade, which worked for the reduction and ultimate abolition of the international arms trade. Speakers outlined different aspects of the trade, but it was the link with poverty that Sara and Simon wanted to understand.

Armed conflicts make the world poorer, they are the leading cause of world hunger, said one speaker, quoting a UN Food and Agriculture Organization source. And the armaments come mostly from Western countries, said another, with Britain, the world's second largest arms exporter, behind only the United States.

British companies, they heard, sell armaments to countries with poor human rights records, such as Indonesia, Saudi Arabia and Nigeria. And it got worse. The UK armaments industry receives government subsidies amounting to over £800 million a year.

During the 1990s alone there were thirty-nine major conflicts, they heard, with more than four million people killed. Nine out of ten casualties were civilians. There were over 200,000 child soldiers in the world. In sub-Saharan Africa there are fourteen heavily indebted poor countries involved in either a regional war or civil conflict. And where had the arms come from to fuel these conflicts? Many from Britain.

They heard how UK armaments exports had risen by over 10% in the last year. Another speaker told of the links between war and conflict on the one hand, and high levels of debt on the other; of how Germany's high levels of First World War debt degraded her economy and provided a breeding ground for militarism and fascism; of how a similar pattern was now being repeated in the poorest countries.

They heard how too much government money in some countries was being used to buy armaments rather than fund vital sectors such as health and education; how in Sudan, where civil war waged relentlessly, the military budget was thought to account for 80% of government expenditure.

A speaker from the CAAT Christian Network said that many churches, including the Church of England, the Roman Catholic Church and the Society of Friends, the Quakers, had taken a strong stand on the morality of the arms trade. A Quaker statement was quoted:

"We believe the arms trade to be morally wrong. It encourages governments to seek military solutions to political problems and adds to the suffering in any resulting conflict . . . the resources spent to manufacture and to buy them are diverted forever from essential human needs such as food and health care . . . the global trade in arms makes the world less, not more secure."

Another speaker, from the Control Arms Campaign, said that his organisation was urging governments to adopt an Arms Trade Treaty. Questions were invited. In pre-Niger, pre-fast days, it would have been Sara who was on her feet like a shot. Instead it was Simon.

"What I have heard this evening has shocked me. But what can we do to stop it, to stop this scandal?"

"Press for an end to government subsidies and support for arms exports," came the reply from a Campaign Against Arms Trade speaker. "Press for the end of exports to oppressive regimes and exports to countries involved in an armed conflict or region of tension; also for an end to exports to countries whose social welfare is threatened by military spending. Also, urge the government to support measures, both in Britain and internationally, which will regulate and reduce the arms trade and lead to its eventual end."

As they travelled home, Peter, Sara and Simon were in agreement. The trade in armaments must become a more central part of the MPH campaign. Sara would write a press release and send a newsletter to all their supporters.

"And talking of trade, don't forget November 2nd, the rally for trade justice at parliament," she said. "Ahead of the WTO meeting in Hong Kong in December, people will be coming from all over the country to lobby their MP. Ours has agreed to meet us at 2.30, probably outside in the gardens as there should be fifteen or twenty of us. I suggest we travel down on the midday train."

And Simon thought of that midday train back in February when they had gone down to see Nelson Mandela – of the way Sara had opened up to him then, and of the surprising events that had happened since.

Sara, for her part, went home and told William about the evening. William listened. But listened in silence. And when she had finished, he said nothing, nothing at all. Sara did not know it then, but William was about to drop a bombshell. Nor did she know that it would not be the only bombshell to drop on her life.

18

Bombshells

It poured down on November 2nd, the day of the Trade Justice rally in London. Sara's faithful flock was nonetheless intact as they boarded the midday train and shook the rain off their coats.

The idea of the organisers was for the campaigners to form up on the roads surrounding parliament, effectively throwing a huge white band around the Palace of Westminster. And people were there from virtually every parliamentary constituency in the land. They formed up in the rain, munched on soggy sandwiches and walked towards the parliament building. Sara had arranged to meet their MP under a large tree in the park close to parliament.

When the MP arrived, the rain was sloshing down; but large umbrellas kept off at least some of it.

"Good to meet you again. What can I do for you?" asked the MP.

"We'd like to speak with you about trade justice and we have a number of specific points to make and questions to ask," said Sara. "First of all, European farmers and companies are still getting paid large subsidies to export food that is then dumped on developing country markets, pushing local farmers out of business.

Do you believe that the EU should agree to an end date for elim-
inating agricultural export subsidies?"

"I do indeed. We agree on this," came the reply. "The new White
Paper on Trade and Investment calls for all EU agricultural export
subsidies to end by 2010. It's our neighbours across the English
Channel and the Atlantic you should really be persuading, not me."

"As a British citizen I cannot influence the French or US governments," said Simon, "that's your job. Other matters on the
trade justice agenda we may not agree on. Free trade, for example.
You keep on pushing this, but it is not the answer for developing
countries. Free trade is damaging the economies of poorer countries, costing them a lot of money. The poor – poor farmers – are
paying for your free trade." Simon's comment was sharp and
damning. The MP, knowing that Simon was a clergyman, was
slightly taken aback.

"I acknowledge the problems faced by small farmers in poor
countries, but protectionism is not the answer," he replied. "If
poor countries keep their borders closed this will not help their
farmers become more competitive in the global market."

"Developing countries surely must have the right to protect
poor farming communities from having to compete with massive
agricultural businesses," said Peter. "Poor countries need the freedom to use policies such as tariffs and quotas. The evidence shows
that protecting poor farmers – whether through subsidies or tariffs –
is an important part of a country's development strategy."

"Exposing poor farmers to the global market will cause massive
upheaval, loss of livelihoods and huge increases in poverty," Peter
went on. "The EU should press in the WTO's agricultural negotiations for developing countries to exempt important food products from any further liberalisation."

"And what about the GATS, the General Agreement on Trade
in Services?" shouted Agnes. "Do you support this? I think that
EU should withdraw its demand that water is included in the
GATS. And it should stop insisting that developing countries
open up their water supply services to transnational corporations.
And we know that many MPs agree with us."

"Yes I have received a lot of e-mails and cards on this matter. However, the great thing about the GATS is that countries are free to choose whether they want to commit their services to its rules or not. And with a billion people lacking access to clean water, GATS is needed to help investment."

"It is just not true that they are free to choose," came in Simon. The MP looked startled at a clergyman virtually accusing him of lying. But Simon went on.

"Many countries are being told that they can only expect to get access to our markets if they sign up to GATS. And one of the major dangers of GATS is that once a country makes its commitment, then under WTO's rules, that decision cannot be reversed."

"I will look into this," said the MP glancing at his watch.

"Another concern we have," said Sara, "is about the IMF and World Bank. They must stop imposing damaging free trade conditions on poor countries in exchange for debt relief and aid. This is the government's responsibility. And Gordon Brown is chair of the IMF's senior policy committee."

"The Government believes that debt relief should be given to those countries that are committed to good governance and poverty reduction. Developing countries have ownership over these policies," replied the MP.

"Yes, but it's the IMF that gets the final say isn't it? And when you say poverty reduction what you actually mean is privatisation, trade liberalisation and deregulation," said Sara.

"The World Development Movement", she went on, "has produced reports on Senegal, Malawi and Zambia which show how conditions imposed by the IMF, including cutting subsidies and tariffs which protected poor farmers, have made poverty worse. How can you claim to defend the right of developing countries to decide their own development policies while the IMF and World Bank are forcing them to cut trade barriers? The IMF forces them to open up, and then the WTO locks the policy in place. Our government must allow developing countries to regulate foreign investment in accordance with their needs."

"Governments need to encourage foreign investment, which promotes development," replied the MP.

"But the evidence shows that the countries that have successfully reduced poverty, such as those in East Asia, have opened up to foreign investment at their own pace," said Peter. "Rich countries are saying to poor countries: liberalise first, then you'll develop. This is not the way that Britain developed. Foreign investment can promote development, but countries should have the right to protect their new industries until they are able to compete internationally. And the government should regulate companies so that they are held accountable for their impacts."

"Regulations must be voluntary. Companies are put off if regulations are mandatory. We can't wrap them in red tape," said the MP.

"The problem is that many companies hide behind public relations," said Agnes. "Surely we need regulations that are legally enforceable and independently monitored if they are to have any meaning at all."

"A final question, I can see that you are looking at your watch," said Simon. "In view of the close link between poverty and armed conflict, would you support an end to government subsidies for arms exports?"

"Oh that's a tricky one," came the reply, "armaments exports earn this country a lot of money. And if we didn't sell them someone else would."

"We'd like to talk with you about that one again," said Sara. "Thank you for meeting us. And we would like to invite you to a rich world–poor world meal that we are holding a week on Friday, Could you come?"

"I will consult my diary and my secretary will let you know."

★　★　★

As the trade justice campaigners arrived back from London and went their separate ways, Simon asked Sara if he could have a

word. They walked back together towards St. Luke's. Simon was
nervous. He was about to drop Sara a bombshell.

"Sara, I don't know if you have ever noticed a pattern concern-
ing Church of England curates?"

"Can't say that I have."

"Well, they tend to move on after four years, maybe they go to
another curacy or they are appointed a vicar or a rector somewhere." He paused and Sara wondered what this was about. They
walked on for a while in silence, Simon reaching inside himself
for courage to say what he had to say.

"Well my four years at St. Luke's is almost over. I will have
been here four years in January, just two months away." As what
Simon seemed to be saying slowly dawned, Sara felt her heart
descend from somewhere near the top of her body down to her
knees. Simon went on.

"Well, just two days ago, I received an offer – to be team vicar
of a large church in Lancashire. Your old part of the world, Sara.
It's actually a bigger appointment than I could have expected at
my age. But it seems the parish council there is strong on social
responsibility. They read of my fast and liked the stance that I had
taken. I shall have three curates, one about my age, the others . . ."

But Sara wasn't listening. She stood still on the pavement and
looked at him, looked at him with the eyes that had first capti-
vated him.

"You're leaving?" The tone was desperate.

"Yes, except that I have not given my final acceptance yet. I
wanted to talk with you first."

"Simon, I need to take this in. What can I say? You've just dropped
a bombshell. I just can't bear the thought of you, well, not being
around. Sorry, I'm being selfish, aren't I? Simon, congratulations,
you deserve it! Of course you must accept. And if this is what you
truly want, I will try, I will try very hard, to be happy for you." But,
at that moment, Sara was much closer to tears than to happiness.

"It's just that our relationship has been so very special," she
said, "I didn't want it to end with you disappearing 200 miles
away to the northwest, maybe for good."

"Sara, I am going to miss you. You know that. But we can still meet. The job comes with a four-bedroom vicarage – just for me! All of you, all four of you, must come and stay. Er, better not just you. .

"There's something else I want to think about too," he went on. "After going to Niger, part of me is still in Africa. I have wondered whether I should apply to a mission society or to an aid agency for a job in Africa, or maybe offer to do Voluntary Service Overseas. On the other hand, I think I should at least give leading a parish a try. What do you think?"

"What do I think? Simon, you ask me to choose between you disappearing to either Africa or Lancashire. Well, I think you should give a vicarage life a try and see if that is for you. You're young. Maybe Africa will be right eventually. But Simon, I feel devastated by this. When would you leave?"

"Early January."

"Early January. So we have only two more months of what has been a very close and valued relationship. A love affair that recognised that a certain expression of love was out of bounds, was beyond reach."

"Maybe if we recognise all the good that has come from it, the way we have energised each other, and yes, the way you saved my life. And to remember that life does move on. We shall continue working for what we believe in, I'm sure. We can stay in touch by e-mail, by phone, etc., still co-operating on the issues that brought us together."

"Thank you, yes, let's be positive," she replied. "Kiss me, please, while you're still here." And they kissed, all too briefly, both aware they were on the pavement.

"The rich world–poor world meal," said Sara, "we need to organise the details. I will be in touch soon."

So Sara went home, trying to be positive. Their relationship was ending, and maybe it was time for it to end, she reasoned, but part of her was aching.

★   ★   ★

The invites had been printed, the MP, the mayor, editor Frank, and the nice police officer who had let them off with a warning, had all been sent complimentary tickets.

"Come to a rich world–poor world meal," said the invites. "As you step into the Methodist church hall, you will have no idea what kind of meal you will be eating. When you arrive, you will pull a ticket out of a bag. A third of diners will get a 3-course meal. The other two-thirds will make do with a bowl of rice. Come to an evening with a difference. It will cost you a fiver – and be warned: two-thirds of you will be subsidising the other third."

And so the MPH committee spread the cooking between them, they organised some music . . . and they watched as people came and drew their tickets and their fate for the evening.

Many of those who drew a rich-world meal ticket looked a little embarrassed. Some even tried to swap their ticket with someone who had drawn a poor-world ticket. Always unsuccessfully. The MP pulled out a rich world meal ticket. The mayor, Frank and the policeman all got the poor. Charley, trust Charley, drew a rich world ticket.

The MPH committee cheated. Especially as they had to serve as well, they decided that it would not be right for them to sit down to a lavish meal. They opted for the rice.

And so the evening started. The rich-world ticket-holders walked up to beautifully laid-out tables with decorated tablecloths, fine cutlery and wine glasses. The poor-world ticket-holders sat down at bare tables. Simon made a few introductory remarks.

"This evening is intended to be a parable of the real world situation," he said. "Let's feel the tension between rich and poor. Feel what it's like to be rich among the poor, or poor watching the rich eat. I would ask that you play out your parts. Rich diners, please do not rush over to the poor and offer them half your food. The real world is not like that. Not yet. In the meantime, be hard-hearted, because sadly that is how rich-world governments are. Other than saying that, well, anything could happen – although a policeman is on hand in case of serious disorder! Enjoy the experience!"

The rich were then served with a sumptuous starter: smoked salmon, salad and crisp bread rolls. The poor sat and watched.

"It would be right," said the MP, positively enjoying his role, "for us rich diners to gather up the few crumbs remaining from our delicious bread rolls and take them over to the poor." So they brushed up the crumbs and took them over to the hungry diners at the bare tables, who ate their crumbs without comment.

The poor-world diners were given their rice. And as they ate, the rich world diners were served with their main course. The mouth-watering smell of a chicken casserole drifted over the poor diners. The poor had finished their rice long before the rich had eaten their casserole. And they were getting restless.

"I think we should go over to the rich and ask them if this is fair," said the mayor.

"Let's stand in a circle round their tables, to symbolise the way the poor are all around them," said Agnes. All nodded. They moved off and surrounded the diners, who were heads down, eating their chicken.

"We are hungry," said the mayor. "We have come to ask if you will share with us?"

"We'll offer you, say, half a carrot," said the MP looking up, "a symbol of the 0.35% of GNP of aid that Britain gives the poor."

"And I will give you some of my sauce," said Charley.

"That's disgusting!" said Peter. "All that food on your plate and you offer us half a carrot and a bit of sauce."

"Tell you what, let's raid their plates!" said another poor diner.

"Yes, let's do it," said another. Mayhem broke out as poor diners started scooping food off the plates of the rich, drinking their wine, trying to take their seats . . .

Hell! There's going to be a riot, thought Sara. But before she could do anything, the nice policeman intervened.

"Stop! Speaking in my self-appointed role for the evening as head of the United Nations peace-keeping force," he shouted, "I command order. Will the poor please return to their tables?"

"No!" said a woman raider. "I am staying here. I am seeking asylum with the rich." And suddenly, the room went quiet. The parable was being played out.

Most of the poor went back, some with their spoils. Then the rich were served with their dessert, a delicious-looking chocolate pudding. Continuing to sense the injustice of it all, the poor began singing and chanting. "We shall overcome" was followed by the chant "What do we want? – Fair shares! When do we want it? – Now, now, now!" The rich finished their chocolate pudding and Simon spoke again.

"I think it's time to draw the parable to a close now. In a moment we are going to bring round fairtrade coffee and tea – for everyone. Thank you for playing your parts so well. I need hardly say that the world does not have to be like this. I'd like to quote something that Sara wrote in her article after the G8 summit: 'Today we know how to make poverty history. We know what needs to be done. Poverty goes on because those with power to end it are not giving it priority. That is the scandal'. I ask you all to continue working to end the scandal we have played out this evening – of hungry people in a world where there is enough for everyone. Defeating hunger and poverty must never be beyond reach."

"Thank you for those words," said Sara to him quietly as they washed up afterwards, "especially the last two. I've heard of 'our tune'," she smiled. "'Beyond reach' seem to have become our words!"

"Words without a song," he responded.

★ ★ ★

William had been in a quiet mood for days. An unusual quietness, thought Sara. Late one evening she decided to tackle him about it.

"Well it's because there is something I need to tell you and I don't quite know how to break it," he said.

A second bombshell was about to fall on Sara. William told her that he had been offered a job with a company that made armaments for export. And that he had accepted the job. He had not discussed it with her, he said, because he knew how she felt about arms exports, and knew she would talk him out of it. The job would pay several thousand pounds a year more – and with the extra money they could perhaps replace their old banger with a green vehicle such as a Toyota Prius. He would start on 1st January.

As she listened, Sara's world fell apart. This was worse, far worse, than Simon's bombshell. For she knew that she could not live with anyone, anyone, who worked in the armaments industry – even William. And she told him so.

"You're bluffing Sara," he responded. "The fact is that if I didn't take the job, someone would. And think of the car . . ."

"William, you are so insensitive! It's December in a few days time. In just over a month we shall be having a party here. What kind of party would it be if I knew that you were starting work the next day for a company that's exporting the means of conflict and making poverty worse – exporting death? You know what's at stake William, you know how I feel – and you never even discussed it with me!"

"As for the car," she went on, "do you think you can bribe me with a car? Every time I got into the wretched thing, I would see machine guns on the wings, firing at every pedestrian on the pavement. Forget it. If you do this William, I warn you, you will wreck our marriage! I'm going to bed."

Unwilling to sleep in the same bed as anyone who planned to work for an armaments company, Sara made up a bed in the spare room. And she lay there, thinking that she just could not live with armaments. She was convinced of that. Tomorrow she would talk to Simon. And talk to him she did, laying it out weepily at the curacy house before a stunned and silent Simon.

"I cannot live with him, Simon, if he goes ahead with this. But the problem is that I couldn't leave him either. Where could I go? What about the girls? We can't come and live with you in your four-bedroom house, can we? Your new parishioners would hardly like that: 'Oh, and by the way, forgot to mention that I

have a married woman and her two children coming with me!'
Not quite on your CV was it? What can I do Simon?"

Silence . . . Simon was a good listener but a hopeless speaker at
such moments, moments when the woman he loved stood crying
before him. It was Sara who spoke again.

"Simon, would you talk to William – please? He might listen
to you. Please?"

"Well er, I am not sure what I could say to him – or whether
he would want to talk to me. I'll think about it." Two more
nights in the spare bed passed, and Simon had still not been in
touch with William. With the atmosphere at the Openshaws well
below freezing point, Sara rang the curacy house.

"Hello," a gruff voice answered. "No it's not Simon, it's Bob
from the drop-in centre. Simon's on the loo. I'll give him a shout.
Simon . . . phone!"

"Sara, sorry, I am finding this difficult. I can't interfere between
man and wife. It's not as if I know William well. I am still strug-
gling with how I can approach this."

"Oh Simon, you are useless," she responded. What was she
saying? Now she felt in danger of falling out with both the men
in her life.

"Please Simon, think of something." The following day there
was a message on the Openshaws' answering machine. It was a
hesitant and garbled Reverend Simon Copplestone, ringing to
speak with William. William returned the call when Sara was out
talking to the local Rotary Club about Make Poverty History. He
did not tell Sara.

A week passed, a week in the spare bed. How much longer can
we go on like this? wondered Sara. It was William who broke the
ice. He wanted to talk.

"Sara, I am sorry I have made you so unhappy. I can see now
that I should have talked over this job offer with you. Of course I
should! Your friend the curate rang yesterday. Poor man, is he in
the right job? I have never heard anyone so garbled, I had to finish half his sentences for him! I expect you know that he feels the
same about the armaments industry as you do. And that he's

worried about the effect on you of – how did his posh voice put it? – the change I am contemplating." They smiled at each other, almost laughed, for the first time in a week.

"I had spoken to Simon about it," admitted Sara, "and asked him to ring you."

"You've very fond of him aren't you? What's more I think you tried to tell me when we were in France this summer. And I was so wrapped up in the cricket, I didn't take much notice. Sorry. The fact is that deep down I love you so much that you could have an affair with him and I would forgive you. I'd just be devastated if you didn't come back! Anyway, today I withdrew my acceptance of the offer – I'm staying put. And only yesterday my present company offered me more money if I would stay! We could think of that Prius after all."

"William, thank you. I am fond of Simon, very fond. If you can be in love with two men at the same time, well that's me right now. I have not had an affair with him. We have both of us recognised that we are – how shall I put it? – beyond reach of each other. And he's off to a new parish in Lancashire in the new year. So he really will be beyond reach."

"It was clear that he was besotted with you, even before you saved his life. You know, I am very proud of you! All you've done this year, the campaigning, the G8, helping Simon and everything. I am not the attentive husband I should be, but you're not easy to live with at times. That's because you care, I guess. Let's invite Simon to our party shall we?"

"I had been thinking we might. And let's include Jean too, you remember, the octogenarian who played chess with Chloe on the bus to Edinburgh? William, just for the record . . . just for the record . . . I would not leave you."

And after the most difficult week of the Openshaws' married life, the bed in the spare room lay empty that night.

19

One 'Beyond Reach' . . .

Sara rang Simon the next morning to thank him. And got a surprise. "Would you be free on December 15th, Thursday evening?" he asked. "I've found a concert I think you'd like. It
centres on Beethoven's Ninth Symphony."

"Great, great! I'll check with William if he's in that evening and
come back to you." But before she did, Simon received an invitation. It read:

Sara and William request the pleasure of your company at
their New Year's Eve plus party, from 9.00 p.m. onwards,
27 Barnlady Road.

Dress: Topical or Tropical

Bring a bottle – of fairly traded anything.

In the bottom right-hand corner was a PTO. And Simon turned
the invite over and read:

> Wine is very life to human beings if taken in moderation.
> What is life to one who is without wine? It has been
> created to make people happy.
> Wine drunk to excess leads to bitterness of spirit. Wine
> drunk at the proper time and in moderation is rejoicing of
> heart and gladness of soul.
> Wine and music gladden the heart, but the love of friends
> is better than either.
> (From the book of Sirach)

He gasped as he recognised the verses – verses from his beloved "bit in the middle" of the Bible.

Sara soon rang back. Yes, she could make it. And Simon thanked her for the invite, thought the verses were great, and that he couldn't think of a better way to end his time here than being with her, even if there would be loads of other people around.

"Simon, those verses. You will never guess who I had in mind when I chose them," said Sara, "with just a little help from Agnes."

A few days before the concert, the World Trade Organization began a ministerial meeting in Hong Kong. Hopes that this might improve the trading position of developing countries, and of the poor, were fading fast.

Trade justice, thought Sara, was always going to be the most difficult to achieve of the three aims of the Make Poverty History campaign. The other two – more and better aid, debt relief – required financial decisions by Western governments, plus a willingness to ensure that additional funds reach the poor. Difficult enough, but trade justice was more complex.

Peter had stressed that justice in trade and related matters required changes in the procedures of international trade. That it challenged organisations with power over the rules, and threatened vested interests, such as those of transnational corporations and large farmer groups in Western countries. And that trade justice called, above all, for changes in Western governments' thinking that free trade is good for the poor.

A day or two into the Hong Kong meeting, the shape was clear. Western governments would consider lowering their agricultural subsidies, provided developing countries opened their markets to the corporations of the Western word. Which meant more water privatisation, more job losses, more injustice, more poverty, thought Sara.

In the midst of this lack of action for justice, they were preparing to go to a concert, she thought. To listen to lovely music, when the music the poor wanted was the music of enough food to eat, a job, dignity, a chance to live not die. And she shared these thoughts with Simon as they met at the station to take the train to the concert in London.

"When I was in Niger, and hardly eating, Sue said to me that it wouldn't solve anyone's problems if I didn't eat. I guess it's the same with music. It doesn't solve anyone's problems if we don't enjoy it. And you have done so much to give the poor a chance to live not die – and you included me. What I think we should do is live intensely in the present moment, in the present time."

The concert began. They smiled and held hands. Carried away by the music, carried away by each other, but both with an ache. That in a little over two weeks time, they might never see each other again. In the interval they talked about Beethoven's Ninth Symphony. Why did Simon like it, Sara wanted to know.

"Well it was a great favourite of someone whose writings I greatly admire, Dag Hammarskjold, the UN Secretary General over forty years ago. There was a UN concert every other year and Hammarskjold would select some of the music. Part of Beethoven's Ninth, usually 'The Ode to Joy', was often included. The year before he died – he was killed in a mysterious plane crash – Hammarskjold gave a brief address before the concert. He explained what Beethoven's Ninth meant to him. He said that in this music, Beethoven had given us a creed that reaffirms the worth of each person. That it includes the promise to practice tolerance and live together as good neighbours – that's why I like it. Why do you like it?"

"Because . . . it's just lovely music. But I shall enjoy it all the more now. And because of the title, 'Ode to Joy'. Joy is what I feel when I'm with you." The concert ending all too soon, they took the train home. The carriage was empty, and Sara put both her arms around Simon's waist.

"You know what?" she said, squeezing him, "William said that I could have an affair with you and he would forgive me. But that he'd be devastated if I didn't come back to him. So how about a mad fortnight of passion in your curacy house? You spoke on the way down of how we should live intensely in the present moment, in the present time. So how about making your walls echo with erotic moanings and . . ."

"Sara . . . it has been a lovely evening, but come back to earth. For a start, the curacy house is a little crowded right now. Bob, Jim and Fred from the drop-in centre are all with me. And more seriously . . . and you are not serious, but if you were . . . well we could have an affair, but in view of the way we feel about each other, where might it lead to? An affair would take us into territory that is unknown. It could deepen our relationship beyond measure, completely beyond measure – so much that you might not want to go back to William. And as you rightly said a few weeks ago, I cannot arrive in my new parish with a married woman under one arm and her lovely young daughters under the other."

"Good picture for your Christmas cards though! Oh I knew you would say something like that! And that's why, I suppose, I made a silly suggestion to you. As love makes it possible to say sorry – sorry!"

"You know I love your flirting, which I see anyway as charm, not flirting."

"What is wonderful about you, Simon," she said, looking at him straight in the eyes, "is that you always put the best possible interpretation on what I do. Thank you," she said, pecking him on the cheek. The train rumbled on.

"Oh, and by the way, talking of Christmas cards . . . I had one this morning from Margaret, the Margaret I told you about," said Simon, "my old girl friend who went off to become a nun. Well, it did not work out. She didn't get past the novice stage. And now she is living in a town quite near my new parish. She had seen the announcement that I was coming up . . . and wondered if we might get together for a drink, when I'm settled in. Oh, and she added – and this will make you laugh – that she is now in training to become a sex therapist."

"Simon, this is wicked. First of all you leave me, and now you tell me you're going off with a sex therapist! You've had one sex worker in your life; now you're preparing to shack up with another . . ."

"I am not running off, I am not preparing to shack up . . . merely a drink. And I don't think a sex therapist would like being classed as a sex worker."

"And you're an expert in these things are you, Simon? Well, I'm as jealous as hell, but you deserve this. Your sex therapist will want to . . . shall we say, engage in all kinds of interesting experiments? Have you got some good times coming to you . . .!"

"Sara, you're leaping ahead." Sara was doubled up.

"Sorry. I could have put that better. But you know very well that sex therapy is a legitimate part of the medical profession."

"Of course I do. At the practice we sometimes refer people to sex therapists."

"Really?"

"Yes really. But if Margaret works out, you may as well enjoy it all the same. After all, you've lived like a monk for so long you must have enough points to qualify for a monastery."

"I had thought of that actually."

"No, wouldn't be for you. You couldn't preach about the joy of sex." She teased and tickled him.

"I could manage. But, seriously, I'm not sure about seeing Margaret. It was some time ago now." Simon paused before looking Sara straight in the eyes.

"There is only one woman I want," he said quietly. "And she is . . . beyond reach."

★ ★ ★

The WTO meeting in Hong Kong ended as expected. Nothing for the poor. Nothing to help make poverty history. Bob Geldof called it a disgrace. And the WTO had not found anyone to host its next meeting of ministers in two years' time. No one wanted it.

The Christmas cards and letters were meanwhile coming thick and fast through the Openshaws' letterbox. And Sara sat down at the computer and decided she would compose a Christmas letter with a difference.

"What a year we have had! All of us have performed so spectacularly this year! Sara climbed Mount Everest in June – in twelve hours, she didn't need a minute longer – and came home and found a cure for the common cold.

"William has invented the all-singing, all-dancing, all-everything ball bearing. He is certain to win the Nobel prize for it. And he's invented a way of walking through a door without opening it!" This was in response to Sara's repeated requests to 'shut that bloody door'.

"Chloe – oh, what can we say? At the age of ten she is already a grand chess-master, and what the future holds, let's just say – check mate. And May, again what can we say – eight and she's the lead violinist with the London Sympathy . . . er wot not.

"And our dog, Odif – that's Fido in reverse he's so clever – well many dogs sit up and beg. When Odif springs up – he jumps right over the house! Oh, and there's one other thing – Sara met a man she fancies the pants off . . ."

She closed it, and thought – well, the last bit's true anyway! It was time for a letter she could send, and wanted to send, to all the people who had been involved in the MPH campaign in the town.

Newsletter
Make Poverty History: How Much Have We
Achieved?

The 2005 Make Poverty History campaign has not made poverty history. No, we didn't expect to wipe out poverty. But when I look back to the start of the year, and to the aspirations we had, I cannot deny that it has been disappointing. But the obstinacy, the duplicity, of government tells us how far we have to travel, how hard we need to push. We must never give up.

The campaign has helped to raise awareness of the issues and persuaded governments to announce increases in aid and debt relief. But not by enough to achieve the Millennium Development Goals. I have to say that our government remains aloof and lacks understanding of how deeply people care about these issues.

It is surely not too much to expect some joined-up thinking from government. For them to ask whether selling armaments to the poor fits in with the anti-poverty agenda they claim to have. They also need to connect poverty and climate change. And do something about the World Trade Organization.

The disappointing end to the year in Hong Kong shows us that the WTO is part of the problem, not the solution. I am coming to the view that the best thing that could be done with the WTO is to scrap it and start again. And develop an organisation that would truly bring the benefits of trade to the poor, that would provide a real development agenda. Sadly our government seems wedded to the dogma of free trade, despite overwhelming evidence that free trade traps millions of people in poverty. The poor pay for 'free' trade.

The achievement of the Make Poverty History 2005 campaign is that there are now tens of thousands more people who are demanding action to end poverty. That must be good news! And it's action, not words, that is needed from government.

One phase of the campaign to make poverty history ends. Another will start on 1st January 2006. It has been a joy to work with you on the campaign this year. It is a joy mixed with heartache that not enough has been achieved. I'd like to quote something that debt campaign leader Ann Pettifor said after a summit of leaders a few years ago.

She spoke of "the joy and delight" of uniting with friends around an issue of justice, of the deep well of love and concern that unites large swathes of humanity, and of the powerful potential of human solidarity. "Above all it gave us hope, courage and energy to do more, and to give more", she said.

Yes, we owe it to 800 million people, the world's poorest people, to do more. But let's go beyond statistics. "Statistics do not bleed", wrote Arthur Koestler. They don't capture the grief of a parent whose child has starved to death. Behind every one of the statistics is a child, a woman, a man.

The campaign goes on. We must keep hope alive. The MPH committee will be meeting soon to decide how to pursue the campaign. I will be be touch. For now . . .

Happy Christmas! Happy New Year!
Love
Sara

Sara and William had meanwhile decided not to buy a Toyota Prius, but rather to sell their old banger and help set up a car-share club in town. With this type of club, they heard from a friend who was a member of one in London, users have a pool of cars to drive. They book in advance through a central office, anything from a day to an hour, pick up a car at a designated parking bay and access it with a smart card. And they paid a monthly fee and were billed for hours hired and miles driven. And Sara was surprised at how many people expressed an interest in joining.

Christmas Day was one of two days in the year – the other was Easter Sunday – when the Openshaws regularly went to church. Well, it was three times for Sara and the girls, as they also went on Christmas Eve to the annual Christingle service, when the children sang carols and were given christingles: oranges with candles.

The Christingle service was always packed to the doors, and this year it was being taken by Simon. But the church was so full, he didn't notice Sara.

As Sara sat in the church, watching her girls collect their christingles, she looked at the side chapel where she had almost lost her marbles over Simon all that time ago. And she looked at Simon in the distance, taking the service. To her, he was a star. Falling for him was weak, foolish, dangerous, but Simon had kept it all in balance, stopped them damaging what they believed in, kept them faithful, helped her to understand love.

He had never tried to proselytise, had never suggested that she might come to church and pray about it with him or anything like that. He had just shown love. In the bargain he had changed her understanding of a number of things, social justice, weakness, opportunity, commitment. In a loving way he guided them, and turned what could have been an explosive and damaging relationship into one that was positive and fulfilling.

And then the next carol was announced: 'The First Nowell'. They came to the line, "The star drew nigh to the northwest." . . . and Sara stopped singing. "My star is going to the northwest," she said to herself, "a banal thought, but how appropriate. I had never noticed that line before. He's going. Will I ever see him again?" And she fought back a tear.

On Christmas Day, they were there again, plus William. Bernard was preaching. He began by paying a warm tribute to Simon, this being his last Christmas at St. Luke's.

At the end of the service, as they left the church, Sara paused to look at same spot where Simon had ended his fast. It looked so different then, she thought, with no decorations, no lights, just bare. She had been alone with him then, and she badly wanted to see him again, alone, before he left for that northwest.

Simon provided the opportunity. He rang a few days later to suggest a drink on the day before New Year's Eve. It was an invitation she gladly accepted.

It was into a very different house that Sara walked, walked for the last time when Simon was living there. The books had been packed away for the move. It all had a bare feeling. Even Simon's guests from the drop-in centre had left, gone to London, explained Simon, to one of the big Christmas centres.

"I see the *Joy of Sex* is all packed away", said Sara cheekily, and then kicked herself. She was not going to flirt today. Simon poured some coffee and they talked, at first about nothing in particular. Then Simon moved up a notch.

"Sara there are a couple of things I'd like to talk about. Firstly I want to say, and this is probably my last opportunity to say it, that you saved my life in more ways than one. Let me explain. It has been said that the glory of God is a human being fully alive. My faith, in the early years of my ministry, helped to bring me more fully alive. But when we met, earlier this year, I hadn't lost my faith but I was in a bit of a rut. I was trying to be clever, using cleverness as a substitute, well, as a substitute for living. Me and the cat, just about summed me up."

"Oh Simon, that's not fair – to the cat." He laughed but didn't want to be thrown.

"You changed that. Your love gave me a new dimension. You brought me more fully alive. Yes, there have been grey areas in our friendship, in falling for each other we were weak, but your enthusiasm for MPH has given me a purpose that I am sure will last as long as poverty lasts. For good measure, there's more. I may have a grounding in theology but it was you who said when we had lunch in June, remember, that you cannot be unfaithful to what you truly believe in. And, in saying that, you set the parameters for our relationship." Simon paused.

"And if you are my inappropriate woman number five, as you once suggested, well, you cannot fault me on consistency." They hugged, tearfully.

"That grey area Simon, you know, at Christmas, a special time for children, it came to me that it's rather larger than I had realised. Yes, I said you cannot be unfaithful to what you believe in. But the way I became besotted with you was hardly being faithful to my role as a mother, and of course as a wife. I feel rather ashamed about it, and ashamed that I've only just seen it. If I'd come to terms with it before, well . . . well, too late now, but it's taught me something."

"Thanks for sharing that with me," Simon responded, "I too should have faced this. Love blinds, I suppose, but that's no excuse. You're right about the grey area. But don't feel guilty, that's no good. Look to the future."

They sat in silence for a while, before Simon went on: "And looking to the future, there is something I want to ask you. We've both recognised that we are beyond reach of each other in a certain way of love. I've been thinking of this in relation to making poverty history. And Sara, I don't find this easy. But when we look at the complexities of tackling poverty, the difficulty of persuading governments to give it priority, their lack of wholehearted commitment to end poverty, their duplicity, when we look at them, and at the difficulty of changing the world trading system, the power of transnational corporations, at wars, arms exports, corruption, human rights abuses, the climate change link with poverty, and so on – as committed as we are, as committed as millions throughout the world are . . . is ending poverty rather like us Sara? Is it also . . . . beyond reach? Are we a kind of parable, both of us standing for the unreachable end of poverty? It's a tough question to ask I know, but is making poverty history beyond reach?"

Again there was silence. This time, a long silence. On Simon's face was a look of lined concern, concern for the response to what he had said. And on Sara's face, a frown of deep thoughtfulness. Finally Sara slowly got up from the chair, stood facing him, and putting her hands firmly on Simon's shoulders, looked deep into his eyes.

"Simon, I will never, ever believe that. I will never believe it. I will never accept it. I will not accept it and neither must you. Ending poverty must be brought within reach. We are talking here of life, Simon, the lives of the poor. You say that I saved your life, how can we not go on believing that the end of poverty is possible? How can we not go on working for that? Life, this is all about life, the very means and meaning of life. It's about the lives of people who are burdened by poverty, enabling them to find life, not lose it. People are not born to live and die in poverty. You know that. Yes there are difficulties, but surely they make the campaigning all the more important. We are campaigning for lives, to enable people to realise their potential.

"You know what – you have just given me the charge I need for next year and beyond. I have dreaded you going, wondering if I could go on without you. Now I believe I can – because of what you have just said. You have challenged me Simon, energised me yet again. You didn't mean to, but you have. You have given me a farewell present, an agenda I shall throw myself into. Thank you." And she flung her arms around him and held him tight. And Simon was at first too stunned to reply.

"You say that I am your star," he said eventually, "well my star blinked just now. Thank you for what you've said. I agree, we must never give up."

"I'd like to give you a farewell present," said Sara. "Peter recommended this book and I bought two copies, one for you," And she pulled out of her bag – 'The End of Poverty: How we can make it happen in our lifetime', by Jeffrey Sachs.

"Simon, this is a really good book. Poverty can be made history, in our lifetime. if enough of us want to make it history. Who was it who said that in great endeavours, to have the will is all it takes? Let's take a 25-year time scale. If the Millennium Development Goals can be reached by 2015, if poverty can be halved by then, and I know it's a big if, then we can think of 2030 as the year to see it go."

"Sara, I agree but I just wonder if those goals will be achieved with our present generation of politicians. They get pushed off course so easily. Any priority they claim to give to ending poverty. . .well it so quickly disappears. Should we not be encouraging committed MPH supporters to join the political party they support, to stand for parliament, making clear their commitment on poverty, and keeping to it when they get elected?"

"Wow, that's a whole new dimension, Simon. You're right. Your star soon picked up. Once again, you are a shining light," she said, pecking him on the cheek.

"Whatever else happens, why don't we agree to meet once a year, towards the end of each year perhaps, and look at progress," he said.

"Great, brilliant idea," she replied. "You are invited to us for this time next year. Bring Margaret. You dare! I am going home to draft a statement of intent about MPH locally to circulate to the committee. See you tomorrow. And don't forget, it's tropical or topical."

"I am coming as topical. But sufficient to the day and all that jazz. . . let me hold you tight." And they hugged for a long, long time.

"I wish this moment could go on, could just go on, for ever," said Sara wistfully. But then she moved on.

"Beyond reach? No Simon. To adapt Oscar Wilde: one 'beyond reach' is a misfortunate. Two would look like carelessness."

E-mail from Sara
To members of the MPH committee
The 2005 campaign to make poverty history will end at national level. I believe that we should go on locally. This draft statement is for your comments.

The local campaign to end poverty
Statement of Intent:

- To campaign locally to end the poverty that affects 800 million people worldwide.
- To work with all who share this aim.
- To campaign on matters directly related to poverty, such as aid, debt relief, trade justice, armaments control and climate change.
- To take the message into the community, by means of talks, marches, exhibitions, petitions, street stalls, street theatre and in other ways.
- To support the Millennium Development Goals, in particular the goal to halve the number of people living in poverty by 2015, as a first step to a world where every child, woman and man is free from poverty. And to work towards 2030 as the day when poverty is made history.

Let's meet soon to consider this. And I have some other ideas I'd like to share with you.
Love
Sara

20

New Year's Eve 2005

"Charley's got a Gong." It was Peter, a very excited Peter, on the phone to Sara while the Openshaws were eating breakfast. "an MBE in the New Year's honours list. She's thrilled of course, I'm appalled. Charley's been admitted to a club that closed down fifty years ago. I'd scrap the whole shooting match. But seriously, I'm over the moon for her."

"That's fantastic news Peter, fantastic. Give her a big hug from me." And Charley wanted to celebrate with them this evening, at their party. They were just off to buy a crate of good champagne. And would bring it with them and come early so the four of them could have a drink together first.

"Let's drink to Charley's Gong," said William.

"What's a Gong?" asked Chloe.

"A bit of metal with no ball bearings. A special bit of metal I suppose. A kind of badge to show you've done something," said William.

As the Openshaws got ready for their party, Simon continued to pack, and to prepare an outfit for the party. Tomorrow he would go to Cornwall to see his parents, and come back the following day. On January 3rd, the removal van would arrive. He would take with him the words that Sara had written and which he had quoted at the rich world-poor world meal. He would print them out in a large size, frame them and hang them in his new study: "Today we know how to make poverty history. We know what needs to be done. Poverty goes on because those with power to end it are not giving it priority. That is the scandal."

Just before 8.30 that evening, Peter and Charley staggered in the Openshaws with a crate of bubbly and a "sorry it's not fairtrade. You can't buy fairtrade champers, well not in town anyway."

The four of them hugged and drank, and looked at each other's clothes. True to the tropical or topical nature of the evening, Peter was wearing a shirt with a picture of Gordon Brown, the words "Under Corporate Control" stamped on it. Charley donned a glitzy Pacific shirt and shorts, Sara a T-shirt showing a large thumbscrew with the words "G8, which way will you turn the screw?" William had not decided yet.

"You don't get a Gong every day," Charley announced, draining another glass of bubbly. It was clear this was one New Year's Eve when her left hand would be nowhere near the top of her glass. By the time the other guests arrived, the four of them were just that little bit squiffy. Which ensured that Sara gave her guests a most warm welcome when they arrived. Especially Simon, who she threw her arms around and didn't care who noticed.

"Simon what are you wearing?" Simon was wearing a T-shirt showing a cross channel ferry with an arrow and words under it: "WTO – this way." He explained it to a curious audience.

"You know that the WTO is in such a mess it can't find anyone to host its next meeting of ministers. Well, as the WTO is all at sea, it would make sense to hold its next meeting at sea – on a ferry."

The champagne-fuelled roar was music to Simon's ears, and as the evening wore on, and people drank more bubbly and fair-traded wine, the shirt got even funnier. Guests were wearing grass skirts, were dressed as pound notes, euro notes. . . .and there was a good smattering of MPH messages. Agnes was wearing a T-shirt showing a leaning chimney marked 'Government priority for ending poverty', and with someone at the side blowing it over with little effort. Jean was wearing a blouse with 'They say free trade, we say fair trade'.

William cornered Simon. "Simon, thank you for ringing a few weeks ago. I did appreciate it. And thank you for taking Sara to that concert. Really good of you old sport. Simon, tell me . . . are you interested in ball bearings? Have you ever considered the importance to our lives of vibration deep-groove radial ball bearings?"

And William was off, with Simon doing his best to look interested. He had not come for this. He had come to be at the side of the woman he loved and who he might never see again after tonight. But Sara was playing the thoughtful host and talking to everyone.

"I'm not boring you am I Simon?" William enquired after some length, some considerable length. "You know what a bore is don't you? A bore is someone who bores others and doesn't know he's boring them."

"Absolutely," Simon replied, "O look, there's a woman over there with a WTO shirt. If you don't mind, I will go and have a chat." Blessed release. The woman was wearing a T-shirt marked: 'I survived the battle at Seattle: WTO 1999'. For Simon, this was manna from heaven. She explained that she had recently moved into the area from the US port of Seattle.

"Yes, I was there," she told Simon "at the tear-gassed WTO meeting in 1999. Like everyone else, I got the tear gas." She laughed at his ferry shirt, but conversation was difficult as Charley was talking very loudly.

"I'm worried about Charley, she's squealing her head off," Peter confided to Sara.

"Sara, Sara, Sara," Charley staggered over and lent on her, "well done, well done you. The G8 – you were spot on. It's bloody outrageous what my lords and masters get away with in the name of spin. You exposed them. They were furious with you I can tell you. Keep on at them Sara, keep on asking that Paxman question – why are those lying bastards lying to me? Keep on exposing them darling. Give 'em a hard time. They deserve it. Oh, what am I saying. . ."

"Charley, come and sit down," said Peter. Charley sat down, . . . and fell asleep.

"She's wrapped up the year, Peter, said it all in one go. Sometimes the drink reveals truth," said Sara as soberly as she could.

"Yes, but that's for tomorrow. Let me pour you this last drop of bubbly." Music was playing, the wine kept on flowing, the chatter was animated. And with around half an half to go before midnight, Sara was sounding as if she was drunk, and Simon was not far off. . .

"Dance with me Simon," she said, pressing herself to him so closely they moulded into one. "I'm squiffy aren't I? Hold me tight or I'll fall over. Thank you darling, thank you. I will never forget this year. You have made it the most amazing year of my life. You have changed my life. You're a star, a star." And they danced and held each other tight, everyone wrapped up in their own conversation, no one taking much notice anyway.

Just before midnight a radio was turned on, glasses were recharged and the chimes of Big Ben echoed across the room.

"Happy New Year everyone," shouted William as they all formed in a circle for 'Old Lang Syne'. And when the singing had finished, everyone went round kissing, hugging or shaking hands with everyone. And last of all, Sara came to Simon.

"Happy New Year Sara," he said, going to kiss her on the cheek. But she turned to face him straight on, put a hand around the back of his head, and with an open mouth kissed him fully on his mouth, searching deep into him. They broke away, and she put her head onto his chest and fought back tears.

"I am going to miss you. . .I am going to miss you so much." Simon turned her round to face a wall so that no one could see her crying. There were no words for a while before Sara picked up.

"Be positive, that's what we agreed and I will try. And who knows . . . if William was ever to have a really nasty accident on his bloody ball bearings, and if things don't turn out with Margaret, who knows . . . who knows. I'd better go and serve some food."

The food was always served just after midnight at the Openshaws New Year's party, around halfway through. People sat on chairs and stools, on the floor, on the stairs, balancing plates on their knees. Simon managed to cram down near Sara. Charley woke up, looked sheepish, and announced that she needed a lie down. And went off to the spare bedroom.

"I'm going to Cornwall in the morning. I'll leave now," Simon said quietly to Sara around two-ish. They stood in a darkened hall and kissed, more soberly this time.

"We will see each other again, I'm sure," he said in a barely audible, breaking voice. And Sara kissed him again, generously, for all she was worth. Sara opened the door and said "bye . . . my star". And watched him walk down the path.

As he reached the pavement he turned, smiled and gave her the tiniest of waves, like the one she had given him by the church door on that Sunday after his fast. And she returned the wave and watched him go, until she could see him no longer.

★   ★   ★

Two days later, at 11.30 a.m., Sara's star left for the northwest. And as he turned the key in the door, and pushed to check it was locked, a child died of poverty.

Author's acknowledgements:

My thanks are due to people who helped with this book in various ways, especially Anne Rodford, Marion Molteno, Robert Molteno, Dimitri Crysto, John Hilary, Rosie Boycott, Ann Pettifor, Tim Lang, David Rhodes, Maranda, Leslie, Carl, James and Alison.

I would like to acknowledge my thanks to the aid and development agencies. Royalties from the sale of this book go to agencies working to eradicate poverty.

Agencies working to end poverty

The Global Call to Action against Poverty. www.whiteband.org

Action Aid. www.actionaid.org.uk

CAFOD. www.cafod.org.uk

Christian Aid. www.christianaid.org.uk

Comic Relief. www.comicrelief.com

Concern Worldwide. www.concern.net

Fairtrade Foundation. www.fairtrade.org.uk

Friends of the Earth. www.foe.co.uk

Jubilee Debt Campaign. www.jubileedebtcampaign.org.uk

One World Action. www.oneworldaction.org

Oxfam. www.oxfam.org

People and Planet. www.peopleandplanet.org

Practical Action. www.practicalaction.org

Progressio. www.progressio.org.uk

Save the Children. www.savethechildren.org.uk

Self Help Africa. www.selfhelpafrica.com

Tearfund. www.tearfund.org

Traidcraft. www.traidcraft.co.uk

War on Want. www.waronwant.org

World Development Movement. www.wdm.org.uk

Information on poverty issues can also be found on the Make Poverty History site: www.makepovertyhistory.org